Lone Star Protector

Lone Star Protector

A Calamity Valley Romance

Jennie Jones

Lone Star Protector

Tule Publishing First Printing

The Tule Publishing Group, LLC

First Publication by Tule Publishing Group 2019

ISBN: 978-1-949707-47-2

Chapter One

NOT MANY WOMEN worried about retribution from their long-dead great-grandfather, but Lauren Mackillop was no ordinary woman.

"Heading to Texas, are you?" the man standing next to her said as they queued for the check-in counter. "You won't know what's hit you."

Oh, but she would.

Born under the stars, with a curse on her head to boot, she was well versed in rugged living and hadn't wanted to go back to any of it. But here she was at LAX, flight booked.

"It's hotter than a stolen tamale in Texas," the man said.

Lauren ran her eyes over the top of his shiny, bald head and smiled her appreciation of his Texan-resident joke. "I know." She flicked the tip of her tongue over her lips, enough to moisten them without disturbing her neutral-blush lipstick. It had cost a fortune and she'd have to make it last now.

"You are not defined by one thing."

Lauren closed her eyes. *"Grandmother, get out of my head."*

"Get your skinny butt back home now."

Skinny butt? It was true, she was slim. Mostly genetics, but she didn't eat much anyway, and in the future she might not be able to afford to eat at all—a fact her grandmother obviously wasn't concerned about. Given what had just happened to her, she was already having nightmare visions of her future. Sad and lonely, eating packet after packet of pretzels. She didn't like to depend on junk food to cure her miseries though, so she hardly ever ate them. Even though they were her absolute favorite.

"Don't dally around the airport," Ava said. *"Or you'll get yourself into more trouble than you can deal with."*

Lauren attempted to shut out the telepathic mental communication she had with her grandmother, but she'd been born with it and it wasn't easy to silence. Especially when Ava wanted to voice her opinions. She'd probably been polishing her runes and knew something Lauren didn't. Not that Ava needed accoutrements to portend someone's fate.

As for trouble! She had a Louis Vuitton suitcase full. Secondhand Louis Vuitton, but still…

"Do you know what the delay is for?" she asked the little man with the bald head.

The line was at least fifty people long. A check-in person at the counter was moving his hands in explanation of something, but she was so far back she couldn't hear what was being said.

"Something to do with a bird flying into the engine of a plane as it was taxiing. Threw a wrench into the takeoffs and landings. Everyone's circling."

Lauren tapped the heel of her ankle boot on the tiled

floor.

"Been in California long?" the man asked.

"Six years." Couldn't he tell by the perfect barely there tan? The hazel highlights woven through the chestnut-brown layered bob, lengths of which framed her face and swung down her back? Couldn't he see the *Vogue* look, played down with a dash of Hollywood urban chic?

Or did he just see a woman wearing another woman's castoffs?

If only she were going home as the successful woman she'd hoped to be when she'd left. Someone who hadn't had her business taken from her. Someone who appeared poised and a little mysterious—although not in an eerie way.

She cast a quick glance at her clothes. She'd needed a classy veneer for her clients and customers but not anymore. So, she'd chosen low-key with her outfit today. She was heading for her hometown of Surrender in Calamity Valley in the Texas Panhandle. There'd be little need of couture.

She sported dark-wash denim jeans, a large leather, stitched-and-tasseled tote bag that had cost its original owner two-thousand dollars and Lauren a hundred bucks, and matching pale lilac suede ankle boots.

"I was doing so well with my business," she told the man, needing to voice it out loud because she still couldn't understand how she'd let disaster through the door and shatter everything she'd worked so hard for.

She'd owned and run the In Need of Loving boutique in Santa Ynez, Santa Barbara County. A mere one hundred twenty-five miles from Los Angeles—she couldn't afford anything *in* LA, although Santa Ynez was pricey enough. Still, her shop slotted beautifully between the historic facades of the businesses on the main street. She'd even acquired a few select customers in LA. Obscenely wealthy women who bought on a whim and discarded on a sigh of discontent. She picked up their preloved, sometimes never-worn, clothing and accessories for a song and sold them in her boutique.

"What happened to your business?" the bald man asked.

"I lost it."

Her shop was boarded up now. Traded on and about to be turned into a steakhouse. They'd probably make a fortune, since it was two doors down from the saloon where her trashy business partner had lost In Need of Loving in a card game.

She never wanted to see another saloon as long as she lived. She never wanted to be reminded of backroom poker games, where sharks with laid-back demeanors bet for fun on people's livelihoods.

She rotated her shoulder, the soft jersey of her pearl-gray scoop-neck top sliding off a little. She pulled her aviators off the top of her head and onto her nose, covering her eyes and resisting the urge to look behind her. She felt as though someone was watching her, and she didn't want to be seen. It was probably just the disturbance of her grandmother being in her head, and everything she now faced—the unknown.

"The name's Frankie," the bald-headed man said, sticking out his stubby hand. "Frankie Caruso."

He didn't look like a Frankie Caruso. He looked like a plain old Bob Smith.

Lauren accepted his handshake. It wasn't his fault he was irritating, it was Lauren's mood. But it might be best to remain anonymous. "Scarlet Juliette Barrett-Bernard," she said, making up the name on the spur of the moment.

His eyebrows shot up. "Is that so? What a fancy name."

It was as far from Lauren Mackillop as she could get.

"Child," her grandmother said. *"Don't put yourself in a situation you can't easily get out of."*

What did that mean? The problem was Ava wasn't a typical granny. She and her sisters were mystics, oracles, and soothsayers and a force to be reckoned with. What Ava had was the gift of insight at its finest. Precognition of the future. Prophetic predictions.

Unnerving, since she'd warned Lauren about the trashy business partner, but had Lauren listened?

She was supposed to have this ability, too, and obviously didn't! Although she'd never wanted the Mackillop gift and was content with the telepathic conversations with her grandmother—which she never spoke about. She didn't want to believe she had greater powers loitering inside her, ready to burst out. She wouldn't know what to do with them, for a start.

"So what's sending you to Texas, Miss Barrett-Bernard?" Frankie Caruso asked.

She offered a wan smile. "I just buried my thieving business partner." The funeral costs had taken a fair whack of her remaining money. "He lost my business in a poker game." He didn't deserve to be buried; he deserved to be left to rot in the street. But Lauren had a conscience. "He was shot in the back by underworld crime lords." That was a lie, but what did a little fib matter now? He'd died choking on a chunk of pineapple—just desserts, if anyone wanted Lauren's opinion. He'd forged her signature on a new contract that gave him 78 percent ownership of In Need of Loving and the means to dispose of it in any way he saw fit.

A poker game!

Frankie Caruso's jaw went slack. "Right. Well—best of luck, and all that."

"I won't need luck. I have my grandmother."

"Looking out for you, is she?"

Lauren wasn't sure if Ava was so much looking out for her as forcing her hand. "Something like that." Her bottom lip trembled and she bit it. She blinked through unexpected tears and turned her head away.

Going back to Surrender under such demoralizing circumstances hurt. But Donaldson's Property Development had been hounding the ninety-seven Calamity Valley residents to sell their land, so her family was working on a last-ditch effort at increasing tourist interest, to prove to people there was no need to sell. Lauren was supposed to come up with an idea for Surrender, since she had a small amount of cash and no pressing engagements in life.

It wasn't that she didn't love the valley and her hometown—she did, with every beat of her heart. It was just that she'd left on a high, business plans pouring out of her. Now, she'd lost that business. Who in Surrender would want to listen to *her* suggestions for commercial growth? She was nothing but a fake, with a suitcase full of other women's designer clothing and exclusive one-offs.

She glanced down at the Manolo Blahnik boots she'd bought from a producer's wife for fifty bucks. Maybe shoes didn't count…

At least she wouldn't be alone in the valley. Her cousin Molly was back in her hometown of Hopeless. Their cousin, Pepper, refused to budge from Arizona though, let alone return to her hometown of Reckless. And here was Lauren, on her way to Surrender, to do—what? She didn't have a clue, but she had a niggling feeling her grandmother was up to something.

A movement in the queue brought her out of her thoughts. A guy in an airline uniform was walking along the line of people, explaining something.

Thank goodness! It looked like they'd be underway soon. All this waiting around wasn't doing anything for her nerves.

She squared her shoulders and inhaled deeply. That wasn't the way to think. She was going home and she had a job to do. Just because she'd made a huge error of judgment in the recent past didn't mean she'd make another.

"I'm sorry, people," the airline employee said, apologetic and defensive all at once. "Traffic is experiencing gate hold and taxi delays are long. There's nothing we can do about it. You've got a five-hour holdup."

Lauren sighed. *Great start to the rest of my life.*

MARK STERRETT WAS used to dealing with whatever came his way. He took life in his stride. But the job he was about to embark on had been forced on him, and he wasn't in the best of moods. Not that his grim expression had made any difference to the guy with the bald head now sitting opposite him.

"It's hot in Texas," the guy said, continuing a conversation that had been mostly one-sided and going on for a few minutes.

Mark picked a pretzel from the bag he'd bought and munched on it. The little guy had taken a seat at the café table in Terminal One, LAX without asking but Mark pushed the packet of pretzels toward him, not wanting to be selfish just because *his* life had hit the pits.

"We get all kinds of weather, mind you. Not just heat, you know?"

"I know." Mark wasn't a true Texan, but he'd been living in Laredo for six years after moving from California and had recently discovered what heat could do to a man. Although he wasn't referring to the weather.

He glanced at the departure board. There was still over a three-hour delay to get through before he boarded for Amarillo, picked up a rental car and got himself to Surrender in Calamity Valley, nestled against the Palo Duro Canyon. Lost and forgotten. But apparently with valuable real estate potential.

"If you're heading to west Texas," the jokester said, digging into the packet of pretzels, "it can be drier than the heart of a haystack and windier than a fifty-pound bag of whistling lips."

"I'll try to remember that."

"Or you might find yourself in the middle of panhandle rain. That's what we call a dust storm. We get four seasons in Texas—all of 'em big ones."

"Thanks for the advice," Mark said and spun the packet of pretzels his way again.

"Wherever you're going, you'll want to watch your back 'cause of the heat."

Mark had cause to take very good care of his back and was only heading to the panhandle in order to protect everyone else's.

"So what were you doing in LA?" the bald guy asked.

"Family issues."

"What business are you in?"

Up until a month ago he'd been a ghostwriter—making up stories for others. More recently—"Property development."

"Looks like business is good," the guy said, raising his eyebrows at Mark's attire.

He resisted the urge to straighten his shoulders beneath the soft leather bomber jacket. Some author had given it to him as added repayment for ghostwriting a biography about a relative who'd flown in World War II. He also owned a cowboy hat purportedly belonging to some cowpoke who'd run a cattle drive from Texas to the railroads in Kansas, and other gear handed over to him in appreciation of his services. He kept these gifts packed away like souvenirs on a high shelf that no one ever dusted, but the jacket he was fond of. He'd worn it so often, it was at that perfect lived-in stage, although it was designer and pricey, and that obviously still showed. It wasn't the sort of thing he'd normally buy for himself.

He didn't see money as the be-all and end-all—although he liked that he had some. He worked hard for what was in his bank account, on his own terms and under his own steam. Some might say it was a wasted talent, giving all those plots and storylines to someone else who'd reap the reward, but that was his preference. Grab a good deal, dollarwise, prove his worth with the written word, then move on. Life was meant for living, not sweating. And after a hard day's writing, there was nothing like a visit to the local bar, or a friendly little poker game with the boys in the back room, to clear a man's head and make him forget about the trials of the day.

But his father had put a halt to all that, so here he was, heading to Surrender. No longer working under his own conditions. The quick trip to LA had been necessary to ensure his mom and three sisters were okay and that they had no idea what was going on, or what might happen to them if Mark messed up in the next couple of weeks.

"Think I'll take a walk," he said to the bald-headed guy. "Keep them," he added as he pushed his chair back to stand and nudged the packet of pretzels the man's way.

"Thanks. See you around, maybe."

Mark smiled but didn't answer. It was unlikely. He'd get this job in Surrender done, ensuring his mom and sisters were safe, then attempt to *not* go find his father and kill him.

Twenty minutes later, he was leaning against a pillar, feet crossed at the ankle, arms folded over his chest, trying not to look at the departure board for the fiftieth time hoping for a positive update.

All around him, people were dozing on hard chairs, mouths open in sleep. Kids were getting scratchy and tired. Parents were making further demands of the now frazzled airline staff as to when they'd get to board a plane.

He ran his gaze over the heads of the many weary travelers until his sight settled on a distant corner and a woman sitting on a row of plastic chairs someone had just put out.

For a second he thought he was seeing things. Was it her?

Lauren Mackillop—the woman he was going to be snooping on.

His heart rate picked up, and any frustration he'd been experiencing got washed away in a rush of adrenaline. Donaldson's Property Developers had given him photos of her, taken from press releases when she'd opened her boutique. They'd given him a brief dossier on all the Mackillop women after he'd agreed to do business with them—like he'd had a choice.

There were three grandmothers, each with a granddaughter, and someone called Momma Marie who ran a hair salon and a takeout in one of the towns. There was a lot of superstition surrounding these grandmothers. Three sisters, known as Wild Ava, Crazy Alice, and Mad Aurora, all with some ability to tell fortunes or weave spells.

What did that tell a guy? Stay clear, that was what. Although in other circumstances, he'd probably make a beeline just for the story.

He studied Lauren carefully. If he introduced himself, would he blow his cover and did it matter? They were going to meet anyway, and he was no longer keeping out of the limelight the way he had for the last month, trying to lay low and figure a way out of the deal he didn't want to accept from Donaldson. Thanks to his father, he'd had no option.

Johnson Sterrett hadn't been in his family's life for two decades, but his latest scumbag act threatened to stab out all the decency his mother had fought for while bringing up Mark and his three sisters on her own. The man deserved to be in jail, but making that dream come true would mean dragging his mom and sisters down, too, so Mark's only shot at ending this nightmare was to accept Donaldson's job.

Mark preferred the word *job* to blackmail. It made him feel more in charge of his fate.

He sauntered toward Lauren, pausing when he got close.

"Heck of a delay, eh?" he said, with a smile. "Just because of some bird."

She glanced up. "I feel sorry for the bird. It died under tragic and heartbreaking circumstances."

Maybe not as coolly aloof as she first appeared.

"Did you get the food vouchers too?" he asked, indicating the ones she held in her hand.

She gave a resigned nod, and held up her vouchers, offering them. "I'm not hungry."

"Really? I'm starving. I was hoping you might tell me the best place to eat. So far, I haven't gotten further than a soda and a bag of pretzels."

She was as slim as a wand, like some model on a runway,

showing the world a fake boredom. But there was a skittishness beneath the poise and Mark also sensed worry.

She looked a bit lost.

"Where are you heading?" he asked, taking the seat two down from her.

"Texas."

"Same. Where?"

"Home."

"Nice."

"Not really."

So she didn't want to go back to Calamity Valley and Mark didn't want to go at all. He slumped a little in his chair and stared ahead. "Same," he said, on a long-suffering sigh.

"Why are you going to Texas?" she asked.

"I've got an opportunity there," he said, still not looking at her.

"What business are you in?"

"Property."

"That's good."

He shrugged. "It's some crummy backwater town. But I need a change and figured I'd get it in this place."

"Which crummy town?" she asked, with more interest in her tone.

Mark threw her a half-smile, half-grimace. "Let's not talk about it."

She huffed out a laugh. "Okay, let's not talk about why we're going to Texas."

He turned on his seat. "Since we've got so much time on our hands, why don't we pretend we're heading somewhere else? Where would you like to go, Miss—" He let the question hang in the air.

"Scarlet Juliette Barrett-Bernard."

He managed to hold on to his laugh. "How do you do, Miss Barrett-Bernard? Pleasure to meet you. Danton Alexandre Dubois."

"French?" she asked, eyes wide.

"On my grandmother's side." Not strictly true, but close enough for his use. Granny Dubois had been an Idaho backcountry logger. Came from Quebec pioneer stock and followed in her granddaddy Dubois's footsteps, running the family firm until she was forced to retire at the age of eighty-three due to arthritis and an inability to swing the axe or type out an invoice. And he wasn't making that up. He had fond memories of visiting her as a kid. She'd been a storyteller too, which was probably why he found himself ghostwriting, moving from one yarn to the next.

"You're not nobility in disguise, are you?" Lauren asked, with a wry lift of her eyebrow.

Her eyes were mesmerizing. Moss green—dark and inviting. She made him feel like he was sitting in the lobby of some grand old hotel, surrounded by the peace and coolness of potted palms and the water music of a courtyard fountain.

She wasn't his type at all. He loathed potted palms and teacups with dainty handles a guy couldn't get his thumb around.

"Shall we pretend we *are* chic aristocrats from Europe?" he suggested. She'd find out soon enough that he wasn't Danton Alexandre Dubois.

She gave a little shrug. "Why not."

He could use this opportunity and gain more intel on what the Mackillop women had in mind to deter Donaldson's salesmen who wanted to buy the valley land. As soon as he had that information, this whole business would be finished and he could get back to doing what he did best—living life *his* way. The casual, take-it-as-it-happens way instead of the constant looking-over-his-shoulder-due-to-being-blackmailed-by-Donaldson way.

"Nice to meet you." He swiveled on the chair and held out his hand.

As she slid hers into his, her skin soft and cool, something fizzed, deep in his gut.

She jolted and pulled her hand away.

"Ouch," he said lightly. "Think we got an electric shock."

She took her focus to the floor.

"Let's pretend we're off to Paris," he said, needing to keep the camaraderie going. "What's the first thing you want to do when you get there?"

She looked up and into the distance. "Stroll down the Avenue des Champs-Élysées." There was a wave of warmth in her voice and she'd answered without hesitation.

"Sounds good." He settled further into the hard seat. "Can I join you? I'll buy the coffee when we get to the Arc de Triomphe." It earned him a glance, and a smile, and small though it was, he was rewarded by its value. He had a feeling she hadn't cracked a grin in a long time, and her response pierced him in his most vulnerable part—the heart.

LAUREN WAS CAUGHT in Danton's gaze, a pleasant sensation of contentment coursing through her.

Handsome as all get-out and looking like a rich guy taking a day off from the frustrations of business, he wore smart yet casual jeans and a white button-down shirt, and while certainly not cheap, the tan-colored leather bomber jacket must have laid him back a cool three thousand. And what a fantastic name. Danton Alexandre Dubois. France—the place she'd always longed to go.

"What do you do for a living?" she asked, imagining the answer. *I sail yachts, mostly.*

"Right now, I'm into that property thing we said we weren't going to talk about."

"Oh, yes." She'd forgotten, too busy trying to figure him out.

His hair was the perfect length of slightly too long, a little mussed, giving the impression he simply had to run a hand through the thick, dark brown strands and he was done.

There was a lazy charm about his handsomeness. Not because he didn't take care of himself, the guy obviously worked out—look at the muscles in his forearms beneath the pushed-up sleeves of his bomber jacket—but he looked like he didn't have to try.

She checked her watch, glanced up at the departure notification board again.

"Want to go someplace more comfortable?" he said. "One of the lounges?"

"They're VIP."

"I prepurchased a priority pass. I'm pretty sure I can take a guest, or persuade them..."

It was tempting. The VIP lounges were quiet, peaceful areas with leather sofas and the aroma of coffee beans and dainty iced cupcakes.

Should she go?

She bit the inside of her cheek and waited for her grandmother to make some pronouncement, but there was nothing in her head but silence.

"Thank you, Mr. Dubois. A decent place to sit and relax would be welcome."

He smiled, and stood. "It's Danton. Let's go, Scarlet. We've got memories to share from our trip to Paris and only three hours in which to make them."

Scarlet. She had to hide a smile. She was suddenly somebody else; she could make up anything about her life and get away with it.

Two hours later, Lauren didn't think she'd ever been more enchanted by any man.

"Stuff like that got a fourteen-year-old beat up where I come from," Danton said as he poured them another glass of chardonnay.

She picked up a white-fudge covered pretzel and popped it into her mouth. They'd eaten their way through a selection of mini gourmet sandwiches, and she had requested a packet of her favorite flavored pretzels for dessert. He hadn't even laughed; just said white fudge was his favorite too.

"So how did you get out of it?" They'd been swapping

stories about their youth, although she hadn't told a single truth about hers, but he wouldn't know that.

"I grew. Suddenly. In a couple of weeks, I was head and shoulders above him. That growth spurt saved my life."

"But why did the boy want to beat you up?"

"He was Suzy Fletcher's older brother. I fancied Suzy—actually, I'd been in love with her since I turned seven."

How gorgeous that he fell in love at such a tender age.

"But Suzy was a year older and didn't want anything to do with a little monster like me."

Stupid Suzy.

"You were still in love with her when you were fourteen?"

He nodded and picked up another white-fudge pretzel. "Crazy of me, I know, but I couldn't shake my love for her until I turned fifteen." He blushed a little and shrugged it off.

What a fascinating man and so gentlemanly. As they'd strolled across the departure floor toward the lounge earlier, he'd slowed his pace so she could keep up with him. She was tall, but he was taller, with long legs, and her ankle boots had begun to crush her toes, being a half size too small—but Manolo Blahnik and only fifty bucks.

Right now, she wanted to kick off her boots and curl her legs beneath her. Not that she'd do that in the VIP lounge, but that was how he made her feel. Welcome and beautiful—and just a little mysterious.

"Uh-oh," he said, turning to look behind him.

Chatter and excitement all around them broke the moment.

He turned back to her, a soft smile in his eyes that also played on his superbly firm mouth. There was a hint of stubble on his jaw now, and she longed to run the palm of her hand along it.

"Looks like this is it," he said, standing and collecting his jacket from the back of the leather sofa.

"Looks like it," she said, rising and picking up her tote bag from the carpeted floor.

People were now hurrying around them, scurrying to collect discarded coats and bags, or searching through pockets and briefcases for boarding passes that were nearly five hours old.

The time had gone so quickly, and so pleasantly.

She walked at Danton's side, reluctant to quicken her pace for more reasons than too-small boots.

At the door to the lounge, he put a hand on her arm to halt her from exiting.

She went with him when he moved them aside, allowing others to tumble out the door and head for their boarding gates.

All the sounds around her faded as she concentrated on his face.

"Thank you for the memories, Scarlet Juliette Barrett-Bernard."

Lauren shivered when he took her fingers and bent to kiss her hand. If this was how they did things in France, she'd be visiting as soon as she got the chance. She could already see herself, strolling down the Champs-Élysées on the arm of Danton Alexandre Dubois.

"Till we meet again."

They'd never meet again; luck wasn't on her side. "Goodbye," she said, sorrow welling. They'd kept their promise and hadn't talked about their lives as they were today, but it was obvious from general conversation that they'd made a connection. She was a little remorseful about having lied to him, but what did it really matter? "Thank you for everything."

He still had her fingers in his hand; he still had his gaze on hers.

Then he bent his head and kissed her on the mouth.

For a second, the air around her was a freshened Parisian breeze, with spring rain tumbling unexpectedly from a teal-gray sky. Umbrellas were blowing inside out all around them, but his lips were warm and she *was* on the Champs-Élysées, she *was* on his arm.

He released her from the kiss tenderly, almost reluctantly.

Something momentarily passed through his gaze. Regret. Because they were parting? Because they weren't swapping cell phone numbers? She didn't know. He removed the expression almost as soon as it arrived.

"*Bon voyage*, Scarlet."

"Passengers for..."

Her breath rose in her chest, her heart still tumbling on that avenue in Paris.

"Flight number..."

"Please proceed to gate..."

"Boarding will commence..."

There was an awful possibility she might cry. She made a move for her aviators on top of her head, but they weren't there.

"My sunglasses," she said, turning. She'd left them on the coffee table by the sofas. "Just a moment, I need to get them." She also needed to get herself under control so she could say a proper goodbye to him once she knew there was no chance he'd see her tears.

She made her way quickly to the coffee table, picked up her aviators, and placed a smile on her face before turning back to Danton.

But he was gone.

Chapter Two

BONE-WEARY AFTER THE five-hour delay, followed by a four-hour flight with an hour's layover in Denver, it was now mid-morning at Amarillo airport and Lauren still couldn't believe Danton had simply disappeared. The first man she'd felt a true attraction to. More than that even—a companionship.

If she believed in the Mackillop curse, she might have thought this was a great big taste of it.

"You're heading right into the curse," Ava said. *"Best get ready for it."*

"It was just a passing thought," she said to her grandmother. *"Just because I haven't had many long-term relationships doesn't mean I'm cursed."*

"How long was your longest relationship?"

"A couple of months, at least."

"Two weeks and four days."

"Okay! So I don't do long term." Lauren stepped out of people's way so she could continue this mental conversation with her grandmother. *"I don't believe in the curse, remember?"*

"You mean you don't want to."

Darn right. There had to be normal reasons why all Mackillop women had found themselves alone since 1939 when the great-grandfathers—referred to as the GGs to show total disrespect for the reprobates—threw down their curse. Manless. Husbandless. Continually bordering on homeless.

That last prophesy was a bit too close to the bone, given that it could be said she *was* currently homeless, having lost her business and most of her money.

"Where have you been?" she asked Ava. *"Haven't you been monitoring my every move since I left LA?"* Not that they had these telepathic conversations every day or even every week, but since she'd lost In Need of Loving, Ava had been very chatty.

"I've been busy. What have you been up to in the last few hours?"

"Traveling." She didn't want to even think about Danton in case Ava caught on.

She obviously had a crush on the man and she'd better forget about him right now. His disappearance couldn't be anything to do with the silly curse. Look at her cousin, Molly. She was about to get married. She'd found the love of her life—and he was still around after three whole months.

But Lauren had made a decision. A *personal* decision. She was going to remain single for the rest of her life. She'd lost everything she'd worked hard for because she'd put her trust in a man. She hadn't been able to hold down a relationship for longer than two-and-a-half weeks, and it was obvious to any observer the only course of action was to get on with things on her own. She'd never trust another man again.

"I've got news for you," Ava said.

"And what would that be?"

"You'll find out."

The curse had lurked in the cousins' lives forever. Everyone in Calamity Valley knew about it, and although no one talked about it, she'd often wondered if that was because they believed it but didn't want to mention it in case something terrible happened again.

There were lots of terrible things happening in the valley right now.

"Don't start trying to scare me with talk of the curse," she told her grandmother. *"I need to keep focused. I'm home to help rejuvenate my hometown."*

"I thought you were home because there was no other choice."

"Gee, thanks for the reminder."

Ava's chuckle was so affable, Lauren's lips twitched. She hadn't smiled in weeks, apart from when she'd been with Danton. They tasted sweet.

"You're home for a reason, child. There's more to this than meets the eye."

"So what's in store for me?"

"Like I said, you'll find out."

Ava left the conversation and Lauren pulled her Louis Vuitton suitcase behind her, making her way over the concourse to the doors.

Outside, the end of a Texas winter hit her at a cool fifty degrees. Spring was on its way though. She smelled it in the air.

She ought to look on the bright side. There were so

many people to see, and hug, once she got to the valley. Davie Little, her adoptive uncle and generally assumed to be the Mackillop cousins' bodyguard, given his towering breadth and height and ferocious Mexican grimace when he thought someone was taking advantage of any of the Mackillop women.

Sweet little Winnie, who helped Molly's mother in the hair salon and the takeout in Hopeless. Momma Marie herself, who'd brought up Lauren and Pepper after each lost their own mothers in freak accidents when the girls were only ten years old.

She rummaged in her tote bag for her shawl and wrapped it around her throat and shoulders. Being home held sensory memories that seeped into her veins more than the day's chill. Memories of her carefree youth and of her mother. Those hurt, but she kept them tucked away, never wanting to forget the mother who'd lost control of her motorcycle on a notoriously dangerous bend in the far south of the valley. Her mother had been as wild at heart as her grandmother.

How come she hadn't inherited that wild spirit, apart from three hours in a VIP lounge?

Suddenly, her ears popped, as though the air around her was pushing down, pinning her to the earth's surface and forcing her to petrify. She couldn't hear the noise of the people around her. Not the automatic doors or the plane taking off above her. Nothing. Not a murmur. But she was watching herself and she was with Danton.

It was raining lightly, and she held a large umbrella over both their heads as they stood on a street corner. He was talking and she was laughing. He had a handful of coins and they were arguing playfully about the exchange rate, Lauren saying fifty French francs was about nine American dollars and Danton insisting it was the most expensive cup of coffee he'd ever bought her.

Freed from the hold of the vision just as suddenly as she'd been bound by it, she hauled in a breath. How weird! She must be more tired than she'd thought. Or maybe it was something to do with the air pressure from the flights, messing with her inner ear.

"Lauren! Over here!"

She found a welcome smile when her cousin waved madly.

"Quick!" Molly shouted. "I'm in the thirty-minute free park, and I've already been here twenty-three minutes!"

Lauren dashed to where her cousin had parked her mother's pickup.

Molly grabbed her in a hug so hard it made them laugh.

"Gosh, Lauren," Molly said, holding her at arm's length, "you are so incredibly beautiful."

"Oh, hush. You're the one with the glow. You've got that *I'm-in-love* look." Molly had always been lovely to look at, with her wide smile, big green eyes, and cascading chestnut-colored hair. Now, she was radiating full-of-beans joy. It was *so* good to see her.

"You'll never guess what," Molly said. "Momma's got Skype. I've got it now too. Once you get it, you, me, and Pepper can hold powwows. In case you need to talk and air your views on everything that's going to happen."

Skype? What progression. They usually held any necessary and important discussions over the telephone. "What's going to happen?"

"Everything! We'll be your backup. You can moan about what's already happened too, if you like."

She didn't want to talk about her trashy business partner, but she'd have to at some point. Her family hadn't known about the hassles she'd been embroiled in until the end. Everyone rallied around once they found out, saying the timing couldn't have been better and it was the perfect opportunity to come home.

"How's Momma Marie?" she asked as Molly opened the passenger door for Lauren to stow her tote bag. "And how's Winnie? And Davie? I can't wait to meet Saul!" Saul Solomon, the man who'd wandered into Hopeless and taken Molly's heart.

Molly grinned. "He is *so* hot. Honest to God, Lauren, I've scooped *the* hottest man on the planet."

"Don't rub it in."

"That's what Pepper said."

"Pepper also told me you can't stop talking about the Mackillop gift—and you're still insisting you've *got* it." All three cousins had been told they had the gift of foresight and soothsaying from an early age, but given their grandmothers' reputations on their heads, as young girls they'd decided to disregard any powers they might have. They often had an ability to know when one of them was in trouble or in need, but that was only because they were close.

"I've stopped talking about that now," Molly said, waving her hand in a brush-it-off manner. "But, you know—I am getting married, so the curse has been lifted off Hopeless. I made that happen. Or fate did. Or something did..."

"What's going on?" Lauren asked, her intuition—the one all women had—suddenly in play.

"Let's go," Molly said, ignoring her question. "I can't afford the parking fee if we go over the thirty minutes, and neither can you. We need to keep every spare dollar for fighting rumors."

"Are people talking about us?"

"They're always talking about us! Get used to it. *Again*," she added with a droll lift of her eyebrow.

Lauren chewed on her cheek. The grandmothers and Momma Marie didn't care too much about what was said of them by those who mocked or didn't believe, but the cousins did. There'd been a lot of name calling in their youths. Especially after the titles Crazy Alice, Wild Ava, and Mad Aurora had been bestowed on the grandmothers. This was why all three cousins left the valley six years ago. To find a place where they could blend in as ordinary women, not granddaughters of soothsayers. Now two of them were back. Was there something in that?

"There's lots to tell!" Molly said.

"Like what?" Lauren asked, snapping down the handle on her suitcase.

"Like the Surrender saloon."

"You mean the bar?"

"Some guy bought the lease, and word is, he's going to call it a saloon."

Lauren frowned. "Old Gerdin sold his lease?"

"He's ninety-one, you can't blame him. Anyway, it was getting to the point where Davie was driving from Hopeless to Surrender nearly every day to stop the bar fights."

Lauren was speechless. Not about the bar fights, they'd been happening for years—a few out-of-towners, thinking they could make use of cheap liquor and start a brawl just for the sake of it. "But apart from the brawlers there's hardly any customer traffic in town."

Molly shrugged. "Didn't stop this new guy. He must be the brave and daring sort."

"He must be an absolute lunatic."

"Don't judge him until you've met him."

A *saloon*! The very thing she never wanted to see again.

She threw her Louis Vuitton onto the tray of the pickup.

"Nice case," Molly said. "Go easy on it."

"Who is this guy?"

"Don't know yet. He's arriving any day. Or any hour…" Molly flushed, and moved to the driver's side, getting in and slamming the door. "You'd best go see Ava."

"Why?" Lauren asked as she slid onto the passenger seat and tugged at the seat belt.

"Can't say."

Or wouldn't. "Molly," she warned, slipping into her I'm-the-eldest role as easily as if she'd never left it behind. All three cousins had been born within a week of each other, but she *was* the eldest, and it meant something.

Her cousin sighed. "I'm not supposed to talk to you about my powers now that you're home, but let me tell you—you've got trouble coming." She fired the engine and pulled from the curb.

It had been odd to hear Molly thought she had the Mackillop gift, and odder still she now wasn't supposed to talk about it. Although Lauren did have that mental communication with Ava—and she'd never told her cousins about it. She felt bad, suddenly. She'd lied to Danton too…

"Woo-woo-woo," Molly intoned in a spooky, mystic's voice as she stirred an imaginary pot. "Trouble and spice and all things not nice. Except," she added, using her normal voice, "there will be something nice waiting for you, after you've been through everything you need to go through."

"You're talking in riddles. You've been spending too much time with the grandmothers."

"Only mine, because I'm practicing my skills and need all the advice I can get. *You,*" she said pointedly, "need to talk to Ava."

Lauren faced forward when Molly screeched out of the airport parking lot and headed for the highway. "I want to get settled before I see Ava." Which reminded her—she didn't know where she was staying.

"By the way," Molly said. "I bet you think you'll be staying with Momma in Hopeless, but you're not."

A prickle of unease wiggled its way through her. "There's nowhere to stay in Surrender." Most of the houses were lived in, a few rented out, and the rest were desolate. Kept up on the outside, so the town had a nice look to it, but empty, dusty, and cobwebby on the inside.

"Sorry," Molly said, not sounding in the least bit apologetic as she plucked three large, old iron keys out of her shirt pocket and dangled them at Lauren.

Lauren recoiled in her seat. "I'm not staying there!"

"Ava's orders."

"My great-grandfather built that place! I'm not living in it." Nobody had. Not for seventy-eight years. Her great-grandmother left it to rot after Lauren's great-grandfather abandoned her, pregnant with Ava. Even Ava wouldn't set a foot in the place, although all the grandmothers had attempted to regenerate their abandoned properties just before the cousins left, but eerie things kept happening, like falling masonry or tiles, and shattering windows, and the builders had left. Spooked out of their skins.

"Sage Springs isn't habitable!" she declared.

Molly dropped the keys onto her lap. "Davie cleaned up the house a little—the part that still has four walls—and Ava sorted you out some furniture and bed linen and whatever."

"Ava went there?" Lauren almost slid off the seat.

"No way! Davie and Momma cleaned up the place. It's habitable now. And at least the house has a roof."

The roof on Molly's hacienda had blown off just before the cousins had been born. The great-grandfathers had done it, according to family lore. At exactly the same time, most of the right-hand wall of Sage Springs's large, historic-styled, mustard-green, silver-turreted monstrosity, had collapsed.

Lauren picked up the keys between her thumb and index finger. They were icy cold. She dropped them into the tote bag at her feet.

There'd been an occurrence of some kind at Molly's hacienda a few months ago, just before she and Saul declared their undying love for each other, and Molly refused to tell either of her cousins exactly what had gone on—but she'd hinted strongly that it was something to do with the great-grandfathers.

Lauren would *not* stay at Sage Springs. Way too creepy. There was also a sense of manipulation in the air that she didn't like the feel of, shadowed by a tingling eeriness that was creeping farther and farther up her spine.

She took her focus to the road ahead. "How are the wedding plans going?" she asked, chaning the subject.

"Momma wants to rope you in for the anchor person for coverage of my wedding, but just tell her you haven't got time."

"What anchor person?"

"The person who sits at the desk and talks to the reporter."

Lauren's eyes widened. "You're seriously thinking of allowing media coverage of your wedding?"

"No way! After everything I've been through with the *Amarillo Globe* and the *Texas Portal*, and all the rumors Donaldson's developers spread about me?" Molly flashed an outraged grimace. "It's Momma's idea. Sometimes I think she's having me on—but you never know with Momma."

Marie was a life-force all on her own. She didn't need any priming, but she certainly knew how to charge up everyone around her—especially when she had a new idea or plan.

She'd started an online *Hopeless Herald* newsletter when

Molly first came home, and it had taken off worldwide as a blog. Lauren hadn't looked at it for weeks, due to losing her livelihood and the stress of all that. Donaldson's had taken offence at Molly's attempt to stop the valley people from selling their land when she'd planned her photography studio at her hacienda in Hopeless, and had spread *terrible* rumors about her.

"We're not sure what type of rumors Donaldson's will spread about you," Molly said, "but we're on the lookout."

Lauren fidgeted on the seat. "I don't like the sound of any of this."

"That's what I said when I first came home."

Molly swung the pickup off the sealed highway and onto the track to the valley, and Lauren's heart melted.

If a person didn't know the track was there, they'd miss it. It was just dirt, weaving its way through a forest of plains cottonwood until the trees thinned and the track widened and became a road.

Within ten minutes, they were well away from the hustle of big-town life.

The valley was beautiful, in an unfurnished, captivating way. Tucked beyond the southwest area of the Palo Duro Canyon State Park, many people didn't even realize it existed. That was how people got lost and stumbled upon any of the three towns in error. Or they wandered too far along the backcountry off-trail areas in the canyon and found themselves in the valley that way.

Lauren might have left Calamity Valley, but her love of their land had never diminished. The valley offered similar well-being experiences as the canyon, although in parts was lusher. Perennial springs and streams meandered through the valley, especially around Surrender. It was their own private hideaway.

No wonder Donaldson's wanted it. They were planning to build luxury cabins and houses, with amazing scenic views of Calamity land, plus the star attraction—the canyon. They'd rent these vacation homes out for a gargantuan amount and make a fortune. Hopeless might be saved, but it hadn't stopped Donaldson's approaching the people in and around Surrender and Reckless. All it would take was one town to sell up, and the rest would have to follow or face serious setbacks.

"Still ours," Molly said as she brought the pickup to a halt when they reached the fork. "We've got to keep this valley and the three towns intact, Lauren."

Yes, but what was failed business owner Lauren Mackillop going to do to help? For the first time since she'd booked her flight, she was apprehensive about more than the loss of In Need of Loving.

She took her gaze to the sign in front of them.

The Happy Hamlet of Hopeless—five miles. Turn left
The Striking Serenity of Surrender—five miles. Turn right
Reckless—five miles. Straight ahead

Hopeless had always been a happy place because Momma Marie wouldn't have it any other way. Surrender was possibly striking, but with the bar fights, it was hardly a place of serenity.

Nobody had ever been able to explain why Reckless hadn't been given a description.

"One day, we'll think of something," Molly said, having read Lauren's mind—not in an eerie way. They'd often wondered why Reckless's creative identity had been abandoned. "The Romantic Reflections of Reckless."

Lauren shook her head. "You suggested that one eight years ago and Pepper didn't like it."

"Well, she can choose something when she comes home."

Lauren laughed. "You won't get Pepper back in a hurry!" Pepper was the cousin with the most disbelief of the curse and the gift. "*I* only came back because of circumstances." Although, she was beginning to wonder about those circumstances.

"Everything has an end," Molly said in a wise, know-it-all tone. "But you won't get there without going through it."

"I can't wait," Lauren mumbled.

Molly turned right for Surrender and Lauren's stomach rippled.

"I expect you're worried about how you can help," Molly said. "That's why you've got to go see Ava. There's a lot of expectation on your shoulders. You've got to lift the curse on Surrender."

The curse she didn't believe in. She was having second thoughts about that, too. "If I *have* to do that, *how* am I going to do that?"

"Can't say."

Now even Molly was sounding like the grandmothers.

Cryptic and secretive. "Molly, this is me. Lauren. Your loving cousin. Please tell me what you know that I don't."

"I can't! Oh—did I tell you? I should get my photo studio finished in a couple of weeks. The hacienda's looking amazing now it's got a roof and Saul is out every day, helping to sort out the hiking and picnic trails between Hopeless and the canyon."

"You're changing the subject."

"Gee—you're quick on the uptake these days."

"Aren't I?"

"Hopeless is doing *so* well," Molly said, continuing with the new conversation. "Last Saturday, we had a busload of tourists."

That got Lauren's immediate attention. A busload? How was she going to compete with that? Surrender had little to offer, apart from the bar.

When they drove past the "Welcome to the Serenity of Surrender" sign and along the main street, Lauren's senses took another hit.

Her town hadn't changed a bit.

It was deserted. Not a single person on the street and only one car parked at the far end of town.

The old marketplace building was plain, whitewashed stone, with the palest pink, smoothly tiled roof, which made it look grander than it was. Surrender always had illusions of grandeur, and did well in the 1880s after the railroad came through Amarillo, but by 1912, when the great-grandmothers had been born, the valley was no longer thriving. They'd gone up and down in the ensuing decades and were currently down. Apart from the kick-start Molly had given Hopeless.

Mrs. Fairmont had expanded the plot of land next to the marketplace, and it looked like a small enterprise. Maybe she'd started selling the flowers she'd always loved growing. Mr. Fairmont was a painter and plasterer, but there was hardly any work for him in the valley.

The cabins lining either side of the main street, built twenty years ago, were still kept up on the exterior. Maybe she could live in one if she cleaned it up. They were pretty, and welcoming, with their blue and yellow painted facades.

Duggan's General Country Store was still open. Generally selling staples like milk, bread, homemade jellies and Momma Marie's famous Hopeless sponge cake. And so was the antique store—which was a junk shop, but nobody dared disillusion Hortense Lockwood. It had been the most fascinating store in the valley when all the cousins were youngsters. Dusty shelves with treasures galore, including real cowboy boots from the great-grandmothers' time, pocket watches with broken cases, chipped pearl necklaces, and feather boas. Sadly, the candlemaker's shop was still closed.

They passed the redbrick archway that had been built in the last century and was covered in the twining woody vine of a coral honeysuckle. It led to the place nobody went. Sage Springs.

"I'll say quick hellos to everyone," Lauren said as Molly pulled up, "then you can drive me to Hopeless."

"Davie's here, somewhere."

"Well, *he* can drive me to Hopeless if you refuse to."

"Guess what's actually going to happen."

"Molly. I'm not staying at Sage Springs."

"Yes, you are. I know what I'm talking about. I'm the one with the gift, remember. You don't have it. Yet."

Yet? She couldn't believe she was having this conversation! "Even if you do have the gift, you don't know how to use it," she argued.

"I'm not perfect, but I'm practicing," Molly said, getting out of the pickup. "And don't forget I'm not supposed to talk about it."

"You're the one who keeps bringing it up," Lauren said as she followed her cousin out of the vechicle.

"That's because it's exciting! I mean, look—see that guy over there? The one grabbing his gear out of the rental car? I bet he's the new saloon owner. And *nobody* had to tell me."

Lauren had spotted the car too, and as it was the only one on Surrender Main Street, and also parked outside the bar at the far end of town, of course it was likely to be the new owner. She turned to check and was about to give Molly a glib response when her heart just about slammed into her stomach.

The man hauling a large suitcase was Danton Alexandre Dubois.

He turned and caught sight of her, pausing for the briefest second. "Miss Barrett-Bernard!" he called, putting the case down and spreading his arms in welcome surprise.

"Miss what?" Molly asked.

Nerves skittered through Lauren so fast she thought she might explode. Danton was walking toward them and she had only seconds.

"Whatever I do or say, don't question it."

"Why?"

"That's Danton Alexandre Dubois. He's French aristocracy—from his grandmother's side." What the heck was he doing here?

"He's what?"

"Isn't this a coincidence?" Danton said with a smile as he arrived before them, eyes on Lauren. "I never dreamed you'd be coming to Surrender too."

"You've already *met*?" Molly asked.

"At the airport in LA," Lauren said, her nerve endings now firing.

"Some crummy backwater town," Danton had said. "Needed a change. Figured I'd get it there."

Molly nudged her sharply with her elbow, making her jump. "Aren't you going to introduce us?"

"Molly," Lauren said, her breath so high in her chest she thought she might choke. "This is Danton."

"Actually, Scarlet," Danton said, deepening his smile and adding a sheepish, slightly embarrassed laugh.

"Who's Scarlet?" Molly asked.

"Lauren!"

Lauren jumped at the booming sound of Davie Little's voice.

He grabbed her in one of his bear hugs, and Lauren clung on as he swung her around.

"¡Estás buscando grandes!" he said as he released her.

"Um... you're looking great, too, Davie!"

Davie beamed from ear to ear. "Let me introduce the new bar owner. Mark Sterrett."

Lauren's heartbeat was now racing. Mark? Plain old Mark? What happened to Danton?

"These are my honorary nieces, Molly and Lauren Mackillop," Davie said, pride in his voice.

Danton—*Mark*—swung his gaze to Lauren.

Lauren stared. What the hell was going on? And how dare he call her hometown of Surrender some crummy backwater place!

"Wonderful to see you again so soon, Lauren," Danton—*Mark*—said, with annoyingly effortless charm.

"Oh, boy!" Molly said to him, oozing excitement. "I never expected this. Welcome to Calamity Valley. Where things happen for a reason."

Chapter Three

MARK HAD HIS hands on his hips as he surveyed his new business.

The bar was ornate in parts and uncared for all around. He could envisage cowboys strolling in not caring if the glasses were clean, but as far as he knew there weren't any cowboys in the valley. He could even see a lost traveler wandering inside, hoping for some respite from the heat, a cold beer, and maybe a map so he could get out of town fast.

But genuine customers?

"What do you think?"

Mark turned to old Gerdin. "Bet this place could tell some stories."

The old man grinned and clicked his dentures. "You made the right choice, son."

There'd been only one business in Surrender up for sale. There hadn't been a choice. "I've got a nose for a bargain."

The bar was wooden, wide, and stretched the length of the back wall, with fancy beading around the edges. It needed a good polish.

Myriad bottles, covered in what looked like decades-old dust, lined the counter on the rear wall behind the bar, their colored glass and contents reflecting like dull gems in the mirror that also spanned the back wall. The bottles were pretty enough, but he made a note to get rid of their contents immediately, before someone poisoned themselves.

He moved toward the middle of the bar where a palm in a terra-cotta pot teetered on the edge. He pushed it back to a safer spot then ran a sleek frond between his fingers. It reminded him of Lauren, and the sensation she'd given him of a serene courtyard in a grand hotel, kept cool by the occasional mist of water from pipes above.

She hadn't been so cool half an hour ago.

He checked his reflection in the mirror behind the bar, which also needed a polish. He was frowning, but it was the look in his eyes he wanted to search.

Yep. He was wearing the look of a man who deserved judgment.

He'd traveled from LA on a completely different flight, with a quick layover in Phoenix. At Amarillo airport, he'd legged it to the rented four-wheel drive waiting for him. He'd wanted to get into the bar before Lauren arrived, so he could take some time to make further plans on how to deal with their eventual and certain meet up. But he hadn't quite made it due to old Gerdin and Davie keeping him in the street, relating tales about the days when things had been profitable. Not the kind of conversation they should have been having with a guy who'd just sunk a pile of cash into one of the businesses in town, but it would have been rude to suggest they take the conversation into the bar. He was supposed to be friendly, gaining people's confidence, going with the flow.

He'd almost broken out in a sweat when Lauren stepped out of the pickup and stared at him. So much for the cool, French persona. It had taken all his willpower to keep up the charming surprise of an apparent coincidence.

So he had a conscience. Well, of course he did, otherwise he wouldn't be here trying to ensure that he and Mom didn't disgrace his sisters. Because if things didn't go well, they'd both be doing time for fraud—and possibly murder.

He shuddered. How in hell had all this happened to him?

He couldn't go to the cops with his sorry tale, because if he welched on Donaldson, somebody out there might find themselves a lot dead.

He looked into the mirror again. It wasn't a two-way but that's what it felt like. As though there was someone inside it, looking out at him. Judging him.

He scrubbed a hand over his face, turned, and surveyed the large front area of the bar, split into two parts by a waist-height wooden railing.

Two men sprawled at a window table were drinking hard liquor, washing it down with a jug of beer. "Who are they?" he asked Gerdin.

"Out-of-towners. They're the types you'll have to watch out for."

Mark hauled in a breath. He had the money to start renovations so it appeared he was genuine. His own money. Like he'd used his own money to purchase the lease. He'd had a fair stash of money—hard cash he'd worked his guts out for—but it was dwindling fast. Ridiculously, he wasn't allowed to pay off the amount his father had stolen from Donaldson. Instead, they preferred blackmail. He didn't know if it was some warped sense of humor on their behalf or if there was something else he hadn't been told. But it was where he was at.

"And who are they?" he asked Gerdin, indicating three men huddled over a far corner table. They hadn't once looked up.

"That's Butch, Doc, and Kid Buckner." Gerdin sucked on his dentures. "Hard gamblers."

Mark did a double take. "They're playing Monopoly."

Gerdin nodded. "Best not interrupt 'em."

Mark continued his appraisal of the bar. In true Old West fashion, steer horns, spurs, and horseshoes decorated the walls. Three wagon wheels, varying in size, had been turned into a fancy, arty-looking chandelier over the bar, and another, ornate—although dirty—glass chandelier hung over what must have once been a dining area.

"Built in 1938," Gerdin said. "Just before the curse."

"What curse?"

"The Mackillops. They're cursed. All of 'em husbandless due to the curse. The whole darn lot."

"Is that so?" There was a lot about this information that ought to put a man off, but his interest was piqued. They were shaping up to be quite a bunch, these Mackillop women. Fortune-telling. Curses. Were they going to use all this as a drawcard for tourists? The sooner he found out and passed the intel to Donaldson, the sooner he could leave.

Lauren was supposed to be the person he got the closest to, since Donaldson's Developement believed it was she who would attempt to turn the town around, the way her cousin had in Hopeless. But he had the distinct impression it was going to be difficult to explain away the "coincidence" of LAX. Dammit! He should *never* have approached her the way he had. He hadn't blown his cover, but he'd put himself on a bit of a knife edge.

Gerdin stepped forward. "I have to say, son, getting your offer was just about the best thing that ever happened to me. Apart from my wife, Ingrid."

Mark smiled politely.

"I guess now you've seen the place, you're full to the brim with notions on how to revamp it and draw in the drinkers."

"I sure am." Closing it was the only thing that had come to mind so far.

"We were right wary about you to begin with. There's developers crawling the valley, trying to get sneaky and persuade us to sell. Sent a few men to snoop on us. One of them offered me a lot of money for the lease on the bar. But I knew straight off they were Donaldson's people." Gerdin sniffed his disparagement.

Mark didn't blink. "You let it go to me for less than you could have gotten?"

"Liked the sound of you. You've got a telephone manner my wife appreciated and I always listen to Ingrid. She's an older woman, did you know that? Got myself an older chick back in the day."

"Lucky man."

Just then, a glass smashed and a fight started. "I'll just see if Davie's still around," Gerdin said.

Mark put a hand on the old man's arm. It was thin and wiry, and although it still felt like there was some muscle tone, Gerdin was ninety-one years of age. "Let me."

"Suppose you better get used to it."

"How did you put up with it for so long?" he asked as he made his way to the window table where the two hard-drinking out-of-towners were pushing and shoving each other, getting a punch in whenever they could.

"Have to put up with the customers I'm given, that's how."

"Bar's closed for renovation!" Mark yelled, a second before grabbing the men's shirts.

Being a notch over intoxicated, both men stumbled and he had no problem dragging them to the doors.

Gerdin picked up a broom and swung it above his head like it was a rodeo rope. "Git!" he yelled, swiping at the air.

After a couple more minutes, they'd swept the men clear onto the street.

Mark waited while they got into their truck and drove out of town.

"I'll call the cops," Gerdin said. "Let them know there's drunk drivers on the road. They'll catch 'em before they hit the highway."

Mark nodded and took his eyes off the dust trail the drunks' vehicle created. The bar was at the far end of the street, so he had a good view of the town.

Spring was in the air, and as the dust settled, shimmering in the sunshine, the light falling through the branches of the plains cottonwood trees lining the street gave the town a whimsical touch. Deep red on the brick archway, pale blues and yellows on the cabins. Natural wood verandas on the few businesses. It was as pretty as the gem-colored glass bottles reflected in the mirror. It just needed a good polish.

Although why he cared what the place looked like, he didn't know.

He headed back inside the bar and looked across to the far corner where the game of Monopoly was still underway.

"What about the Buckner boys?" he asked Gerdin.

"They're like fugitives. Hiding out from real life. Eldest one worked on some building renovation that was started some years ago, but everyone ran off and it never got finished. He stayed in town. Rented a house on Water Street from Mr. and Mrs. Fairmont. Then brought his brothers here."

"What do they do for a living?"

"Whatever they can. They've got a truck, but find it hard to gain employment due to not having no proper schooling. They're wizards with their hands." Gerdin pointed to the wagon-wheel chandelier. "Made that for me and Ingrid one night after we bought the Monopoly board and set it up in their corner."

"How come they skipped the education system?"

"Their daddy was a horse's ass," Gerdin said in a hiss. "Doc, the middle brother, he had the most schooling. He can get right fancy sometimes. Big words and all."

"Thanks," Mark said, and made his way to the Buckner brothers, Gerdin following.

"Afternoon, gentlemen. Just wanted to introduce myself. Mark Sterrett."

"He's the dude who's bought the lease," Gerdin said. "The one I told you about."

The middle brother stood, a polite expression on his face. "Name's Doc. I'm thirty-seven. I'm the spokesman for the family."

"How do you do, Doc?"

"This here's Butch, he's the eldest. And this is Kid. He's just a kid."

"I'm not. I'm twenty-one."

"I'm forty-three," Butch said, in a deep bass voice, looking up at Mark.

"I'm thirty-one," Mark replied, taking the eldest brother's hand and thinking it best if he joined in with the age game in case there was some importance attached to it that he'd missed.

"If you're closing the bar," Doc asked, "can we perchance borrow the Monopoly board?"

"It's all yours."

"I'll miss my apple juice," Kid said grumpily.

"We'll get Mrs. Wynkoop from Hopeless to bring you some over," Gerdin supplied. "She's got an orchard. Four apple trees," he informed Mark.

"Impressive."

"I like my hard liquor," Doc said. "But in moderation, so I reckon I won't miss it too much."

"Man after my own heart," Mark told him with a smile, clocking the one shot glass on the table.

Butch stood. Ponderously, like a sleepy grizzly bear. "I like beer, but I limit myself to one a day. Gotta keep a clear head for the Monopoly. Reckon I can go without for the duration too."

Mark smiled. "I've heard the Buckner men are good with their hands. I might be looking to employ three good men. How would you be fixed for time?"

Doc pulled his shoulders back. "We are currently free and can be engaged in employment."

Butch nodded agreement, still expressionless.

Kid looked like he'd been given his first lollipop. "Heck," he said. "Real jobs."

"We've got a deal then." Mark shook each man's hand, something about the earnest expression in their faces incredibly rewarding.

The Buckner brothers. Possibly the nicest hard gamblers in Surrender.

They packed up their game, straightened the chairs around their table, and left.

"I'll leave you to it, then." Gerdin handed Mark the keys to the bar. "Oh, and by the way. There's a big iron gate at the end of the bar's rear yard. It's locked. Don't open it. Don't go through it."

"Why not?"

"It leads straight to Sage Springs."

"What's that?"

"It's the house where young Lauren's going to be living.

Wild Ava gave it to her." Gerdin shook his head. "That curse. It'll likely kill us all off before Donaldson's get a chance to make another move on us, or send some slimy fella down here to spy on us."

Mark maintained his expression but a little heat crawled under his collar.

Chapter Four

"THANKS FOR THE lift, Davie." Lauren only just managed to halt herself slamming the cab door as she got out on Hopeless Main Street. During the short drive, she'd become more and more exasperated with herself.

Just because she'd had a shock.

She'd left Surrender ten minutes after arriving. Fortunately, Davie had recognized her edginess and had driven her to see Momma Marie. Molly had insisted Lauren quickly tell her everything that had happened at LAX and then she'd fled back to her hacienda and her hot fiancé.

"I'll run you back to Surrender whenever you're ready," Davie said.

She gave him a hug, penitent about the frustration that had settled on her like a heavy, drab canvas. "Sorry I'm not very talkative."

"You've got a lot on your mind."

Didn't she? Mark Sterrett and his lies for one. Not to mention the lies she'd told him in the VIP lounge. Plus, a *saloon*—in her hometown!

"We can't wait to hear about your ideas for resurrecting Surrender, Lauren."

"Neither can I." Whatever she might have done, everything had suddenly changed. If she'd come home *only* facing her rundown, wall-less inherited house, she wouldn't now be wondering what the heck to do about absolutely everything else.

Davie laughed at her wry tone and clapped a gentle hand on her shoulder. "You'll work it out."

"How's business?" she asked, glancing at the window on his art and craft shop which was a riot of Mexican color. Pottery. Sculptures. Paintings. Baskets. She'd never seen the window so full.

"Going so well I've had to hire help."

"That's wonderful!" Over the years she'd known him, he'd sold his beautiful works to stores all around Texas but hardly any from his shop in town—due to nobody visiting to buy them. Mostly, she remembered him playing bouncer at the bar or bodyguard to anyone who needed looking after. Their valley really had been practically dead. Surrender and Reckless still were.

"Everyone's beginning to see some profit now," Davie said.

She glanced up and down Main Street. There was bunting in the trees, a tourist board with maps of walking and cycling trails, and a brand-new parking lot that wasn't full, but she'd never seen more than one or two vehicles in Hopeless before now and there had to be at least ten cars parked. People were wandering around town, browsing shop windows or sitting at picnic tables in a new park area, eating a slice of Momma Marie's famous Hopeless sponge cake and sipping a takeout coffee.

Hopeless had ambitions. Lauren had Surrender.

"Molly and Saul's photographic studio and hiking business has given our people employment, too," Davie said. "It's fired up enthusiasm for just about everything. Life in Hopeless is looking good."

"I'm so pleased for you all."

It wasn't that her town was in a sorry state. It was just the same old Surrender it had always been. Except it wasn't. Not anymore.

"Davie," she said, halting him as he turned for his shop. "What do you think of that Mark Sterrett guy?"

"I like what I've seen so far. Ingrid Gerdin gave him a thumbs-up, and you know how particular Ingrid is."

Should she tell everyone what she knew? That he was a liar and a fantastic kisser. If he hadn't turned up in town after wining and dining her at the airport, she wouldn't feel so uncomfortable about the part she'd played at LAX, glibly lying her heart out to a very attractive man she'd had a bit of a crush on. The focus being on *had.*

"He looks the kind that's too good to be true." That wasn't saying anything bad about him, but it was putting the question into the air, where it might hover until she got an answer. "I wonder why he chose to buy the lease on the bar?"

"Maybe the guy just needed to get away from something. Start afresh."

In Surrender?

"Call me when you want a lift to Sage Springs," Davie said, taking a step back and obviously eager to get back to his art and craft shop.

Darn. With everything else going on she'd forgotten about Sage Springs. She'd gotten off the plane with one problem—humiliation due to losing her business. Now, the problems were stacking up.

A sense of unease crept up on her as she stood alone on the street. Not about the lying Frenchman this time but about herself. She shouldn't have left Surrender just now. She should have stood her ground with the new bar owner, demanding to know what was going on. She should have made the effort to say her hellos to her townspeople, many of whom she loved dearly. She should have chosen a cabin and started cleaning it so she could live in it. Or had coffee with Mr. and Mrs. Fairmont. Or bought some groceries from Duggan's General Store.

But she hadn't. She'd run.

She made her way to the hair salon. She'd only been home an hour and already everything had gone haywire. She could do with some family comfort.

"Marie!" she called as she pushed through the multicolored strands of the plastic blind on the salon doorway and inhaled the aroma of shampoo, hairspray, and cake and coffee wafting down the corridor to the takeout.

"Sugar!"

The sound of her adoptive mother's vibrant voice as her heels *click-clacked* on the tile floor from the takeout had Lauren's heart pumping. A second later, Momma Marie appeared from the corridor, dazzling and radiant, arms spread as wide as the smile on her perfectly made-up face.

Lauren's own smile hurt her cheeks. Marie was dressed as she usually was, head-to-toe in varying shades of pink, her stunningly highlighted chestnut hair piled high on her head. Marie was 1960s all over, with a dash of modern Chanel, a whole lot of glamour, and a disarming charm like none other. Which a person had to watch out for.

Marie hugged her, kissed both cheeks then leaned back and ran her gaze from the top of Lauren's head to her Manolo Blahnik boots. "Why those developers spread a bad rumor about your cousin Molly is beyond me. Her beauty is entirely innocent and wholesome. But yours—Lauren, you have the body and the looks of a woman built for sin."

"Marie!"

"A scarlet woman, that's what you look like."

Scarlet? Had Marie heard about her experience at the airport? Only Molly knew.

"You're like one of those French models, Lauren. You're all Parisian-fied."

Molly *must* have said something. But when? Surely there hadn't been time—not with that hot fiancé waiting impatiently for her return. "I'm actually wearing other women's clothes. I don't own many of my own."

"Sugar, you'd look good in a tattered nylon nightie. Why some good man hasn't snapped you up is a conundrum."

Her whole life was a conundrum. "How come you're using such big words?"

"I'm full of them, sweetness. It's because I'm a reporter." Marie snapped her fingers. "You know what? Donaldson's might make something of your incredible good looks. I'd better put it on my list of possible rumors."

"You've got a *list*?"

"Don't underestimate them. They're not around yet, but I'm watching for the first sneaky move they make." Marie turned for the salon counter, opened the lid on a strawberry-pink laptop, then paused. "What are you doing here, anyway? You're supposed to be at Sage Springs."

"Oh, well, I, um…"

Marie sighed the sigh of a patient mother. "Sit down and tell me *all* about it."

"I'm not sure where to start."

"At the beginning." Marie settled on a stool and smiled broadly. "How was the funeral?"

Lauren flung her tote bag onto the counter. "It happened."

"Trash, that's what that man was. What were you thinking, taking him on as a partner? No! Don't tell me. I expect it was the same as Molly—running from your homes and trying to get away from the curse hoping you'd be normal. I've got news for you, sugar. You're not normal. Do you know what you've got coming? The battle of Surrender, that's what. Have you seen Ava?"

Lauren pushed out a sigh. "She's busy." She sank to the hair chair. It was *the* chair in the salon. Pink with silver trim and Momma used it for serious beautification matters.

"How do you know she's busy? You haven't been back long enough to see her."

Lauren drummed her fingers on the arm of the chair. Maybe it was time to edge into the curse, the gift—and the telepathic conversations with her grandmother she'd never told a soul about.

"Molly's insisting she has the Mackillop gift."

"And it's confusing you, and neither you nor Pepper want to believe her."

Lauren blinked. "Does that mean it's true?"

"Of course! She's got the works. The whole Mackillop ability. She just doesn't know how to use it yet."

Wow. Molly *did* have the gift. It wasn't that she hadn't believed her, more like she hadn't wanted to believe. Because if Molly had it and was prepared to accept it after all these years of denying it—did Lauren have it, and was she going to accept it too?

"Do you think having some strange ability to hold a conversation with someone in your head is a part of the Mackillop ability?" she asked.

"Undoubtedly."

Heck. Marie hadn't even paused before answering.

"Do *you* have the gift?" The cousins had always assumed Marie was the only daughter of the grandmothers who'd missed out. Lauren and Pepper's moms had it, but they were gone now, leaving only Marie, whose nurturing had always been maternal. A guiding female force in their young lives. She'd let the grandmothers explain the history of the Mackillops, hardly ever talking about the gift or the curse.

"Sugar, I'm far too busy sorting out people's lives on my blog."

"Do you believe in it, Marie?" Lauren persisted. "The curse?"

"I only believe in what's in front of me. I never look behind unless someone's following me. Get your gorgeous skinny butt up that hill to see your grandmother and ask her the questions. She's the soothsayer."

Ava lived a twenty-minute walk out of Surrender, if a person took the back route from Sage Springs. "Do you know what she's got in mind for me?"

"She wants you to rejuvenate the house in the only way you can."

"What only way?"

"*I* don't know, sweetness! I'm just making assumptions you'll come up with an idea that is the *only* idea. How do you think I managed to get fifty-nine thousand blog subscribers hanging onto my every word without prodding them now and again?"

Lauren clutched the arms of the chair. "Fifty-nine *thousand*?"

"Tell me about it! All those email addresses on file has just about busted my cloud storage. I wouldn't be surprised if NASA called me to say I was interfering with their space shuttles."

Lauren leaned forward, remembering what Molly had told her. "By the way, I don't think I'll have time to be your anchor woman, and I'm not sure we ought to be showing Molly's wedding video on your blog."

Marie brushed it off with a wave of her hand. "I like to yank her chain now and again. She's so into that gorgeous man of hers, she gets distracted when she needs to be focused." Marie paused, gauging Lauren with a slight frown.

"Talking about distractions…how was the journey home?"

Lauren hoped she wasn't blushing. "Long."

"You didn't get the feeling someone was around you at the airport? Someone you've never met before. A journalist? A guy after a story? Some odd little man?"

"No." Only Mark Sterrett, and there was nothing little about him. He had to be a couple of inches over six feet.

"What about the cops? Were they onto you for any part they think you played in that trashy business partner's worthy demise?"

"The police questioned me, but only about the 78 percent of In Need of Loving it looked like he owned. I got to keep my 22 percent, and I didn't talk too much about the gamblers he'd lost my business to because they weren't the type you'd want to annoy."

"I still can't believe he forged your signature on a new agreement."

And worse still, lost the business. He'd obviously intended selling it without her knowledge and reaping the monetary reward. If he hadn't gone gambling, she might have discovered what he'd done and been able to put a stop to it.

She edged the hair chair farther toward to the salon counter. "Did you hear about the new guy leasing the bar?"

"Pfft! Did you meet him?"

"Briefly." A few minutes on Surrender Main Street and a three-hour sojourn in a VIP lounge where they'd shared chardonnay, white fudge pretzels, and lies. It was the lies that bugged her most. Who was he? Why was he in the airport the same time as her, and what was he really doing in Surrender?

"Let's not talk about him," Marie said.

"Why not?" If he was here for some nefarious reason, her people and her family needed to know. "He's into property development. Hasn't anyone got anything to say about that?"

"He's after making a quick buck."

"In Surrender?"

"Or else he's in need of respite." Marie pursed her mouth in thought. "Maybe he's a man with a brilliant future, forced to change his life in order to—I don't know—save his family? Have you considered that before you go dissing him?"

"It's unlikely he'd be forced into anything he didn't want."

"How do you know if you've only met him briefly?"

Lauren swallowed. "I'm just making an assumption." She'd told Molly about the airport meet up but didn't want to discuss it with Marie because the whole episode now made her feel like some pathetic, lonely woman who'd been desperate for a man's good opinion.

"Find out what his plans are," Marie said. "Maybe you can help him."

"Help him? I don't trust him!"

"There you go—dissing him again. Maybe he'll help *you.*"

Unlikely.

"Lauren, you said you know nothing about him, but you're in the same position as him. Use that. You've got insider information on what it's like to change your life."

"How do you know he's changing his life?"

"Guesswork, sweetness! Momma's intuition." Marie shook her head. "Oh—let's forget him. Did you see the Buckner brothers?"

"I didn't have time to say my hellos. I wanted to ask you if I could stay here until—"

"Sweeter souls you'll never find. I hope he treats them right when he hires them."

"Mark Sterrett? He's hiring them to do work on the bar?"

"Isn't he going to call it a saloon?"

A saloon. It still got Lauren's goat. There'd be little call for fancy cocktails or wines. He'd probably hire a dozen scantily clad dancers and build a beer fountain.

"I thought you didn't want to talk about him," she said.

"We aren't. We're talking about the Buckner brothers."

"Oh, right."

"I guess old Gerdin told him about their skills, and I bet he's gone behind your back and hired them before you can."

Lauren frowned. "I'm not going to hire them."

"So how are you going to get that wall back in place on Sage Springs?"

She hadn't gotten around to thinking about it.

"You can't just let this man walk all over you, Lauren. You have to fight back."

"I don't know what I'm fighting! If he gets the saloon up and running, what happens to Sage Springs and whatever it is I'm going to do with it?" She was supposed to be the one to rejuvenate the town, not him. There was no way she'd be able to work *with* him. Sage Springs would have to shine and somehow knock his bar off the planet.

Marie flexed her shoulders. "I'll help as much as I can, sweetie, but let me tell you—I'm getting exhausted here! I'm stuck to my laptop twenty-four seven because of my blog followers. I'm in constant touch with my reporter colleagues so I can ward off any underhand play from the developers, and I'm still doing hair and beatifications—but only on Fridays and Saturdays, given the stretch of my time."

Women traveled from as far as Lubbock for one of Momma's fancy updos. She was as famous for her ability to tame and tease the most difficult hair as she was for her sponge cakes, and now her blog was taking priority, along with the necessary needs to keep the valley safe. It wasn't fair Marie had so much on her shoulders. Lauren *had* to find a way to help.

She chewed her inner cheek. One thing she'd learned from the grandmothers was that events that happened strangely or remarkably at the same time, without apparent reason, didn't necessarily make a coincidence.

Old Mr. Gerdin had sold his lease because he was ninety-one and plum tired—that was reality.

Lauren was back in the valley because she'd been blasé about her business, thinking her future was sewn up and secure. She'd been wrong and was now forced to start again from the ground up—that was reality.

But the meet up at LAX? There was room for doubt about it being a coincidence and she was sure she'd been played. Down on her luck and hooked by all the masculine laid-back charm—but if he had known who she was, why would he play her? What would he gain?

I guess I'll find out. But not by sitting around Hopeless.

"So what are you going to do?" Marie asked.

She met her aunt's gaze. "Get my skinny butt to Sage Springs." Not because she didn't have a choice, but because she wasn't going to surrender to anyone or anything ever again.

"And?"

She scooted forward on the chair, excitement spreading in her veins. "I'm going to engage and retain employment for Sage Springs's renovation so *he* doesn't use it all."

"Pfft!" Marie said. "*Him*! He won't know what's hit him."

"That's right!" Lauren said, stabbing the air with a finger.

"Then what are you going to do?"

"I'm going to rebuild the wall on Sage Springs." She had twenty thousand dollars from the pittance she'd supposedly legally been left with after what she considered to be the unlawful sale of her boutique.

"Then I'm going to do something wonderful with the house so it helps the whole town. Every single person who lives in Surrender."

This was a bit of a shady area, given the way the house looked and its reputation.

Marie sucked in a breath. "It's going to have to be good, sugar."

The first thing anyone outside the valley would suggest

was a guesthouse. *Spend the night with a ghost. Spook yourself stupid at Sage Springs—will you last the whole weekend?* But that would only be catering to the nonbelievers and fuel more gossip about Crazy Alice, Wild Ava, and Mad Aurora—who weren't witches or fortune-tellers out to make a buck but genuine soothsayers, each using their abilities to help people, not hoodwink them.

"Sage Springs is going to be a *brilliant* drawing card," she told Marie. "Not just for Surrender, but for the whole valley." Danton Alexandre Dubois had made her feel worthy in that VIP lounge. A woman of interest and maybe a little mystery. Turned out he was the mystery. But this was her opportunity to be that woman for real. "It's going to outshine and outdo *anything* Mark Sterrett does with his horrible saloon."

"Atta girl!" Marie cried as she stood and lifted her hand for a high five.

Lauren accepted it. *Smack.* Done. Suddenly she had a plan. Just like that!

She beamed, a little bemused, but with passion firing every which way.

She only hoped it wasn't going to be a case of—atta singed butt.

Chapter Fi e

LAUREN STOOD OUTSIDE the large, old iron double gates to Sage Springs, looking up at the fancy rusted metalwork.

The fascinating thing about talking to Marie was that a person left her presence filled with a renewed energy for the challenges of life—but Marie didn't give definitive advice, she somehow suggested. That was a true gift. No wonder she had fifty-nine thousand blog followers.

"There's starlight and wonder awaiting you," Marie had said when she dropped her off five minutes ago. "Go get it, sugar."

Lauren took her focus beyond the gate and up to the evening sky.

The stars were out in the dusky night, seemingly just sitting around, doing their thing. But they weren't, they were moving, and living, and exploding and traveling through space at great speed.

What could they do, the great-grandfathers? Ava wouldn't send her into the house if there was danger, but there had to be trouble waiting. Trouble Lauren was meant to sort out.

The curse had been on their heads for years and she was forced to accept there might be some truth to it. But had Molly really ended it for herself and her hometown? Or only dented it? She was engaged to be married—but the wedding hadn't happened yet. Her photography business wasn't fully up and running and neither was Saul's hiking business. There were still a few weeks before the grand opening of both. Anything could happen in that time. Which meant Lauren had to make her plans for Sage Springs and make them fast to help deter whatever trouble was lurking out there. The better armed against the great-grandfathers or the developers, the more chance the Mackillops had of coming through whatever storms were heading for them.

She shivered, the air colder now, and dropped her tote bag on top of her suitcase, then took one key off the ring of three.

"How come you're not talking to me in my head?" she asked her grandmother.

"Maybe I don't like the conversation you're having with yourself."

Lauren found a smile. *"I'm at the gate. I've got the key in my hand."*

Ava didn't answer.

"I'm going in. I might not come out alive, and it'll be your fault."

"Watch your back, Lauren."

"Hello, Scarlet."

She almost jumped out of her skin at the sound of Danton's voice.

She spun around and glared at him, hoping her heartbeat couldn't be heard because it was pounding in her ears. "I think we can end the pretense—*Mark*."

He gave her a slight shrug. "At least we'll always have the memories of the Champs-Élysées."

And a shower of spring rain, with a flurry of umbrellas a moment before he kissed her.

His voice might be as low and mellow as a tumbling brook but any cozy, romantic thoughts she'd had about him were dead in the water.

"Why did you do it?" she asked.

"The pretense? It was fun. Why did you do it?"

"Nothing better to do." She wrapped her thin shawl more securely around her throat and turned her attention to the gate, thrusting the key into the lock, but it refused to turn.

"Want a hand with that?"

"What I'd like is for you to get off my property."

"I'm standing on the boundary of *my* property."

It was a demarcation line too close for comfort. She glanced over her shoulder. "What are you doing out here?"

"Taking the evening air, then I saw you here at the gate and thought we ought to have a little talk."

She looked him dead in the eye. "I'd be grateful if you didn't mention how we met at the airport or what happened." It was best to get that said upfront. There was little value in everyone in town knowing they'd already met. It would fuel rumors and she had enough on her plate.

"You mean the memories we made together?" he asked,

his brown eyes teasing. "What's so wrong with what we did?"

"People might take it the wrong way."

"Do you always worry about what people think?"

"You would too if you were a Mackillop."

"So you're brushing me off because you're trying *not* to live up to your family's reputation." He gave her a hesitant smile. "I've heard about the grandmothers."

"You leave them out of this. There's nothing wrong with them."

"I didn't say there was."

"And you?" she asked. "I suppose your family doesn't have a reputation. I suppose your family is flawlessly well-respected."

He didn't move a muscle, but she thought she saw a momentary darkening of his eyes.

"How did you make up the French name?" she asked when he didn't respond.

"Dubois *is* a family name, on my mother's side."

"What about Suzy Fletcher? The girl you were in love with."

"Absolute truth. What about you?" he asked, tilting his head. "You told me you came from a big family. You said you were an only daughter with five brothers."

"I knew you were lying, so I lied too."

"You didn't have a clue I was lying—and I wasn't, remember? Granny Dubois existed and so did Suzy."

"Suzy had a narrow escape, and I bet Granny wasn't a true Frenchwoman. So where did the names Danton and Alexandre come from?" This was her chance to ask as many questions as possible and seek out the truth or catch him out on a lie, and she was going to take her opportunity.

"I made them up. What about Scarlet Juliette?"

"Just a make-believe name from when I was a kid. How come you were able to make up French names so quickly?"

"I'm a writer. I make things up all the time. Why did you need a make-believe name when you were young?"

"Because I was a little girl! I liked fairy tales and precious things, like plastic pearl necklaces and grown-ups' high-heeled shoes."

"I liked Scarlet."

They stared at each other in the depleting light. What had he seen in Scarlet that was so different from Lauren, the real woman?

She really ought not to care.

She returned her attention to the key stuck in the lock, jiggling it hard.

"If you're not going to let me help you, you'll be sleeping under the stars. Here." He shrugged off his bomber jacket.

"Why the sudden courtesy?"

"You mean I wasn't courteous in the VIP lounge?"

She'd felt the onslaught of many emotions when she'd been with him in the lounge. Like it was okay to run wild across a field, or tap dance down Main Street, and not give a damn what others thought. Things she'd done as a child but never as a woman. She hoped to regain that touch of devil-may-care spirit one day, but there'd be no singing and dancing until she discovered what he was up to.

"I don't trust you," she informed him. "Just so you know

where you stand."

"Fine, but come on. You're cold."

Without waiting for a response, he draped the jacket over her shoulders.

The heat from his body warmed her instantly. There was the merest fragrance in the leather. Aromas of bergamot, mint, green grass, and fresh mountain air. It smelled like adventure; strong, earthy, masculine. It smelled of money, too. More money than Lauren had at her disposal. Could he really turn the old bar into a profitable saloon?

She cringed. He'd ruin the ambiance of her town, the one Surrender already had beneath its rundown state, the one they were going to enhance. However they were going to do that.

"I'm not sure I'd trust anything around here," he said, reaching for the key in the lock. "I've been hearing all sorts of things about the town and the valley. Gerdin told me about the property developers trying to buy your land."

"They're offering way below value. They're trying to steal it, not purchase it."

"What do you think these developers are going to do next?"

"What's it to you?"

"I've just bought into the town—there's a lot at stake."

"You didn't know about them?"

"Nobody said a word before I signed the lease."

Suddenly a cell phone rang, vibrating against her hip.

"That's mine," Mark said and shoved his hand into the jacket pocket, pulling out his phone.

Lauren stepped away, her heartbeat a little fast. Under other circumstances, she'd welcome a little body-shock reaction to the slightest touch from an attractive man she'd kissed, but not now that she knew who he was—or rather, who he wasn't.

"Sorry," he said as he stuck the phone in his jeans pocket.

"You aren't going to answer it? Don't mind me." Whoever it was, his slight pause between looking at the caller ID and deciding not to answer made her wary. What was it Marie had made up about him? *Maybe he's a man with a brilliant future, forced to change his life.*

"What are you really doing in the valley?" she asked.

"I'm snooping on you. I'm writing a novel about your town. I'm going to turn the bar into a flower shop. Take your pick."

He got the key unstuck and pushed it back into the lock.

"Did you know who I was?" Lauren asked. "At the airport?"

"I took a lovely lady named Scarlet to a late supper in a VIP lounge." The key turned with a groan, and the iron gate creaked open.

Mark handed back the key. "Want me to see you to your front door?" He nodded at the other two keys in her hand. "They're large. What sort of house is it?"

"One without a wall. One with a curse. One that's haunted by my great-grandfather. Take your pick."

A shadow of a smile played on his mouth. "Can't we be friends, Lauren?"

"I don't make friends with people who are up to no good."

"I'm surprised you've got any true friends, to be honest, since there's a curse on your head. Gerdin told me that, too. Is that why you came home? Is there going to be trouble?"

"I came home because of a company called Donaldson's." She waited, but he didn't flinch, blink, or move a muscle. "They're mean, underhand sharks."

"I'm more interested in the curse." He stuck his hands in his pockets. "Tell me about it."

"Why?"

"I like a good story."

Was there someone around you at the airport? Marie had asked. *A journalist? A guy after a story?*

"What sort of books do you write?"

"I write other people's books."

"So why suddenly buy a bar?"

"I'm looking for a change."

"And you chose a crummy backwater town?"

His smile held a chagrined apology. "It's actually not so bad. Certainly not from where I'm currently standing."

His flirting gave her an instant reminder that she'd wanted to kick off her shoes and relax while she was with him, like any woman might do while getting acquainted with a man who oozed warm, masculine sensuality in bucketloads.

She looked away. She had to stop remembering the occasion that way. She no longer had a crush on him.

"I'd like to be friends," he said. "Especially as our properties are so close. If you're planning to open a business, we might need to come to some agreement about access."

"There's a dedicated access road to my house. Nobody need set a foot on your saloon property."

"Yeah, but it's the long way around. Quicker if people use the land at the rear of the bar. I'm a little worried about what you're planning, too. If you're going to open a hospitality business, perhaps we can join up in some way."

She almost laughed out loud. "I wouldn't join two pieces of bread together to make a sandwich with you."

He grimaced. "This isn't going well, is it? I think I liked us better when we were chic aristocrats from Europe."

"The only thing I liked was the pretzels."

"Ouch." He took a step back, hands in the air. "Okay, I'll quit trying to make friends with you. From now on, I'll watch my back, you watch yours."

Darn right. And here was something to make him twitch.

"By the way," she said sweetly. "My great-grandfather built the bar. So don't joke about the curse on my head, because you might have just bought into your own curse."

She grabbed her Louis Vuitton and walked through the gate, dragging the suitcase behind her. "Good luck with that," she called as she made her way up the gravelly driveway without looking back.

A FEW MINUTES later she was standing at the bottom of the steps to Sage Springs house, trying to focus on her next task. It had been one hell of a twenty-four hours. She was tired, longed to soak in a bathtub of hot, bubbly water, and knock back a glass of wine.

She tapped the heel of her boot on the ground as she studied the lead-glass front door.

She was going to go in—she was. In a minute.

She glanced up at the house towering above her. It should have a romantic feel with its three-story steeply pitched roofline, its double turrets, brick chimneys and fish-scaled shingled spire. But the sickly green paint on the weatherboard along with the mustard-colored patterns and cuts of the access trims made a person want to turn around and go somewhere else.

What on earth was she going to do with it?

It was Victorian in most parts, and nothing more than a showcase of her great-grandfather's wealth. He'd been a fancy pants. Except it had been the Mackillop family's money, not his. He'd inveigled his way in, like all three great-grandfathers had done. They'd fathered, then run off when the going got tough and hadn't gotten their own way.

She released a sigh.

The house looked like someone had transported it here and set it down because it was too heavy and too cumbersome to cart any farther.

Her heart melted a little. *Poor old house.* There was a ballroom inside. Only a small one, but she'd danced in it as a girl, sneaking into the house with her cousins and playing out fairy tales.

She gripped the keys in her hand, lifted her suitcase up the steps and rolled it across the floorboards of the wraparound porch until she got to the front door. Which was open.

What are you frightened of? Ghosts can't hurt.

She pushed the door wider.

Lamps were glowing and the aroma of sage infused her nostrils. Marie must have lit the lamps earlier that day. At the far end of the hall, the kitchen door was open, and the pine table held a bowl piled high with fruit, an oval china dish with a flynet over it, which was most likely supper, and what looked like a boxed Hopeless sponge. Undoubtedly, a vanilla cake with a white-fudge frosting—her favorite.

Sage Springs was named for the bushes that led to the waterfall by the lake and Marie had placed dozens of branches of sage in old tin and glass vases and bottles, the herby aroma taking away the musty smell of dust and cobwebs. Nobody went to the lake anymore. The only way was through Lauren's fenced and gated property, down a long winding trail that began at the far side of the house, and nobody came to Sage Springs. Not after a man was nearly killed here.

She'd always thought the grandmothers decided to attempt renovation of the three houses six years ago because they'd known trouble was around the corner with the developers. But had they been working to a different plan? All three cousins had left after that, determined to find a new life away from all the name calling. Each of them wanting to be someone other than a "wacky Mackillop."

Was it the curse that had drawn her and Molly back? Or were the grandmothers up to something?

She parked her suitcase and dropped her tote bag on top of it, then walked down the hallway. She paused outside the open double doors to the ballroom where she'd twirled in her borrowed high heels, catching glimpses of herself, hair flying, in the mirrored sections on the paneled walls.

The house hadn't frightened her then. She'd snuck inside many times, either with Molly and Pepper or on her own. It had been her turreted hideaway. What young girl with a vivid imagination wouldn't want it?

She turned from the ballroom. What was she feeling, back inside again? No chill. Nothing eerie or untoward encroached on her senses. Instead, a kind of awe spread through her.

Starlight poked into the house. There wasn't an outside wall on the right-hand side of the imposing staircase that led to the first story, so she could see the stars. It was as though they were inside with her.

Somebody had hung clear plastic sheeting over the gaping hole, the cracked and broken bricks and plaster hanging behind the sheeting like flotsam on some shipwreck. Davie had done that, probably.

Her family had welcomed her home with bunches of sage, gentle lamplight and weatherproof plastic sheeting. Molly, Marie, Davie. She might not have her mother, but she wasn't without family. Even the townspeople were her family.

And her grandmother.

It was late and she should get something to eat, find out which bedroom had been made up for her, take that bath and try to get some sleep. But she wasn't going to do that.

"Ava?" she called mentally. *"I'm coming to see you."*

"I know," Ava replied. *"Don't forget to grab a jacket. It's cold this evening."*

Lauren started as the fragrance of Mark's cologne, entrenched in the leather of his jacket, encompassed her. She'd totally forgotten it was draping her shoulders, warming her.

Chapter Six

AVA LIVED IN a two-room stone cabin, with four picture-perfect windows, two at the front, two at the rear, and a yellow-painted front door. But she spent most of her time outside, sitting on the Adirondack chairs by her fire pit and her cauldron of magical stones, gazing over the Palo Duro Canyon.

Heading up the valley walls on the rough track to her grandmother's cabin in the sky had always been a climb filled with expectation. Of stories, of teaching, and of some arguing too, as Lauren got older and a little teenage angst had shown up. But her grandmother had always fed her spirit, not dampened it.

She paused beside the cabin. She'd always been able to inhale the wonder up here. It had the same effect now for the woman as much as it had for the child. Not that she could see the canyon—it was too dark—but the sun would rise, revealing four geological layers of a bronze vista, glinting as it came to life, waiting to stun its visitors with the hues of an earthy-colored rainbow.

She really had come home, and this whole valley was her home, not just the town she'd been born in.

She'd lived in Surrender until she was ten years old when her mother died, then with Marie in Hopeless but, when she turned seventeen, Ava said she was responsible enough to live on her own in Surrender. She'd rented Mr. and Mrs. Fairmont's house on Water Street. They were fancy enough back then to own two properties. But now, they'd rented the house to the Buckner brothers, and Lauren wasn't about to kick those sweet gentlemen out.

She'd worked for just about everyone in town. The general store, the candlemaker, Hortense's junk shop—her favorite, although she never got out of the place without being covered in dust.

She switched off her flashlight and pocketed it in the checkered wool coat she'd found in the wardrobe at Sage Springs. It was Molly's, so Momma must have dropped it off with all the bedding and food.

Walking toward Ava, she didn't call out. Ava knew she was there.

She had an old copper cauldron, fixed above her fire pit, hanging from a chain on a tripod. The fire was never lit, even in winter, although the earth was always warm around the pit, and the air tepid, like a slow end to the first day of spring, as though the sun's warmth didn't want to budge now that it had shaken off its blanket of winter.

Lauren glanced at the cauldron, filled with stones—which moved. Although nobody saw them shift. A certain stone would settle on the surface and be poignant to the person who was seeking guidance. They could blink and where a gray stone had rested, nestled by others, a small purple-hued rock would be in its place.

"I saw Marie earlier," she said as she settled into the Adirondack chair next to her grandmother. "I was all charged up."

"What happened?"

"I had an argument with someone." She smiled. "It's lovely to see you in person," she said as she leaned across the narrow divide to kiss Ava's cheek, which was paper thin and as smooth as one of the stones beneath the waterfall at the lake, sluiced with the clearness of continuous falling water. "Although it's not like I got clean away from you," she added with a tease. "You've been doing a lot of talking this last month."

Ava smiled and tugged at the brim of her Texas Longhorns cap. She lifted one jean-clad leg and rested her boot on the rim of the fire pit, hands together on her stomach, her long, thin fingers interlaced. "You'll have the ability to talk with your own granddaughter in the same way we do."

"Don't forget I'd have to find a man to help me make a daughter before I got a granddaughter."

"Or he's got to find you."

"And then he's got to stay."

Ava nodded at Molly's coat. "What happened to the one you were wearing?"

Lauren shifted on the chair. "It was borrowed." She'd give it back to Mark tomorrow. "So, I suppose we need to talk about the saloon owner."

"The man you argued with."

Lauren nodded at the hessian bag tied to Ava's belt.

"What do the runes tell you?"

"They're telling me there's a woman sitting next to me who thought her independence and business acumen would define her as a woman of merit and worth, but who made an error in judgment and has now lost her courage."

Well, that was to the point. "I was trying to forget all that."

"You have to face it, not forget it."

Lauren looked out to the canyon. Even up here, in the darkened night, its spiritual power reached her and she had a need to be truthful.

"I met him, Ava. At the airport. I told him I was someone else."

"Did he lie too?"

Lauren scrunched her nose. "Not exactly." He hadn't told her which crummy town he was doing his property developing in because they'd made a pact not to talk about why they were going to Texas, and she had to grudgingly admit he probably did have a French background, from Granny Dubois. But still. "He's going to be a problem."

"He's got his own troubles. You might want to cut him some slack."

"Do you believe he's here to change his life?"

"No, because he's not. But changing his life is what he'll end up doing."

Just the thought of living in the same town as him for the rest of her life was enough to make her shudder.

Ava lifted her other leg to the wall of the fire pit and crossed her feet at the ankles as though settling in for a nice little chat. "Why did you lie about your business partner's death to that little bald man?"

"Because he deserved to be shot in the back. Choking on a chunk of pineapple doesn't have the same ring to it."

"I told you not to trust a man who says he can solve your problems unless he first proves to you he can."

"He talked about process improvement and implementing new procedures."

"You got scammed. You're a spiritual person. There are scammers out there who prey on people like you."

Lauren leaned on the arm of her chair. "That's why I want to talk about this new bar owner."

"You and he are intertwined."

"I know! He's opening a saloon, and I haven't got a clue what I'm going to do with Sage Springs."

"Santa Ynez," Ava said with a scold in her tone. "LA. California. It was the wrong place for you to sell your second-hand gear."

"It was hardly 'gear.'" Lauren pulled Molly's coat around her a bit tighter. "So, shall we talk about the guy who bought the bar?"

"What does he make you feel?"

Vulnerable.

"I knew he was coming," Ava said.

"I wish you could say you knew when he was going."

Ava chuckled. "I do, actually."

"What?" Lauren sat up straighter. "When?"

"Can't say."

Lauren slapped the arm of the chair. That meant she

knew but *wouldn't* say. "Why am I the only one worried about him?" First Marie didn't want to talk about him, now Ava.

"Could be because he sees the real you, and as you don't know who the real you is anymore, he makes you feel exposed. Weak. At risk. Scared out of your fancy Manolo Blahnik boots that you're going to mess up again."

Lauren burst out laughing. She couldn't help it.

Ava laughed with her. "That's better."

"I guess I'm not comfortable in any man's company right now," Lauren admitted. She also better woman up and admit she might now believe in the curse, or, at least, see how it might have come about and the notion of it stuck. "The great-grandfathers—they can't really do serious damage, can they?"

"They can, child. They're a dark force."

That wasn't the answer she'd been hoping for. "Is Molly safe?"

"She's learning how to protect herself and her man."

Her man. Lauren's gaze drifted to the cauldron of stones. "I can't imagine that kind of happiness."

"You can't imagine it because you haven't got it on your wish list."

One big thing on her list right now was the question of what to do with Sage Springs. "Marie mentioned something about me heading into the battle of Surrender."

"There are any number of sorry souls around us, and each of them might be heading into some sort of battle. You'll be the one to bring that battle to us."

"I wouldn't do that!"

"Not intentionally, but growth means upset. You'll need help."

"Can't *you* help?" She hated asking, but when in need, why not use the family connection to fate and all it portended? If she knew what was going to happen, she could arm herself against it before it even looked like occurring.

Ava recrossed her feet at the ankles. "If I were able to do that, I'd have gotten rid of the great-grandfathers long before now."

"What happened at Molly's hacienda? Did they visit? Did they try to hurt her?" It didn't seem possible that ghosts could do such a thing.

"It's not your time to hear answers. You've got to find your own questions first."

"That's so cryptic, it's not funny."

"Everything has an end."

"But we won't get there without going through it." It was what Molly had said too. It must be a soothsayer's expression. "Do you mean you can see the end, but you're not sure how the middle is going to pan out?"

"You're catching on quick, child."

She glanced at the cauldron as a glint from the moon rested on a green stone. "Does that mean something?" The stone was larger than the others, which were varying shades of ochre, granite blue, and lavender gray, and she was sure it hadn't been there before.

"It's not for you."

"Who's it for?"

"Never you mind. Let's get back to the matter at hand. You need to trust someone. I'm sorry to tell you it's a man."

"I trusted a man in Santa Ynez. Look where that led me."

"It led you home."

"Are you talking about Mark Sterrett? He won't solve my problems. He'll create more." He already had.

"Try. You might be surprised." Ava glanced Lauren's way, her olive-green eyes all-knowing. "What wildness of spirit will you discover inside yourself now that you're back, I wonder."

Lauren pushed out a wry laugh. Her mother's death had hurt like the sting of a whip, but Ava had struck a deal with fate. She had the motorbike fixed and had ridden it everywhere since, whether to get supplies from town or to visit her sisters. Nothing frightened her. She took fear and squashed it by facing it. Lauren wasn't sure she had the same makeup as her mother and grandmother.

"Your momma had the gift, just like me," Ava said softly. "Almost exactly like me, and we crossed swords occasionally but never for long."

"Do you miss her?"

Ava nodded. "Life is a battle, Lauren. Each day, each minute—even when we're smiling."

"I'd like to laugh again. I had dreams once, and I can hardly remember what they were, but they made me happy. Maybe I'll find them—once I figure out what to do with Sage Springs." She glanced at her grandmother, hoping for a suggestion.

"The only way our town will survive is through you.

You've got work to do."

Lauren rested her boots on the rim of the fire pit and crossed her feet at the ankles.

Problem was, this meant she had to play nice with the saloon owner and she'd just gotten him offside.

What if she got everything wrong, like she had with her boutique and the business partner? What if Sage Springs never operated as a business to begin with because she couldn't think of what to do with it? What if Mark's business was better than hers?

She shouldn't have argued with him. The professional way to handle it would have been to remain aloof but open-minded. How else was she going to discover what he was up to?

As her mood tumbled, she noticed the green stone had disappeared, and in its place was a white, diamond-shaped stone.

She reached for it.

Ava shot forward and took her hand. "If you take it, you have to keep it. It holds your wishes."

Lauren closed her hand around the stone, taking possessions of it. It was meant for her, and maybe its power would help her make all the decisions she needed to make.

"You're forgetting about your wishes," Ava said. "You can't make anything work without hope, or a wish, and maybe a prayer."

Lauren shook her head. "I don't know what I want. It's all gone wrong."

"You misplaced your loyalties, that's all. You'll find your wishes. Someone will show you."

She must mean everyone in Surrender, all the people Lauren had grown up with. They wanted their town to do as well as Hopeless. They were feeling left out and wanted to shine. Were they putting their faith in Lauren?

"Do you mind if I stay tonight?" She felt closer to family here. Closer to her mom.

"I'm not going inside," Ava said. "I'm staying here."

"I'll stay out here with you." She lifted the collar on her wool coat and settled back in the hard, wooden chair.

Ava picked up a cushion from the ground, beat it on her legs to get the earth off, and handed it to Lauren.

Silence filled the night, until Lauren's eyes tired of trying to see into the dark, and into the future, and she let her head fall back on the pillow.

It was still warm and there was a kindness in the air.

She was drifting to that safe place where bears didn't growl and wild dogs didn't bite when she felt the warmth of a blanket fall on her, and her grandmother's hand brush across the top of her head.

"You're not alone, child."

But she was. Deep inside her. She swallowed loneliness every time she took a breath.

Maybe she was already asleep and dreaming, but the vision in her head was vivid. She was looking up at a man whose obvious adoration of her was reflected in his brown eyes and his steady smile. He took her hand and held her fingertips, then drew them to his mouth and kissed them, never once losing eye contact with her.

Mark Sterrett.

Chapter Se en

MARK THREW DOWN the polishing cloth, stepped back from the counter beneath the mirror, and studied his work. Not bad. Dust free and he'd kept a few of the now empty colorful bottles with fancy labels, since they enhanced the look of a saloon.

"You're getting a clean too," he told the mirror. Or maybe he'd take it down.

He'd had the strangest vision of Lauren earlier that morning. *In* the mirror. He was tired, yes, and a lot stressed, but the hazy images through the smears of grime had looked real and had sent shivers down his spine. Was there a curse in that mirror?

He didn't scare easily, and plenty guys would laugh, but Mark wasn't plenty guys. He was a writer, and his brain sparked at any possibility of a story.

Or it had, until recently.

He kept his eyes on his reflection. Did he look like his father? Not on the outside; Mark favored the Duboises on his mother's side. Tall, broad-shouldered men and tall, lean-limbed women. But on the inside? Did he have any of his father's traits? He hoped to hell not.

Johnson Sterrett was a typical older man wannabe playboy, with more chutzpah than ready cash of his own. He'd lived in Bermuda for the last decade, enjoying balmy breezes, any woman who was looking for some holiday love and willing to pay for it, and working as a property manager for Donaldson. *The* Donaldson, the reclusive multi-millionaire who owned more than one property development company in America. Donaldson was a wannabe philanthropist. Seemingly a great guy. Unless someone crossed him. Or stole from him.

Over the last two years, Mark's father had embezzled close to a half a million dollars from Donaldson, and now Donaldson was playing with Mark. Taunting him. He'd set up a crime scene in California and planted enough evidence to see Mark's father, Mark, and possibly his mother, convicted of fraud and murder. All that was missing was a dead body and an anonymous call to the cops.

Mark thumped a fist on the counter, making the bottles rattle. He was the one who'd detailed this plot. It was *his* crime. He'd given the setup and the scenario for what he thought was a screenplay and handed it over to a man he'd communicated with only on the telephone, until he'd been given an email address in order to send the screenplay—which was now closed down. No physical address. No personal meetings. Just a guy with a booming Texas accent.

Foolishly, he hadn't been concerned about the secrecy. There were plenty of would-be writers out there who liked to test the waters without getting their feet wet. Get a ghostwriter to give them a plotline or a full storyline, and take the glory for it—*if* it sold.

This one wouldn't sell. It had been a ploy from the start. But it might play out for real.

Donaldson wasn't interested in the money Johnson Sterrett had embezzled. Donaldson wanted revenge, and he'd chosen to use Mark and his mother as his means to get it.

Mark wasn't having someone's death on his hands or his conscience which was why he'd had no alternative but take this job, but he'd walked right into this mess like a schmuck. He'd even enjoyed writing the murder scenario and had put his all into it. Now, he had to get out of this situation, and somehow protect not only his mom and his sisters—none of whom knew what was going on—but also the people here, in Surrender. Because Donaldson's men were vicious, given what he knew personally about their tactics.

He wandered to the coffeepot he'd put on at six a.m. and poured the last of a dark brew, adding sugar.

His buy-in to enter this poker game was the biggest he'd sat down to. He wasn't at a friendly five-dollar table, with fifty bucks at stake—he was playing with the big boys. He was all-in. Every chip he owned in the pot.

Who were the Mackillop women? What were their strengths and weaknesses?

When he first approached Lauren at the airport she'd looked unnerved about something. When Davie had formally introduced them, she'd shown surprise and unease, but there had been a glint in her eye that made him wonder if she was going to start a fight right then and there.

He blew out a breath, pissed at himself for telling her last night he'd watch his back and she'd better watch hers. She was supposed to be the one he got closely acquainted with.

He picked up his cell phone from the bar. It was time to call in. He couldn't let it go any longer, but he'd report his findings carefully, without giving anything away. Not that he had much intel on the Mackillops yet, but one of them had gotten under his skin.

He wasn't used to having a conscience, having never done anything to intentionally hurt someone. Now here he was, getting embroiled with the nice Buckner brothers and the dull sparkle of Surrender. But what real harm could he do the people here by discovering their intentions for the town and reporting it? Surrender had survived. It was a bit broken up, but still here. They'd sorted out Hopeless, from what he'd been told. Could Donaldson's seriously coerce them into selling?

It was Mark's job to ensure they did.

He hit the recall button on his cell and waited three rings before Boomer—the nickname he'd given the man he spoke to—picked up.

"Where were you last night and why didn't you answer my call?"

"I was getting better acquainted with the woman I'm shadowing."

"Get as well acquainted with the little lady as you want to. Women tend to give out all their secrets in the bedroom."

Boomer's deep, rough laughter put his teeth on edge.

"I called you twice this morning too. Where were you?" Boomer said.

"Taking a leak."

"Don't get smart or someone will get hurt."

"You stay away from my family." His mother and sisters didn't know where he was; they thought he'd dropped into California on a whim and had gone back to Laredo. But his mother had been a little suspicious when he'd questioned her about the car.

Three weeks ago, she'd won ten thousand dollars cash and an imported SUV worth around forty. She didn't remember entering the raffle, but as she entered any number of them for charity, she didn't think anything of it and was thrilled with her win. She didn't check where the ten grand came from when it hit her bank account either, because it was deposited by a company with a charitable name. A fake company. It came from an account Donaldson set up in Johnson Sterrett's name. Mark's hardworking, family-loving mom sold the car, banked her additional forty thousand, then shared her money, giving some to her daughters and a lot to her charities. Mark hadn't wanted any; he'd had enough of his own money.

If Donaldson went ahead with the murder and placed that anonymous call to the police, they'd find Johnson Sterrett's fingerprints, along with Mark's signature on the setup for the crime, and now also his mother's seeming acceptance of fifty-thousand dollars, all of which originated from a fake charitable company run by her thieving husband.

It was unbelievable Donaldson would spend another fifty grand—and God knew how much more—after losing nearly half a million, just to get his revenge.

"I've been here only one night," he told Boomer. "I haven't got any intel; I'm calling in to advise you of that. You have to give me time."

"There is no time, Sterrett. We're sending a posse down, and we'll be setting up a property development campaign board in front of the bar."

"You can't do that! How am I supposed to make it appear normal? I've just arrived in town."

"You'll think of something. Advise the numbskulls we're there to be friendly. Give us a good word."

"I'm not supposed to know anything about Donaldson's."

"Use your brain. You're a writer. Plot your lies in the bedroom with the leggy brunette."

Mark gritted his teeth and tasted bile.

"Get close to her," Boomer said, his voice taking on a low-toned, aggressive growl. "Discover what she intends to do with that blowhole town."

Mark threw his phone onto the bar when Boomer cut the call. It slid along the now polished top and crashed against the potted palm. He grabbed it before it fell and pocketed it.

Taking his coffee outside, he wandered along the wooden veranda and leaned his forearms on the railing, forcing himself to calm down.

There was some activity on Main Street this morning. A lady in a wide-brimmed straw hat was tending the flower patch next to the marketplace building and talking animatedly to a man wearing painter's gear.

The few businesses were open. A general store, which sold flowers but not decent coffee, so he'd have to drive into Amarillo to get some. A junk shop with a fancy title of Hortense's Antiques. An old place with a broken sign, Candlemakers, which looked like it hadn't been open for a decade. And the redbrick archway, with a faded, lopsided, cracked wooden sign saying Sage Springs and the Waterfall.

He was going to have to attempt rejuvenation of the bar, but along with some interior reno work, what else would a keen businessowner need to dc to get the townspeople on his side? Offer them something. But what would middle-aged and elderly residents want? There weren't many young people around. So far, he'd only come across Kid Buckner. What was there to keep anyone alive and kicking in Surrender?

He pulled himself up. He was supposed to be snooping on them, not figuring out what they wanted.

A movement caught his eye.

Lauren walked through the redbrick archway, his jacket draped over her arm, and headed for him. The archway led to her house, and to some waterfall, but he hadn't used that track last night. He'd gone out the back of the saloon, wanting to see where the two properties met. The end of his land, the beginning of hers.

She was wearing jeans again today, with a thick, black leather belt and a soft white shirt. She had a lemon-colored long scarf wrapped around her throat, the fringed ends ruffling against her thighs as she walked. She was tall and slim, with an elegant gait, but she wasn't smiling and there was power in her stride.

He'd kissed her at LAX. He hadn't intended to—it just happened. Why the hell had he done that? She wasn't his type.

He picked up his coffee. "Morning," he said as she got closer. He wasn't able to gauge her mood from her moss-green eyes because she had her sunglasses on.

She came to a stop on the other side of the railing. "Thanks for the loan of your jacket," she said as she hooked it over the top rail.

"You're welcome."

"Are you hiring the Buckner brothers?"

He paused, caught off guard by the unexpected question. "Is there a problem with that?"

"Only that you got to them before I could."

He threw her a smile. "So you've got plans for Sage Springs?"

"They're under wraps until I've sorted out the various aspects and how it's going to affect everyone."

"Makes commercial sense. But the offer to chat about business propositions is open, regardless of what I said last night."

"I'm not in the least bit interested in partnering up with you."

"You might be, if my business takes off and yours pales by comparison."

She laughed, as though surprised by his effrontery, and it was so genuine sounding, Mark smiled with her.

He tipped his coffee mug her way. "At least we're talking." He'd imagined he'd be the one doing the chasing today, but she'd walked right over. She needed something from him. Cooperation? Or was she worried about what his business might do to hers?

"Actually, I do see sense in discussing *your* plans," she said, "and how they might affect mine."

Bingo.

He raised his eyebrows. "So it's all about you?"

"You won't stick around. I'm here for good."

"And what makes you think I won't stay?"

"Intuition. What are you intending for the bar?"

"I'm keeping my plans under wraps too. You open up, then I'll open up."

He gave her the chance to fold in this verbal game playing, but she didn't—she didn't know what she was going to do with her house any more than he knew what to do with the bar.

"Let's get back to the Buckners," she said brusquely. "I want to hire them too."

"To do what?"

"Fix a staircase and build a wall. If you give them any grief about taking on additional work, like firing them, you'll be answering to me."

All her lean-limbed gracefulness could fool a person. He had little doubt she'd haul a forty-pound bag of cement mix across a worksite without any trouble if she had to.

"But I hired them first," he said.

"I suggest you have them one day, and I have them the next."

At least they were negotiating. "That's going to double the time it'll take to renovate Scarlet Sage Saloon."

Her draw dropped.

Mark's almost did too. He hadn't even thought about renaming the place until now.

"You can't do that!" She took a step back. "My house is Sage Springs, and the lake and the waterfall have the name Sage in them too. Are you trying to be funny?"

He put his coffee down and leaned his hands on the railing. "Look, let's not fight about it, but let me get this right. You're going to take my builders, just because you think you have a right to. You're going to open a business that backs onto my property. We're the only people in Surrender who are interested in growing a commercial enterprise, and you think you're top dog. As far as I can see, you want it all your own way. That's not fair."

"Life isn't fair!"

She'd gotten that right. But it was time to try a different angle. "Why did you return home, anyway? What made you come back here?"

"My business partner ruined me before choking on a chunk of pineapple. I love my town. I haven't got anywhere else to go. Take your pick."

"Lauren," he said patiently, "I think we need to sit down and discuss our plans, professionally and politely."

"Why?" she asked, her voice barely there. "Why Scarlet?"

"It just came to me," he admitted in a voice equally soft. He gave the moment a beat. "I haven't spoken to anyone about Paris. You asked me not to." Perhaps she was feeling humiliated about their interlude at the airport, but if she'd just laugh it off, it would help make him feel better about his hand in the duplicity.

She licked her lips and glanced away. "I *can't* trust you," she said, almost to herself.

"You won't know if you can trust me until we both let up a little."

He hadn't known about Sage Springs, and perhaps the developers didn't either, because they hadn't mentioned it. Only that she had about twenty thousand dollars and was undoubtedly going to start some business, so they'd sent him in to grab the lease on the bar before she did.

He'd wandered back to the boundary of Sage Springs late last night and walked through the still-opened iron gates. The house was a monstrosity in the moonlight, with its turrets and silver-tinted spire. The sort of place where Victorian potted palms and dainty teacups would feel right at home.

"Come on—let's give in," he pleaded. "Or we'll be fighting it out on the street."

She lifted her sunglasses and pushed them onto the top of her head. "We might just be doing that."

Her moss-green eyes were luminous in her face, and in an instant, he was captive.

"Wild Ava," she said, "my grandmother. She knew you were coming."

Mark hauled himself out of the daze. Was she bewitching him? "I'm looking forward to meeting her."

She gave him a rare smile. "Be careful what you wish

for."

He desperately wanted to scrub a hand over his face, and somehow release himself from whatever hold had gripped him. How could this Ava possibly have known he'd arrive in Surrender? Unless there was some truth in the abilities of these grandmothers.

"Lauren, let's sit down and talk. Let me help solve some of your problems."

"Hah!" Her eyes flared as she pushed out a laugh, but it was a hollow sound. "*That*," she told him, "was the wrong thing to say."

She turned and marched toward the center of Main Street.

Mark slapped the veranda rail. If only he *hadn't* approached her at the airport. But it was no use crying over spilled milk. He had another problem now. If she talked about him to her townspeople and tried to put them off him, he was going to have a difficult time persuading everyone he'd just been contacted by Donaldson's—out of the blue—and had agreed to have their campaign board outside the front door of the bar. He wasn't supposed to know who Donaldson's was, but Lauren had spoken about them last night, telling him what they were up to, so he couldn't spin that one.

He took a deep breath.

He'd met only a handful of the townspeople and thought he'd gotten along with each of them, but how was he going to appear genuine when this news got out?

Chapter Eight

LAUREN WAS OUTSIDE Duggan's General Country Store saying her hellos. It was the best place to catch everyone. If she personally visited one person before another, she'd be accused of favoritism.

"Saw you talking to the new bar owner just now," Mrs. Fairmont said as she shifted a bunch of yellow roses from one arm to the other. "What's he like? He's *very* handsome."

Lauren managed a smile.

"I'm dying to meet him. Do you think he'd mind if I just knocked on his door? He's closed the bar for renovations."

"Oh, go ahead and bang on the door," Lauren said. "Why not get a group of women together and take him cake?"

"How exciting that he's arrived! I wonder how he's going to change the bar?"

"We won't find out until we all ask. By the way"—she fished out a check from her back pocket—"here's another four months' rent in advance. Just between us, Mrs. Fairmont. As usual."

"Haven't said a word. Not in all these years. Those

Buckners, they're good tenants."

Lauren didn't pay the whole rent for the house that had once been hers, just half. She felt responsible for the Buckners, since work on Sage Springs house had been put on hold because of her great-grandfather's ghostly apparition, and the brothers had gotten stuck in Surrender.

"Shame they can't get more work," Mrs. Fairmont said. "I blame their daddy. He was a real horse's ass."

Lauren smothered a laugh at polite Mrs. Fairmont's words. "Horse's ass," she agreed. "But they'll be getting quite a bit of work now. I'm hiring them, and so is he." She flicked a thumb toward the bar down the end of the street. *Let me help solve some of your problems.* Huh. Who did he think he was, the Lone Ranger?

"And what have you got lined up for us with the house?" Mrs. Fairmont asked.

"Ideas are spilling out of me!" she said with a smile.

"I just hope we get as many tourists as Hopeless. Imagine that!"

She had trouble envisaging it, but nodded.

"I'm hoping my husband will see some employment too."

"Oh, he will! I'll need a painter and plasterer for Sage Springs—and I'm sure the new bar owner will need his services too. Pop a business card off to him. In fact, why not collect everyone's business cards and drop them all off at once? We don't want him employing people from outside the valley."

Mrs. Fairmont paled. "Oh, dear. I'd best get onto this

right away."

"And forget about the cake," Lauren said. "He said he prefers savory. His favorite is highly spiced chili—with beans."

Mrs. Fairmont's eyes widened in astonishment. "*With* beans?"

"As many as possible, apparently," Lauren said, then added a shrug. "Not a true Texan, that's the problem."

Mrs. Fairmont rushed off toward her house on Water Street, and Lauren fingered the diamond-shaped white stone she'd put in her pocket. For luck. She had no doubt the women in town would try to get into his good books by cooking him what they thought he'd like. By the end of the week, he'd be drowned in spicy chili with multi-colored beans.

Scarlet Sage Saloon. How dare he! He'd done it on purpose.

Maybe she'd have to open a haunted house after all, just to get something up and running fast. Except there weren't any lingering souls waiting at the house when she'd returned earlier this morning, just the aroma of sage and the sun shining on the clear plastic sheeting covering the lack of a fourth wall in the hallway. Later, she'd unpack and settle herself in. Davie had carted all her old stored belongings to the house. If she spread her things around, it would feel more like hers.

The air cracked in her ears and, no more than a beat after, she was in another place.

Sage Springs, in the attic space, but it wasn't the house as she knew it. It was light and lived in. She could even smell wax polish.

Mark was at a desk that used to be in the hallway. There were open books spread around him, about Texas and the Palo Duro Canyon, and about saloons, the Old West—and Calamity Valley.

In the vision, she wanted to approach him as he frowned over his laptop, reading what he'd written, but with a familiarity the real Lauren didn't understand knew he needed to work in peace.

"Lauren Mackillop!"

Lauren came out of the vision with such a big jolt, her aviators fell off the top of her head.

She put a hand on her chest to still her heartbeat. What was happening to her? Her imagination was in overdrive! She'd have to find some way of destressing or she'd end up in hospital.

"Lovely to see you again, Mrs. Gerdin," she said shakily as she bent to pick up her sunglasses. "You're looking well." At ninety-three, she looked amazing.

Ingrid crossed her arms over her scrawny chest. "What are you going to do with the house?" She was stick thin and angular, with a mop of white hair that curled around her large ears. "I'm hoping for something happy and productive. Maybe some dancing."

"I'm putting my business plans into place—"

"Well, don't take all week. We need to show Hopeless what we've got. They're pretty stuck-up right now, full of their success."

"But we don't want to be in competition with them—"

"Saw you talking to Mark earlier."

Lauren stepped closer and lowered her voice. "What do you think of him?"

"*Very* handsome. Utterly charming."

Was that really all they saw? "You don't have any regrets?"

Ingrid paused, her mouth twisted in thought. "I've gotten used to our lazy ways in town, and truth be told, there was hardly any upkeep needed for the bar, so I don't miss it too much, although having Gerdin home all day is driving me insane." She let out a sigh. "I just wish I could use my brain now and again."

Lauren wished hers would work faster.

"The men have got hobbies and workshops and whatever for when they retire or for when they haven't got work," Ingrid said, "but we women just have housework whether we're employed, unemployed, or retired. It's not fair. You know what I mean?"

"I do." And it wasn't fair.

She took her focus to the main street.

Surrender was quaint. It could be elegant, with a bit of work. She could see bookshops and quiet cafés working nicely. But they were now going to be hosting a saloon. What was that going to do to prospective businesses or those already established? It might overshadow everything with its gaudiness and loud music.

Regardless of what the town already had or could offer, would he charge in with his bold ideas without giving the slightest thought for Surrender's residents?

She couldn't let that happen.

"Mark wants to know everyone's opinions on what to do with the bar," she said to Ingrid, "and whether or not you all really want a saloon."

Ingrid slapped the palms of her hands together. "I knew that man wouldn't let us down. Knew he was a good sort right from when I took his telephone call about the lease."

"He's a little worried it'll make him look like he can't make up his own mind if he asks us what he should do though."

"Typical man! Wanting to do it all himself."

And in his own way.

"This is what I call excitement!" Ingrid said. "Me and old Gerdin have got the money from the sale, and now we've also got the chance to use our brains and express our opinions." She glanced at Lauren. "You don't think he'd mind?"

"Not at all," Lauren said. "Express away!"

"Oh, good heavens," Ingrid said. "Here comes Hortense. I'm off. Don't forget now—I want happiness, I want to use my brain, and I wouldn't say no to some dancing."

"It's all on the list!" Lauren assured her as Ingrid loped off at a great speed, given her age.

"What was *she* talking about?" Hortense Lockwood said with a scowl.

Lauren produced her loveliest smile. "We were discussing the new bar owner and his saloon."

Hortense made a grumbling noise. "He needs to draw decent men into town, I hope he knows that. I'd like a choice of between the ages of thirty and fifty-two. Me, I'm only thirty-three and a quarter, but I'm not choosy if they're younger or older."

Hortense had been twenty-five when Lauren was a kid, and a real flirt, but kind with it—it was Hortense who'd given her the long string of plastic pearls. She was just occasionally on the antagonistic side. Then her boyfriend left her and her world collapsed. She'd been thirty-three and a quarter ever since.

"You need to talk directly to the new owner," Lauren told her. "Let him know exactly what you're hoping for. He said he could do with some input from us. You know, general ideas about how the bar can be redecorated. I think he's going to pull down all the furnishings and just have bare white walls."

Hortense grimaced. "Modern."

For a second, Lauren thought she was going to spit on the ground.

"You might want to have your say, Miss Lockwood."

"I will. Don't you worry. Where's he from again?"

By the look of her drawn, plucked eyebrows Hortense was beginning to think it might be outer space.

"Not sure, but he's not a Texan. He loves chili, spicy—but with as many beans as possible."

"Beans?"

"A few of the women are getting together to make him some."

Hortense pulled a frown. "I don't cook. Look at these hands," she said, holding them out. "They're ruined due to all the artifacts I'm constantly shifting around the shop. Nobody would want these hands to have cooked anything."

Hortense was always clearing the heaped shelves to make room for more stuff she found in the cavernous back storeroom. Where she'd gotten it all from, nobody knew. Although her mother had been a traveler and lots had come from overseas.

"I don't want to miss out if everyone's going over to the bar to discuss what he's doing," Hortense said.

"You won't!" Lauren assured her. "If he's moving stuff around, you're the person who can tell him exactly how to do it, and if he's decluttering, you might want to buy some things off him for your antique shop. But don't pay over the going rate, Miss Lockwood. He's not a real Texan, remember."

Hortense pushed her hands into her trouser pockets and grinned. "Never known it so hectic in Surrender. Pretty soon, we'll be getting busloads like they do in Hopeless and my shop will be thriving. I can practically hear the cha-ching of my old till."

Oh, dear.

"What business are *you* going to be delving into with the house?"

Lauren scratched her head. The way things were going, it was likely to be The Ghostly but Happy Dancing Dating Restaurant—with hand massages on the side.

"Uh-oh," Hortense said as a bright pink camper van drove into town with bold wording on the side panel.

MommasHopelessBlog.com

Lend me your ear!

Marie threw a cheery wave out the open driver's window. "Morning, sweetie! Hortense, honey—you look like you've been pulled through a mesquite hedge backward."

Lauren tensed. Marie and Hortense had never seen eye to eye.

"Don't 'honey' me," Hortense called out as Momma got out of the camper van. "There's men coming to town. I'm the one likely to catch one and keep him. You Mackillops lose all your men."

"At least we still have our beauty," Marie said sweetly as she walked toward them on raspberry-colored kitten heels.

"Miss Lockwood is hoping the new saloon will bring lots of decent, single men our way," Lauren explained.

"I'd definitely like to make my choice from those men," Hortense said. "But there's others coming. Haven't you seen this morning's *Texas Portal*? Donaldson's developers are planning to come to town—and they're not the sort of men I want to see."

Lauren forgot all about hand massages and dating agencies. The *Texas Portal* was a rag distributed all around Texas, mainly full of classified ads, but they loved to splash tacky news on the front page. They'd spread horrible rumors about Molly, which they'd gotten from the developers. What could they possibly be saying about Surrender and where could they have gotten a story from?

She glanced at Marie, who looked like she didn't know what this was about, either.

"Look at the time," Marie said, lifting the sleeve of her Chanel-style jacket and examining her watch. "I have to check my blog. Come on, Lauren."

"Try some coconut and lavender oil on your hands," Lauren said to Hortense as she backed away, following Marie. "It works wonders!"

Lauren climbed into the camper van, ducking her head, but it had a pop-up roof so she could stand up straight. "I don't think you're supposed to drive with the roof popped up, Marie."

"We haven't got time to worry about that now! The *Portal*!"

"You haven't seen it yet?"

"Haven't picked up today's newspapers yet. I've been busy gathering stories for my blog." Marie typed fast on the keyboard of her laptop that sat on a desk. "It must have happened while I was driving. I need a hands-free laptop system!" She glanced at Lauren. "Do they exist? Or have I just invented one? I wouldn't put it past me."

"There it is!" Lauren said as the laptop screen fired up with the front page of the *Portal*.

Wackiness on Our Doorstep Once Again

The residents of the weird and eerie town of Surrender in Calamity Valley are seeking to rebuild their town's image. Donaldson's Development is heading to town and taking their army of salesmen with them.

The oldies of Surrender will sure get their permed curls in a knot over this one.

It should be a good fight! Texas-style.

"Oldies? How dare they? And I haven't got short-range plans."

"Sugar, you haven't got *any* plans."

"How do they know we've even gotten to a planning stage?"

"Oh," Marie said, waving a hand distractedly. "Word gets out. But Lauren, did you read it all?"

Lauren bent to the screen again.

Meet Donaldson's developers at the Surrender Saloon.

Lauren slapped the desk so hard, the laptop bounced. "You've *got* to think he's up to no good now!"

Marie raised a hand. "Don't cast a man as guilty until you know for sure he is."

"I spoke to him just ten minutes ago, Marie, and he said nothing about them turning up in town! And last night he approached me outside the gates of Sage Springs after you dropped me off. He wanted to know what business I'm planning but wouldn't tell me the first thing about his own plans. I mentioned Donaldson's to him."

"And?"

"Poker-faced, as though he'd never heard of them."

"And the very next morning, the development company he's never heard of is planning to camp out on the veranda of his bar." Marie tapped her finger against her mouth. "Truth is, I'm a bit sad about all this. I was hoping he might turn out to be the man of your dreams. No! Don't scoff. How many good-looking men have wandered into the valley in the last six years? One—and he's Molly's."

"How could you possible think I'd be interested in *him*?"

"Stranger things, Lauren—and we know how many strange things go on around here."

They were beginning to slap her around left, right, and center.

Maire closed the lid of her laptop. "I'll speak to him, but I don't want to go in hitting him hard, and then spend the rest of my life apologizing, so tell me straight—are you sure you can't see him as man of your dreams?"

"Positive. Decisively so."

"Because every woman has a man of her dreams, Lauren. They don't always read the signs or even get to meet the man. Sometimes they're a figment of an overactive imagination."

"I've met this man. The signs are negative." Man of her dreams! Although, he was in her visions, those strange moments when she was carried elsewhere. But that *had* to be stress.

"What should I do?" she asked. "Should I call the *Portal*? Should I call Donaldson's?"

Marie patted her hand. "Let me deal with the press and with Donaldson's. I'm not going to let anyone spread rumors about you, either. At least, not ones that will stick."

"What can they possibly say about me? They don't even know I'm here."

Marie colored up. "I might have blogged about you yesterday. Your homecoming and all the trials you're facing."

"You *what*?"

"It's a new reporting angle I'm trying. There are a lot of

people out there, all over the world, begging for my help."

"I wasn't actually one of them."

"You're so touchy about people knowing personal things about you," Marie scolded.

"You didn't mention my business partner and losing my business, did you?"

"Of course I didn't!"

That was a relief. The press would have a field day. Nobody would trust her ever again. She'd be a laughing stock. Mark would be in his element, the whole of Surrender at his feet.

"You just concentrate on your plans for Sage Springs, sugar, and let me handle the press. I understand how they think."

"The press at the *Portal* doesn't think. They act on any absurd thing they hear. And I'm no closer to having a plan than I was yesterday."

"Sugar, the solution is all around you. Are you listening?"

Lauren paused, but there was only white noise in her head. She hadn't expected such intensity to get the town rejuvenated so quickly. She hadn't thought at all! And she hadn't expected to see Danton—*Mark* ever again. "I'm lying to the townspeople about plans I haven't got, and everyone's talking about what they want and what's best. It's a mess."

"It's a battle, all right. Sorry souls, that's what our people in Surrender are. You need help. A deputy sheriff. Someone who can rally the troops on your behalf. Leave it to me. I'll find you one."

"I think it's best if we don't involve anyone else." They

were currently up to their elbows in subterfuge and lies. If she didn't put a stop to Marie's interference—well meant or otherwise—they'd be up to their necks.

"We're all involved, sugar. Everyone in the valley is under threat until you get your brain into gear." Marie slapped the desktop. "You've got to get this Mark Sterrett on your side and discover how he knows Donaldson's."

Lauren winced. "Might be too late for that." Any moment now, Mark would be surrounded by vats of chili and people asking him for work or offering suggestions for what he should do with his bar. "I thought I'd have more time," she said, fisting her hands at her side. "More time to think. More time to plan."

"You mean you hoped for more time to smell the roses!"

"It would have been nice to have a tiny, miniscule break from everything that's happened to me!" Now she'd have to bend. Not a little, but a lot. She'd have to apologize to Mark for being curt, which he'd see as unprofessional. She might have to own up about the chili. She could see him now, watching her, his brown eyes teasing as every word she uttered gave him the upper hand.

"I'll talk to him," Marie said. "Leave it to me."

A rush of panic whooshed through her. "I'm not sure that's the best idea. He's very good at lying."

"And I'm good at getting information out of people. Good job the advertising on my blog pays so well." Marie straightened her jacket. "We reporters always need something in our pockets to pay off informants."

"You're going to pay him to tell you what he knows?"

"Not with my hard-earned money." Marie picked up a cake box from the desktop and marched to the door. "Don't worry. I know what I'm doing."

"Marie! Wait!"

Was she doing the right thing by letting Marie handle this? She could talk to him herself and accuse him outright. But he'd shut up and she'd get nothing out of him. Especially once the chili started piling up and his visitors began telling him what they wanted and how he should go about doing it.

She didn't have much choice. Maybe Marie could pave the way. "Just don't tell him anything personal about me."

"Pfft," Marie said. "As if I would!"

Chapter Nine

MARK PRESSED THE heels of his hand to his eyes. He hadn't had a drink, but maybe he needed one.

This is not real.

So how could it be happening?

He let his hands fall and looked into the mirror behind the bar.

It was still happening.

In the misty rivulets of years-old dirt and some sort of cloudy haze, a little girl about eight or nine, with long, chestnut hair tumbling around her shoulders, was dancing.

Lauren.

She wore high-heeled, rose-colored shoes that were too big for her, and had a long string of pearls around her neck. So long, the single strand was touching her knees.

"This is absolute craziness." He couldn't possibly be seeing this, except it was right before his eyes.

The door of the bar opened with a bang against the wall. He turned fast, ready for anything untoward, and looked straight into a woman's piercing green eyes.

A ghost? They didn't normally wear fake Chanel—did they?

"Can I help you?" he asked after clearing his throat to find his voice.

"Honey, I'm hoping so."

It spoke. Ghosts didn't do that—or did they? He glanced at the mirror, but the vision was gone. Maybe he ought to get his eyes tested when he was in Amarillo picking up decent coffee.

"Chocolate sponge with strawberry cream cheese filling," the woman in pink told him as she put a cake box down and slid a cake knife out of the side flap. "I'm Momma Marie Mackillop." She pointed the knife tip at him. "You can call me Marie."

It was Lauren's aunt—Molly's mom.

He ran a hand through his hair while he gave himself time to get his act together. "Nice to meet you. You live in Hopeless, don't you?"

"You'll find me wherever I'm needed."

"Davie told me you make the best cakes in Texas."

"I dabble in a lot of things, when I'm not reporting for my blog. Now, here's the thing, Mark."

He hadn't given her his name, but by now, everyone in Calamity Valley would have heard about the new guy buying the lease on the bar.

"Where are you from?" Marie asked. "Who are your family and why did you decide to move to Surrender?"

He took a breath. *Stay as close to the truth as possible.* "I needed a change. Family issues. I'm not getting along with my father."

"At least you have a father."

He wished that wasn't the case. "He didn't stick around."

"Neither did mine." Marie threw him a light smile. "You'll have heard about the curse on us Mackillop women by now."

Her eyes were green, like Lauren's and Molly's, but they were also sharp and sassy.

"I don't hold any credence with it." It didn't seem polite to admit he'd been wondering about it—along with the possible curse on his bar.

"You should," Marie told him. "It's true. Look at Lauren. She's got to be the loveliest woman alive, don't you think? But can she find a man?"

"Is she looking for one?"

"Pfft! The *right* one, Mark—can I call you Mark?"

Hadn't she been calling him by his first name since she walked through his door?

"She's a willow branch in a storm, a delicate flower, like all we Mackillop women."

He didn't get the notion Marie was delicate in any way whatsoever, regardless of the rosy, feminine look from head to toe. She was a straight shooter, and possibly a wily one.

"She needs a man who understands her, Mark. Her roots. Her rhyme. Her reason. She's a Mackillop. That means something around here."

Was Marie warning him off Lauren? There was no need. There was currently an apparition of an eight-year-old Lauren in his mirror, scaring the socks off him. Not to mention the living Lauren—a very attractive lady but not his type—who hated his guts. "I can assure you—"

Marie held up the cake knife, its tip facing him. "Never make assurances you can't keep. Just like I won't color a man guilty until he's had the opportunity to prove his innocence."

Ouch. What was going on here?

"I know about men like you, Mark. You've got so many opportunities in front of you you're not sure which door you want to walk through."

Right now, he ought to walk out the front door and never look back. But he didn't have the pleasure of options. "Best opportunity for me is this bar," he said, with a smile.

"You mean your… *saloon.*" Her lips puckered around the word as though she were about to bite it off and chew it up.

"Not a raucous saloon. I think you've all had enough of bar fights. I was thinking more—" He hadn't thought at all. "Well, to be honest, I've had a number of ideas but not a particular one that grabs my attention."

"There's only one thing you can do with the place, and I trust you'll come to that same conclusion."

Couldn't give me a clue, could you?

"Some people say there's a curse on this bar," Marie said, glancing along the countertop—and at the mirror.

Something that felt like it had eight legs in hobnailed boots took a walk down his spine. "Would they be right?"

Marie turned a serious look his way. "There's only one curse to worry about, and its name is Donaldson's Property Development."

She paused, maybe waiting for a reaction. Mark didn't give her one.

"We're on the lookout for a real shady character. A low-life. No doubt pretending to be someone he's not."

"I'll keep an eye out for him," he said, offering her a frown of concern.

"You'd best do that, honey, because whatever he's got planned, he's out to ruin Lauren."

If anything, he wanted to solve Lauren's problems. He might as well, since he was stuck in town while attempting to solve everyone else's! Except her problems were in direct contrast to his little problem—blackmail.

The blade of the cake knife glinted as the sunlight streamed through the windows.

"What's all this about you allowing Donaldson's to set up a campaign on the front veranda of your saloon?" Marie asked.

That stumped him. How did she know? Boomer had only cut the call a half hour ago. "I'm sorry, Marie. I'm not sure what you mean."

"It's all over the *Texas Portal.* Donaldson's is visiting Surrender, apparently with your blessing."

Damn them! They hadn't even given him a chance to get his story right.

"They called me this morning," he said. Talk about thinking on his feet! "I didn't realize it would be such a bad thing."

"Oh, it's a terrible thing, Mark. They're duplicitous. They've probably wound you round their little fingers."

It was more like a noose and his neck was in play, not his fingers. "They said they wanted the opportunity to meet people."

"When are they arriving?"

They hadn't told him. "I don't know." He stepped forward. "Look, if they're coming anyway, it won't matter where they stick their campaign table, so let them use my veranda where I can keep an eye on them. I mean, what can they do? You've gotten Hopeless up and running, from what I've heard. I'm sure Surrender will follow."

Marie stared at him for what felt like an eternity.

"You see that plant down there on the counter?" she asked, nodding to where he'd placed the potted palm. "Are you the kind of man who can nurture things that need tending and care about people who have gotten lost? Because that's the kind of man we need in our valley."

She was really boxing him in. He didn't even own a house plant apart from two plastic ones his apartment's previous owner had left behind. "I'll do whatever it takes to help our town. I've got a stake in it now, too."

"Don't forget that, Mark. Because otherwise, you're going to lose everything."

That was already looking like the truth. He *did* have to ensure the bar worked as a viable opportunity, because when this was all over he had to sell the joint to recoup some of his money. The only way to do that was to sincerely help the town rejuvenate, which was what Marie was asking.

He pulled his shoulders back and attempted to ignore the heat gathering behind his shirt collar. His life had just gotten even more complicated. Helping the townspeople put him in a great position to know what was going to happen, and a bad position regarding the real reason he was in town—to tell Donaldson's what they were planning.

"What can I do to help?" he asked.

Marie bathed him in a warm smile. "Well, Mark, since you ask…"

Chapter Ten

"WHAT HAPPENED?" LAUREN asked when Marie stepped inside the blogmobile.

Marie took off her jacket and draped it over her desk chair. "He's a charmer. *Very* handsome."

"Yes, but what did he say?"

"He said he likes you. He thinks you're a smart woman and hopes you can both get over your differences. He's really sorry about that, by the way."

"Is he sorry about letting Donaldson's use his bar?"

Marie stuck a hand to her heart. "He's beside himself! He said if he'd known how bad the feeling was, he'd never have allowed it."

Lauren grunted.

"Give him half a chance, sugar. If Donaldson's is using him, he'll be roped in good and hard."

They were going to be camping on Mark's front veranda. Which meant Lauren had to stick around, too, to make sure he didn't say anything about whatever it was they'd eventually be doing to rejuvenate the town. It was imperative Donaldson's didn't get a whiff because they'd try to ruin their plans. Not that she any plans yet, but—

A memory struck. Before she'd gone to LA her original intent had been to stay in Texas and settle in Dallas, believing the city to be the place where she'd lose herself in the crowds and eventually discover the real Lauren. The woman without an unusual past.

There'd been this cute three-room building for lease on the edge of Bishop Arts District. She'd wanted it from the moment she spotted it, empty and forlorn. Its owner had passed away and there'd been a fight over who was taking on the lease.

She'd known the moment she saw it exactly what it needed to fit in with the quaint hideaway and the rhythm of the district that was heavily populated by women, all in shopping, relaxation, and curiosity mode. All looking for the next best thing, many thinking they'd never get it.

She couldn't afford the startup costs, and back then she hadn't had the required acumen or retail experience the stakeholders wanted. But she'd still put forward her proposal.

In Dallas, she'd found a wish. A dream for her future. A desire to work toward.

Then lost it. Because of a board made up of men who had no foresight and thought of her as nothing more than—a woman.

Could she rekindle the Dallas idea and shape it to work in Surrender?

"Who are these Donaldson men?" she asked. She knew next to nothing about them and she'd better arm herself now by learning as much as possible.

Marie brought up their website on her laptop.

"That one," she said pointing to a broad-smiling man with jet-black hair, "is Leonard D'Prichia—" She bent closer to read his surname, then shook her head. "Some fake Italian guy. We call him Leo D'Pee. Now that one," she said, pointing to a man whose mouth and eyes were so thinned and narrowed he might have been doing an impersonation of a shark, "is Ty 'Slick' Wilson." She scrolled down. "There's also a Bob Smith, but we don't know anything about him, and there's never been a photo of him up on their website."

Bob Smith? The name sounded familiar.

"He's just an underdog," Marie said. "He probably does the accounts or something."

No matter how many underdogs they had, they were trouble, and the townspeople were going to be demanding more amenities for prospective tourists. She'd have to think more broadly than just what she was going to do with the house.

"We're going to have to be careful, Marie. I don't want our townspeople getting sidetracked by anything Donaldson's offers as a bribe." She didn't want them to get close enough to smile at any of her townspeople, let alone offer them incentives to sell their land.

"Dear Mark came up with a brilliant notion of how to get around that," Marie said. "He's going to let them use his veranda for their campaign—and I honestly don't think he's got a choice—but he's going to stick to them like glue and make sure they don't get a chance to trick anyone."

"And what is *dear Mark* really doing in Surrender? Did you ask him?"

"He has a little problem with his father, and he needed to get away to clear his head—and let me tell you, my mother's intuition told me he's under serious pressure."

Like having to ensure his lies weren't discovered. "What's he going to do with the bar?"

"He's going to let the townspeople help him figure out the best way forward."

Lauren's mouth dropped open. Wasn't that exactly what she'd put into play? Not that it was supposed to have helped him, quite the opposite, but suddenly, everything was at cross-purposes. It would just be her luck if it turned out dear Mark *loved* extra-spiced chili swimming with beans.

"How come the townspeople aren't helping me with ideas for the house?" she asked.

"Because they haven't thought about it. But funny you should mention it. You know, just standing next to that very good-looking man, I discovered ideas popping into my head, one after the other."

Uh-oh. Lauren crossed her arms and waited.

"Sugar, I found you your deputy sheriff! Mark said he'd happily be your second-in-command. You and he are going to hold a town meeting, and together you'll sort out everyone's needs."

"We're *what*?" Lauren uncrossed her arms, shoulders tensing. "That means I'll have to practically work *with* him!"

Marie flung her hands in the air. "How else did you expect this to work? By magic?"

"It would help!" She covered her eyes with her hand and gave herself a minute to think. Before Molly took control of

Hopeless, all the valley residents were keen to sell due to the sweeteners the developers were throwing at them, like free white goods and other fancy wares. But now that Hopeless was basking in some glory, Surrender and even Reckless wanted the same. What if the developers upped the price they were willing to pay for the land? If one town sold, it would be the end of the whole valley. The last thing she needed was disjointed communication between the towns.

"The town meeting is a good idea," she said to Marie, "but I want you to know I'm not happy about his involvement."

"Keep him close, that's what I say."

There was sense in that, too. Marie was certainly popping out the good ideas. Thanks to dear Mark.

"I'm in charge of the meeting though," she said to Marie, to clarify. "Yes?"

"He's just your backup. He's happy for you to take the lead. I promise, sugar—next time you see him he'll be eating out of your hand!"

MARK HAD MORE than one headache and would have loved to get out of the bar to inhale some good, fresh Texan air. The place didn't feel like his with everybody hanging around or wandering in to see how progress was going.

They'd brought sustenance, too. There was a pot of extra-spicy chili bubbling on the stovetop in the kitchen—crammed with a variety of beans, some of which he hadn't known existed. No one in their right mind would eat chili with beans in Texas. He'd been in the Lone Star State long enough to know and was comfortable sitting on the no-beans side of the fence, so why think he would want them? And so many of them!

He also had a pocket bulging with business cards. People he was supposed to employ. What could a florist and a junk shop owner do for him? As it turned out, quite a lot. All he needed now was for the candlemaker to walk through the door and he'd be convinced the bar had no need of electricity.

"I think you ought to consider a jukebox," Ingrid said, feather duster stilled mid-air. She'd arrived earlier to tell him she felt bad about leaving so much dust, and to offer him examples of what he might do with the bar.

He'd never met a woman like Ingrid. She'd been a synchronized swimming star in 1935 and had shown him every coordinated move she'd ever made, advising him to imagine she was in a swimming pool, when in fact, she'd been on the other side of the bar, standing on one leg, knee bent, with only the other leg and her head and arms visible.

He wasn't sure he'd ever remove the image from his head.

"I'll think about it, Ingrid."

"It could go in that alcove over there, if you take out the shelving and replaster the wall."

"Good opportunity to employ my husband," Mrs. Fairmont said.

Another cost. They were mounting up. But diplomacy was the order of the day, so he kept his mouth closed. What did it really matter what happened to the bar?

It was *his* money paying for it all that was what!

He figured the floral arrangements Mrs. Fairmont was designing for the many copper and brass spittoons might set him back—what? Fifty bucks? A hundred? How much did flowers cost?

"What are you going to do with that?" Ingrid asked, indicating the dining area across from the bar, cordoned off with a waist-height wooden railing.

"I've got a few ideas." Not that he thought any of them would be listened to, so it was good he actually didn't have any.

Be grateful for the little things.

"Gonna share 'em at the committee meeting?" Ingrid asked.

He wasn't supposed to be getting this involved, but Marie had told him that was what he was going to be doing. Being on the Rejuvenate Surrender committee would put him center stage, high on a dais, and he'd wanted to keep close to the ground. No chance of that happening fast. Not now.

"When is this meeting?" Doc Buckner asked. He was up a ladder, removing a large moose head from the wooden staircase paneling above the bar. Nobody had wanted to take it down until Mark argued it would frighten the kids.

That had sent another round of questions his way about whether he was going to be offering family entertainment. He didn't know; he'd said it off the cuff. But it wasn't a bad idea to include space for kids, say, in the dining area. There was also a big rear garden.

But what was he thinking? That would mean more money on kids' play equipment.

The other Buckner brothers stopped what they were doing and waited for Mark's answer. Butch was fixing new signs to the restrooms. He'd found them in the junk shop. Miss Lockwood had come over earlier and started moving the ornaments and furnishings around. Then she'd asked to buy some and Mark just handed them over. What did he want with more wagon wheels, saddles, and spurs? But she'd gotten riled at the thought of being a charity case, so she had taken Butch over to her shop and he'd come back with more gear than Mark had originally gotten rid of. Like the spittoons.

He glanced at Kid, the quietest person in the bar, and wanted to hug him.

Kid was scrubbing the mirror. Hopefully washing away the curse while he was at it.

"I'll be talking to Lauren about the meeting," Mark informed everyone. "It's going to be a fantastic opportunity for you all to air your thoughts." Marie had put him in charge of generating enthusiasm, as second in command. She'd said Lauren knew all about it, but he wasn't sure Marie hadn't played him.

Wouldn't be the first time.

"I'll get that jukebox alcove cleared now," Butch said, pacing the floor with his ponderous stride, a sledgehammer over his shoulder.

One slam and five of nine solid wood shelves broke in

two, wood splintering to the floor.

So, that was definitely where the jukebox was going.

Mark turned and checked his phone. Nothing from Boomer. He'd sent a text asking when Donaldson's were turning up and was waiting for the answer. Hopefully he'd have a few days, at least.

Marie had unknowingly helped him out by suggesting he tell the townspeople straight up exactly how he'd been duped by Donaldson's. She didn't have a clue how much, but he was grateful to her. As soon as everyone arrived at the doors earlier, he'd been given his opportunity to explain his error, and assure them he was on their side.

They'd fallen for it, like all good souls.

If only he could rewrite the script or write a brand-new story. One that saw his family safe, his father behind bars, and his bank account as full as it had been before all this began.

He was going to have to contribute the minimum amount of information to these developers in order to continue playing his hand. After he'd accepted the job, Mark had threatened Boomer again, telling him he'd go to the police and blow the whole thing. But Boomer had played his trump card.

If you do that, Sterrett, some woman out there is going to get killed.

Donaldson's was putting Lauren at the front of this, believing she was the one who would attempt to negate any underhand deals Donaldson's offered her townspeople.

Would they hurt her physically? Or just in a business

sense?

He glanced at the mirror Kid was cleaning. Maybe he'd been shown those visions of Lauren as a warning. This was who she was. She was a child who had dreams and wishes. She grew into a beautiful, spirited woman.

Now she was dead.

Chapter Ele en

LAUREN WAS LYING in the ironwork four-poster in the master bedroom at Sage Springs, chewing on her cheek.

She'd hardly slept a wink.

Would her plan from Dallas work in Surrender?

She hadn't intended settling in California. She'd thought it best to stay in Texas, so had headed for Dallas with all her hopes. She'd found herself in the Bishop Arts District simply because she was being a tourist but kept going back and had met any number of women and chatted to them in stores, or had coffee in the cafes. But from the moment she'd seen the wall mural of a redbrick archway with a pathway meandering toward a lake, she'd been reminded of the home she'd left. Maybe it had been homesickness or fear of what she was heading into in the future, all on her own, but in that instant, she'd known what the petite, three-roomed premises should be. Even though she hadn't stood a real chance, she'd been daring enough to pursue a dream.

So could she fulfill that dream here?

She'd need to find a way for her idea to work around what Surrender already offered, plus the businesses she hoped to rejuvenate, not to mention the saloon.

Then there was the house itself. It was large, overly ornate in places, and drafty. Obviously, she'd need a wall up first. Some parts would have to be redecorated too. She loved the hardwood floors and the solid oak half-paneling, but the thick, dark green, floral wallpaper above it would have to be stripped. She'd need a lighter, more serene ambiance.

And how was her great-grandfather going to take all this enterprise while his house was overrun with women?

"Tough," she told him, looking up at the ceiling in case he was hovering around, sticking his nose into her business.

Was there some way to get rid of his spirit and the bad sensations that had descended on the house like a thick cobweb over the years? Could a person shift the wheel of fortune or govern the power of fate? It looked like she was about to try.

Her ears popped and the air around her stilled.

She was trapped again. She struggled against it, clutching at the cool, silky bedspread, attempting to push it off, to move, to run. But the air calcified and she was carried to another time.

It was an early-summer day, the sun bright and her long hair flying as she ran across the grasslands toward the lake. At her side was a child, holding her hand. She was the image of Lauren as a little girl. It was her daughter, and the little girl's name was Juliette.

Behind them, Lauren's husband was laughing at something their other children were saying. He held the little hands of twins Danton and Alexandre firmly as they ran with him, two-year-old chubby legs almost airborne as they tried to catch up with their mother and older sister.

Mark.

Lauren gasped for air as the vision faded, clutching at her throat.

What was at the back of her mind, slinking in her subconscious, to make her see things like this? It wasn't a muddled daydream. She'd been on those grasslands, she'd felt her child's fingers in hers, and the wind on her face.

She sat up, dazed.

Was it because she'd made the decision to push away all hopes for a normal, happy life after what happened in Santa Ynez? Did she really want to be single for the rest of her life? Was that why she was envisioning Mark and her together?

Perhaps she *was* a little attracted to him. Not the man who'd bought the bar but to the man who'd wined and dined her. The man who'd taken her to Paris. The man who'd preferred Scarlet to Lauren.

Was there really a difference in the two women? Had Danton seen Scarlet as spontaneous while Mark saw Lauren as uninspiring?

She was going to prove him wrong. Not because she wanted him to like her, but because she needed to believe in herself, be happy with herself, no matter what life threw at her.

Although, it was currently throwing quite a bit.

She hadn't closed the heavy, damask curtains last night, and a bright glint of morning sunlight pierced the window. As its beam hit the Victorian dressing table, it bounced off something shiny. The white, diamond-shaped stone. It had been in her jeans pocket yesterday. How had it gotten onto the dressing table?

"You *are* crazy!" she said as she flung the bedsheets aside and got out of bed.

She was a Mackillop. Daughter, granddaughter and great-granddaughter of soothsayers. She'd had the ability to hold conversations with Ava in her head since she'd turned seven. That wasn't normal! *She* wasn't normal—and she never would be. But what had she done? Turned her back on it.

The stone had moved because of forces she'd ignored. Forces that were inside her. Forces she'd inherited from her Mackillop ancestors.

Her heart was pounding and her brain firing in all directions.

"Ava!" she called telepathically. *"I know what I'm going to do with Sage Springs and my guess is—so do you."*

Boy, did she have a few things she wanted to say to her grandmother. But she wasn't going to do that.

She pulled her laptop out of her Louis Vuitton suitcase and set it up on the Victorian dresser, then looked out the window onto the wanderlust gardens as something caught her attention.

The topiaries were no longer topiarized, just great big blobs of green leaves, overgrown and trailing along the stone walls on either side of the entrance pathway to the house. There was nothing there. No noise. No movement—but an image of Mark's face was reflected in the pane of glass in the window. He was smiling at her, perhaps taunting her.

This was getting ridiculous!

She pulled her sunglasses off the dresser and slid them on. It was like he was following her around, spying on her.

It took her a few minutes to work the Skype program, since she'd never used it before, then suddenly, Molly's face appeared onscreen.

"Hey! You got Skype! Why are you wearing your sunglasses?"

"Don't ask."

"Hang on! Don't say a word until Pepper gets on."

She waited, tapping her fingernails on the dresser. They'd never once had a conversation about the valley or the curse without all three of them being involved.

Pepper's shining face came onscreen.

"Hey, girls! What's new? Why have you got your sunglasses on?"

"I'm having a bit of weird time."

"Ooh," Pepper said, hunching forward. "Tell."

Lauren took a breath. "I'm having strange visions, and I need to talk to you about some other things too."

"Visions about what?"

"Me and Mark Sterrett."

"I knew it!" Molly said. "It's happening."

"Who's Mark Sterrett?" Pepper asked.

"I never thought I'd genuinely be asking this question," Lauren said to Molly. "But the gift. What happens to you?"

"I can't talk to you about that or how it works because we have to experience it individually."

"The gift? You two," Pepper said, shaking her head.

"Can you hear yourselves?"

"There's something else I want to know," Lauren said as she pulled off her aviators and plonked them onto the dresser. "What happened at your hacienda? What did the great-grandfathers do?"

"The GGs? Can't say."

"You mean you won't. Come on, Molly! I need backup here."

"Um," Pepper said. "Can I just remind you both—the GGs are *dead*. And who's Mark Sterrett?"

"Pepper," Molly said. "Just listen. It'll help when it's your turn."

"My turn to what?"

"Find the man of your dreams!"

Pepper rolled her eyes and ripped open a packet of popcorn.

"She's eating junk food again," Lauren said. "Are you stressed, Pepper?"

"Totally. Molly goes home and starts saying she has the gift, now you're home and suggesting *you* might have some of the spooky abilities. I'm definitely staying in Arizona."

"Look," Molly said to Lauren. "There is something I have to tell you, because you need to be prepared."

Even Pepper stilled.

"Be careful when Mark's at Sage Springs."

"There's no bad feeling here at all."

"That's because *you're* in the house. You're clearing the air, but when Mark's there, you'll feel the change. The GGs don't want him around you. They'll try to get rid of him."

"Is that what happened at the hacienda?"

"It'll be different for you. I'm just warning you to take care."

"Mark hasn't been here," Lauren said, "and he's not likely to visit."

"Well get him over there! Test the waters. Just make sure you're dressed," she added, pointing to the short, flimsy tee Lauren wore to bed, "or you're going to be giving him ideas."

"*Now* the conversation gets interesting!" Pepper said. "Is he good-looking?"

"Very handsome," Molly said. "If you like that sort of sexy. Me? I've got my own kind of handsome and he's more than sexy enough. My satisfaction levels are off the scale."

"You're showing off again," Pepper said, digging into her popcorn. "Don't get too enamored with this Mark guy," she told Lauren. "He's not going to stick around, remember."

"Mine did!" Molly reminded her, with a smug smile.

"Girls—I'm not enamored!"

"Well, you're the one who says you're having visions of him," Pepper reasoned. She leaned in closer to the screen. "What's he doing in these visions? What are you and he doing *together*?"

"Not what you're thinking."

"I bet he's good at it though," Molly said. "You can tell with some men that the experience is going to be—otherworldly." She giggled. "Pardon the pun."

"I like those type of men," Pepper said, thrusting her hand into her packet of popcorn. "Except they don't exist."

"I hardly know this man. And I don't trust him."

"That's too bad," Molly said. "Since I heard he's on your town committee."

Lauren had given more thought to that overnight. If he was up to no good, being on the committee would give him ample ammunition to do whatever it was he was here to do. She'd have to keep a very close eye on him.

The battery light flashed on her laptop.

"I'm going to lose power any second! What else do I need to know, Molly?"

"Just get that man to Sage Springs!"

The screen went gray, then black.

Lauren slapped her thighs. But it was her own fault for not charging the laptop last night.

The sun shone through the windows and made the stone on the dresser sparkle.

She picked it up and held it. What had Ava said? *You can't make anything work without hope, or a wish, and maybe a prayer.*

Luck wouldn't go amiss, either. She clutched the stone. From now on, she wouldn't go anywhere without it.

She yanked off her tee and pulled on fawn-colored skinny pants, threw an ivory, long-sleeved sweater top over her head, then dug out a bright yellow belt and lemon-colored sandals from her suitcase. The sun was shining, spring was in the air and it was time for a splash of color. She had a plan for the house, plus a committee—and a deputy sheriff to expose.

Chapter Twelve

"HOLD YOUR HORSES, child!"

Lauren pulled up just under the red brick archway in town. *"I've got a bone to pick with you,"* she told her grandmother. *"You knew all along what I was going to do with the house!"*

Ava chuckled.

"You could have given me a heads-up. A hint."

"The clues were all around you."

She had to relent on that one. Marie had been right, too. Lauren hadn't been listening.

Sage Springs
A Place of Discovery
Arrive Tired, Leave Inspired

The women in the valley were worn out, working long hours to make ends meet if they had a job, then going home to housework. At other times, they were miserable because there was nothing to excite them.

That was going to change. Sage Springs would give women the opportunity to learn. She'd open up the ballroom and invite select speakers to talk about business skills, marketing, and female empowerment. She'd hire someone to teach them chutzpah if necessary—the very thing men had with an automatic command that many women, even those in powerful roles, lacked. Men carried self-assurance into a job interview even if they didn't know how to handle the job. Women were more grounded, and honest, and though just as inventive and capable, their apparent lack of self-confidence held them back.

"You still there?" Ava asked.

"I'll charge low rates for the valley women," Lauren said, still caught in the grip of exhilaration. She'd offer anything and everything to assist them in whatever they yearned to do. Whether it was starting a small business online from home or opening up a retail space. *"I'll give them discounts and easy-pay options. I'll find a way to subsidize them. And I'll give credit points if I end up using the services they've devised from my enterprise—but everyone outside the valley will pay."* They'd pay through the nose once word got out and the town became successful. She knew it like she knew the beat of her own heart.

She'd also give women a chance to retreat and indulge. A little time out in fine company, with good conversation where every woman counted. She'd offer wine and cheese tasting on the veranda, a book club.

Try yoga in the gardens.
Take tea in the atrium.

She'd even throw in hand massages!

"I was thinking of renting out one of the cabins in town and

turning it into an information office," she told Ava. She didn't expect visiting tourists to book a spot there and then, but she'd tantalize them, surprise them with an opportunity for growth. *"I'll create a welcome packet for Sage Springs. A business card, a leaflet of classes and opening times, but I'll add a posy of sage, or a small, fragrant candle. Something feminine. Something useful for themselves and their homes."* After visiting Surrender and discovering what was on offer at Sage Springs, those women would be dying to make an appointment. They'd feel rejuvenated just thinking about spending a couple of hours in the company of other women who are taking time out for themselves and learning as they went.

"And?" Ava said.

"I know. I've got to bring it all together. The house, the local businesses, the atmospheric appeal of our town and its historic feel—but with a contemporary touch." The Welcome to the Serenity of Surrender sign might mean something once she got her enterprise going. The house would offer relaxation and peace too, for those women who wanted it. Good wine and fine teas—and those hand massages.

"This is all going to appeal to the ladies," her grandmother said. *"What about the men?"*

"I guess they'll have the saloon."

She glanced at the bar, where the doors were flung open. Stepladders, paint tins, and a moose head were cluttered on the veranda.

She was going to bring prosperity to Surrender, no matter what it took. But him—Mark. What was it with the meet up at the airport and then his arriving in the same crummy backwater town Lauren had been born in? Not a coincidence. So what was the connection between the curse on the Mackillops and Mark Sterrett's sudden arrival?

"Ava—I have to get him to Sage Springs."

"Molly tell you that?"

"Yes, but she wouldn't say anything else. It's my great-grandfather, isn't it?"

"It'll be different for you," Ava said, her voice taking on a reflective tone. *"You'll be safe if you brave him."*

Lauren blinked. *"You mean I have to stand up to him?"*

"In your own way—that's important."

"But I don't have a 'way.'"

"It's your gift, Lauren. It's with you. Nurture it. Listen to it. It'll get you through. And your bar owner is going to be drawn into this, whether he wants it or not."

"He's not mine."

"Get him to come see me."

"You're going to warn him but not me? Honestly, Ava—I could do with a clue on this one."

"Be careful he doesn't see those blushes, for a start."

"What blushes?"

"You color up every time his name is mentioned!"

She admitted to her face heating up a few times when under his teasing scrutiny, but—*"Do you think people have noticed?"*

Ava chuckled, and Lauren pictured her pulling at the brim of her Longhorns cap. *"So has he."*

Oh, Lord. She turned her back on the bar.

She'd need support from him for Sage Springs. The marketing of a saloon and what she was going to offer hardly went hand in hand.

"I remember you telling me about Dallas," Ava said. *"I know how heartbroken you were when they pulled the rug from beneath your feet."*

Lauren sighed. *"I wish I'd been able to stay there. I mightn't have gotten into so much trouble."*

"But then you wouldn't have learned the lessons you were supposed to learn."

"Everything has an end," she said before Ava got the chance to remind her. *"I just have to go through it."*

"Wise words, child. Don't forget them."

Did Ava know about her visions involving Mark? She might know the outcome of whatever was going to happen, and she might pop into Lauren's head for the odd chat, but she never encroached on her granddaughter's personal space.

"Ava?"

No answer. Her grandmother had gone.

She turned to face the bar.

Was Mark supposed to help break the curse in some way? Why would that involve visions of beautiful children and a loving relationship with him?

She certainly wasn't going to marry him to find out. But she had some unbending to do. He hadn't told anybody his plans, and that proved he was here for no good reason—yet the nagging doubt was there. She hadn't once sensed any badness in him. He wasn't mean. He wasn't spiteful or callous.

She'd have to play it nice with him. Not *too* nice. She didn't want him getting the wrong idea, but she had gone at him hard so far, even though she was the only woman in town who thought he was up to no good.

The women were right though. He *was* handsome. He was also reasonably engaging, if one fell for a charming glow in a man's eyes and a whole lot of gallant masculinity.

She forgave herself for once having had a tiny crush on him, and headed for the bar.

Just don't let me blush.

She paused in the doorway. The aroma of chili wafting up to the rafters was so heady that remorse took a hold. Would it be extra, extra spicy?

The bar had been cleared. Dust sheets covered the tables and chairs which were stacked in a far corner. Mr. Gerdin sat on a barstool reading a magazine, seemingly oblivious to the bustle of activity around him.

Ingrid was dusting. Mrs. Fairmont was flower arranging. Butch wrangled shelving, Kid was cleaning the mirror, and Mark was pulling at his earlobe as Doc spoke to him.

Then he looked up and spotted her.

Lauren tensed and ignored the smell of spicy chili.

"I hope you're not after the Buckners this morning," he said as he came up to her. "They're kind of busy."

He held out his hand, indicating she come inside.

"There's certainly a lot going on," she said, walking forward. "I'm glad to see you've got your plans underway."

"Glad?"

This was it. The unbending. The part where she was nice.

"I was wondering if you'd like to visit Sage Springs. I

thought we could have that chat about business propositions after all."

"I'm honored. What happened to yesterday?"

What *had* happened yesterday? So much she could hardly sort it out in her head.

"When you were so standoffish with me," Mark explained.

"I had a vision," she told him, unable to keep the news to herself.

"Was I in it?" he asked, with a tease in his voice.

More than he'd want to know…

She turned for the door. "Shall we go?"

"Right now? Can't we hold our discussion here?"

"My business plans are quite distinct. I need you to see the house."

"To ask my opinion?"

"I don't need your opinion."

He stuck his hands into his pockets. "Why am I getting the impression you're up to something?"

"Me?" she said, striking a hand to her breastbone. "You're the one who won't tell anyone what your plans are for *Scarlet* Sage Saloon."

He had the grace to look abashed. "I could be persuaded to change the name and not use *Scarlet.*"

"But you'd keep *Sage.*"

"Hey, I've got a business to run too. Although my plans change every time someone walks into the bar and offers another idea."

That had been Lauren's doing, along with the chili.

Don't let me blush.

"This town holds history," she told him. "It's got the architecture, for a start, and that's why I want you to see the house. We need to use the historic feel of Surrender, not try to cover it up."

"We? Is this you negotiating?"

"Take it or leave it." He had to be dying to see inside the house. Probably so was everyone else in town. Nobody had been in it for six long years.

"I'll take it." He pulled his hands out of his pockets and gave her a dazzling smile. "One-sided negotiation is better than not talking at all. And who knows, maybe you'll let me get a word in now and again."

He was scrutinizing her, regardless of his smile. Observing her as he looked directly into her eyes. What did he see?

It was a shame she'd left her sunglasses at home.

"We also need to talk about this committee we're on, and how it'll be run," she said.

"Well, first off, yes—you're in charge. I don't usually interfere in arguments, business or personal, unless I'm involved directly."

"You bought the lease on the bar. You are involved. What happens if the townspeople sell their land? Who are you going to serve drinks to?"

"I didn't say I wasn't going to sit on the committee, I'm just saying let's go easy. See what happens. Take it as it comes."

"You must be as worried about these developers as we are."

"Oh, believe me, I am. I'll be keeping a close eye on them while they're in town."

His tone hadn't changed, he was still wearing his smile, but something in his words struck a chord of concern.

"You have a personal interest in Donaldson's?"

"Like you just pointed out—I have a business interest. What is it with them, anyway? Do they call you? Pester you?"

"That's what you're doing for them, isn't it?"

"No, come on. I mean it. Have they contacted you? Have you ever felt like someone was following you?"

Lauren shivered. "Are you trying to scare me?"

"If something odd happens, let me know, would you?"

"Why?"

"We're the committee. We're fighting this thing together."

He was still smiling, but *was* there a warning in his words? What did he know about the developers she didn't?

Maybe he's a man with a brilliant future, forced to change his life…

"We need to arm ourselves against them before they camp out on your front veranda," she said.

"I agree."

"So when are they arriving?"

"They didn't say."

"We have to blindside them."

"Aren't they shrewd businessmen? How are we going to do that?"

"You're a writer. Can't you think of something underhand?"

His smile softened. "I'm beginning to think I'd prefer it if we went back to not talking."

"He's just your backup," Marie had said. *"I promise, sugar—next time you see him he'll be eating out of your hand!"*

He was. But in a way that kept him slightly apart. As though he were playing two sides of a game.

"Hey, Mark!" Ingrid called. "We need your final decision on where all the photos of the town are going. I say above the bar where the moose head was, and Doc says on the side wall, but like I told him, they'll only get splattered with food and grease if they're in the diner area."

"You make the decision," he said. "We can all discuss its pros and cons later."

"You're opening the diner?" Lauren asked, glancing at the cordoned off area.

"I've no idea," he said, shrugging. "I wasn't even aware I was going to have photos on the wall. I'm getting a jukebox, too, going in that space Butch carved out. Oh, that reminds me—I had a word with the Buckners. They're all for spreading out the work between your place and mine."

It was irritating that he'd gone ahead and "solved" one of her problems, but since she hadn't had time to speak to the brothers about work at the house, she cracked a smile. *Cooperation. Be nice.* "Thanks."

"You're welcome. They're a helpful lot, your townspeople. Couldn't believe it when they all trudged in this morning, offering suggestions."

"Small town. We get involved in each other's business."

"It's just that it happened so fast. It was unexpected. A bit like an invasion."

Lauren cleared her throat. "There are plenty of things you'll discover. We're no ordinary town. This is no ordinary valley."

"I'm beginning to understand. There are lots of stories right here in Surrender."

"And one of them is yours." She cocked an eyebrow. "How will your story play out, I wonder?"

"Depends on whether you meant it when you said there was a curse on my bar or whether you were just being a smart-ass. Depends on whether the sudden assistance I'm getting is genuine or on whether everyone was told I was floundering and needed help." He tipped his head, staring her in the eyes. "Maybe by someone who has an axe to grind? Someone who is also going to be opening a brand-new business in town."

Don't blush!

"Sage Springs?" she said.

"Yeah. Let's go. Ingrid," he said. "Popping out for a while."

"We'll be here when you get back, Mark."

"I bet you will," he mumbled, with a laugh. "And someone might want to check the kitchen," he called. "Smells like supper's burning." He turned to Lauren. "They're cooking chili. Real spicy. I wonder why they added beans though. Reckon someone is trying to tell me something?"

He was too darned clever and she was beginning to hate the tease in his brown eyes.

He indicated the door with a sweep of his hand as he beamed down at her. "And I warn you, if I get back and discover I'm going to be adding a nail salon and a shoe shop to my bar—I'll put full blame on you."

Chapter Thirteen

MARK FOLLOWED LAUREN up the steps to the mustard-green monstrosity then checked that his cell phone was on silent while she had her back to him.

He was still sweating. He hadn't expected her to turn up at the bar with an inquisition, and it hadn't been easy keeping up that humorous demeanor while having to ask her if Donaldson's had contacted her. Or some strange guy with a booming Texan accent.

It hadn't taken him long to figure she'd been the one to instigate the overwhelming assistance and the chili though.

It made him smile. In her shoes, he'd have done the same thing.

"Nice," he said as he looked up at the wooden boards of the veranda ceiling, painted a light cream that stood out like a ray of hope next to the other drab, Victorian colors.

It was another place that needed a good polish. Perhaps a miracle.

He followed her through heavy wooden front doors, with lead-glass windows on either side, and looked around the hallway.

He had so many questions he didn't know where to

begin.

"I ought to tell you straight away they say this house is haunted by my great-grandfather."

"Do you see him?" he asked, relieved she hadn't asked for an opinion on what he thought about the house so far. It was either imposing or impressive; he hadn't seen enough to make up his mind.

She shook her head. "I don't even feel his presence here. Do you?"

"Haven't been inside long enough."

"I'll give you the tour." She headed off, perhaps not wanting to know what his first impression was.

He followed her through the rooms, absorbing the atmosphere.

There were glass door handles, and antique light fixtures everywhere. The real deal. He pushed a button and a chandelier lit up. "They work."

"Electricity and plumbing were upgraded a few years ago."

"Your renos are mostly cosmetic then. Well…" He paused. She hadn't mentioned the plastic sheeting covering the gaping hole in the outside wall or the broken banister on the wooden staircase next to it, so neither would he. He'd already gotten the idea she was only going to give him information she thought he needed and she'd give it in her own time.

He looked up at the ceiling. It was covered in fancy plasterwork, hand-painted and stenciled. Elaborate enough to be on a wedding cake. Perhaps that was what she was going to do—open the house up for weddings.

He followed her to the kitchen, which had a pressed tin ceiling, then back down the hall to a dining room and a couple of reception rooms, with more cake decoration ceilings. The doors and frames throughout the house were solid oak, as were the built-in cabinets. He'd counted seven fireplaces so far, all oak with cast-iron fireboxes and grates.

There were plenty of windows letting the light in, and any number of fancy lamps and light fittings, but the ambiance was oppressive in some way. As though a heaviness shrouded each room, regardless of the natural light pouring in.

He shook the sensation off. It was probably just the stress in his life making him feel like he was trapped.

"The atrium," she said as she showed him a glassed room with a black and white tiled floor.

This was where the potted palms and dainty teacups would fit in.

He smiled. He didn't know where he'd gotten the notion of coolness the first time he'd met her. She'd been under pressure, having just lost her business, although he had no idea how that had happened, but of course she hadn't been open to a guy's apparent flirting. Although she'd been comfortable with him, eventually.

He'd charmed Scarlet, but now that he knew more about Lauren, he liked the real woman.

In other circumstances…yeah. He'd make a play.

"Why do you keep smiling?" she asked.

"Just taking it all in. What's in there?" he asked, nodding

at closed double doors in the hallway.

"The ballroom. I'll show you later. This," she said, indicating the solid wood broken staircase and the cavernous hole in the wall, "is where the Buckners come in."

"You certainly need them."

She didn't offer any explanation and he didn't ask. He wasn't sure he wanted to know how the destruction had happened. Cannonball was the first thing that came to mind, but given this house was a Mackillop residence, it was more likely to be the ghost of her great-grandfather sending down his wrath with repeated lightning strikes from the barrel of the devil's shotgun.

Normally, he'd be at the computer by now, using all the stories he'd learned and plotting for a book. Someone else's book, but he thought of it as his while he was writing it. It only ever became someone else's property when he handed it over and got paid.

And now? He swore to God, he'd never write another book as long as he lived.

"You don't use these stairs, do you?" he asked as he gripped the remaining banister rail, testing its solidity. The entire bannister on the gaping-hole side had fallen in one piece to the floor.

"Of course I do. My bedroom's up here."

"It needs a structural engineer to check it out."

"Doc will know what it needs. Just keep to the left-hand side."

A tread groaned behind him, a few steps down, and he looked over his shoulder.

A cold chill drifted over his face and neck. There for a second, then gone. Like a puff of icy mist.

He checked the plastic sheeting. It mustn't be properly secured to the wall, although there was no wind outside today to create a draught.

"I'll arrange for the Buckners to fix the staircase first," he said, continuing up. "I'll let you have them every day until it's done."

"Why thank you, but *I'll* make the arrangements with the Buckners," she said from the top landing. "I'd like to arrange the town meeting, too. Tonight. Seven o'clock. Your bar."

He held up both hands in surrender mode. "I'm at your command." He was sure she almost smiled before she turned away. "I can even offer everyone supper. A great big vat of spicy beans with meat and chili peppers thrown in."

Now, *that* was a laugh. Smothered but a laugh.

Damn it, he wanted to flirt with her. Wanted to know if she was attracted to him as much as he was beginning to think he was to her. No, he didn't wonder about that. He was attracted.

He was also stressed to the eyeballs. Boomer wasn't returning his calls so he had no idea when Donaldson's would turn up. He was desperate to call his mom to see if she was okay, but that would be one call more than his usual weekly and she'd smell a rat.

But why couldn't he take five minutes off to flirt with a beautiful woman?

There were five bedrooms upstairs and three bathrooms.

She showed him each. They were furnished but not lived in. Dust had gotten trapped in the folds of the heavy curtains and on the glass lampshades.

They wandered along the hallway to the far end and the last door, which was open.

He paused outside.

"My room," she said, and pulled the door closed.

He'd only managed a glimpse. A four-poster bed, unmade, the imprint of where her head had been still on the pillow. French doors that opened out onto a balcony, where a hammock was strung on the rafters.

"You sleep out on the porch?" he asked. "It's not quite summer. Hope you dress warmly." And not in the flimsy looking lightweight tee he'd spotted over the end of her bed. A short tee, not a knee-length. Maybe not even thigh-length.

Damn. That was going live with him.

Their gazes met and held.

He wasn't sure what he wanted to say, but it would be something soft. Something romantic like, *Hey, you're looking lovely today. Meant to tell you earlier.*

"There's an attic," she told him. "I'd particularly like you to see that."

Fine. She didn't want romance. Truthfully, he wasn't sure why he was suddenly so keen to give her some. Perhaps because they were alone, in a fairy tale kind of house.

"It's a nice space," he said after they'd climbed the stairs to the attic.

It was more than nice. It was *great*. A hideaway. Crammed with broken furniture and boxes of junk, but if he hadn't made the decision to quit writing, this was where he'd have his study if the house was his.

There was no claustrophobic feeling up here and he took a bit of time looking around until he felt her scrutiny and turned to her. Why was she looking at so intently, as though waiting for him to pronounce some judgment on the attic?

"Where next?" he asked, taking his thoughts off the unlikely scenario of ever having a space like this to call his own.

"There's only the ballroom. If you really want so see it."

"Might as well. Seen everything else."

She led him down the main staircase. He paused behind her and tested the tread of a few steps, waiting for the groaning creak he'd heard earlier.

Nothing.

He glanced at the plastic sheeting. No draft crossed his face, either. Maybe he'd imagined it all.

Downstairs, she opened the double doors to the ballroom and let him go in first.

He took his time, walking to the center of the room, examining the wallpapered and mirrored panels and the ornate chandeliers overhead, giving his heartbeat time to settle.

This was the room she'd danced in as a child, with her borrowed cloak, high heels, and a string of pearls that reached her knees. It was the room he'd seen her in in the mirror at the bar.

There had to be a feasible explanation for that. Even if it turned out to be brain damage.

"Lauren?" He waited for her to focus on him. "Do you granddaughters have this Mackillop 'ability' or whatever it is?"

"Molly has it."

"And you?"

"I don't know."

He'd never been out with a woman who could read minds or tell fortunes. Yet he wanted to take Lauren out. For real—as Mark, not Danton. He wanted them to have a chance to see where it would go. He wanted to know what sounds she'd make as he made love to her, his hands caressing her body and his mouth pressing kisses all over that lovely, expressive face.

"The house has a nostalgic feel," he said. He wasn't sure what he thought about the place, to be honest. It was grand, impressive, and would be immensely attractive once it had been redecorated with lighter hues and tones. But still, the oppression surrounded him.

"There's no nostalgia here," she told him. "Nobody's lived here. Ever."

Maybe not, but he still felt it. She'd been in this house as a child. Perhaps those moments had been captured in this ballroom. "The house must hold some tales."

"It does. But it doesn't hold any memories."

"How come?"

Again, their eyes met and held.

She broke first, by blinking. "You're being very good about all this, Mark. Ghosts, curses. Thank you."

She'd called him by his name and he liked hearing it. He thought perhaps she loved this old house, probably because of her childhood years, and that she was worried he'd say he hated it—along with whatever business idea she'd come up with.

"I'm actually flirting," he said, attempting to lighten the mood.

She blushed and his heart pinched.

Before he could stop himself, he held out his hand. "Let's dance."

He wanted her in his arms. Wanted to know if she'd fold against him or sink into him. Whether she'd feel right, up close to him.

"There's no music."

"Let's pretend there is. Let's make some memories."

"Haven't we made enough?"

"Paris? Come on. Dance with me. Let's make new memories." Ones where he wasn't double-crossing her. Memories where his mom and sisters were safe, his father in jail, and Donaldson's a distant recollection.

LAUREN TURNED IN the doorway and walked back into the hall. She hadn't expected to be unnerved in this manner. Nothing weird or ghostly had happened, and he hadn't suddenly broken out in a chilled sweat of terror, screaming because apparitions were hounding him. She'd watched for it and was sure nothing untoward had occurred. But her nerves were on alert anyway, because they were alone together.

Was he trying to catch and hold her gaze on purpose? Their eyes had met a few times, and in those briefest of moments he'd made her feel like Scarlet. As though he were trying to say, *"Hey, I actually like you."* And each time, for a second, she might have admitted she actually liked him too.

"Wild Ava wants to see you," she said when he followed her out of the ballroom.

"Is she going to tell me off for flirting with you?"

Her heart gave a little jump. *Had* he been flirting? For real?

"I don't know what she'll say to you. It'll be between you and her. But let me tell you, she can spot a fake a mile off."

"So can I."

That brought a laugh. "You expect to find a fortune-teller asking you to cross her palm with silver before she tells you all about your love life? You're in for a shock."

"My love life is pretty dull at present. Has been for a while now. I doubt Ava will even mention it."

Was he telling her he hadn't had a relationship in a while in order to let her know he was free?

She really ought not to care.

He was wearing his bomber jacket again, his button-down shirt open at the collar, his throat tanned and wide, his shoulders squared with the ease of a confident man. He gave off the sense he could discern the strengths and weaknesses of those around him, but in a reassuring way, not an antagonistic one. Even Lauren, manless due to a personal decision more than the curse, had recognized his attempt at gentle seductiveness when they'd been on the upper landing outside her bedroom, and she'd almost fallen for it. And again, just now, when he'd asked her to dance.

She cleared her throat. Okay, so he *was* attractive. But

she needed to concentrate on realities. Why he was here and his connection to Donaldson's. Then there were the abnormalities and the unknown. Some faceoff with her great-grandfather. The ludicrous visions of her and Mark with beautiful children. She'd thought those a result of some psychological imbalance—and who could blame her for having a few kinks she couldn't iron out, given her record, past *and* present? Now, she wasn't so sure.

He'd liked the attic space. He hadn't said so, but he'd relaxed in the room, looking out the window, studying the stored junk, and running a finger in the dust on the desk chair and chest of drawers, as though mentally furnishing the room to his taste.

It was the room she'd seen him in during her last vision. Poring over the books on his desk. The woman in that vision had understood him. The woman standing in the hallway at the bottom of her broken staircase didn't.

"The craftsmanship is amazing," he said, running his hand along the banister and the carved sage bushes, the sparrows, starlings, and white-winged doves. "The Buckner brothers are going to love getting their hands dirty with this. With the whole lot."

She'd been so deep in thought she hadn't noticed him moving. He was halfway up the staircase. "You hate it all?"

"The house? No. Surprisingly, I don't. Not sure exactly what I think, but it's got—something. Can't find the right word."

"I've got to modernize and freshen it up. I loathe all this dark, heavy wallpaper. It makes a person feel the walls are closing in. I want to open all the windows and let the air rush through."

"It kind of does already, since you've only got three walls in the hallway."

There was amusement in his tone.

"What happened?" he asked, nodding at the plastic sheeting.

"I'll try to make it short. There are any number of people in town who can fill you in on the hearsay and superstitions."

"Intriguing."

She headed into the story of her ancestors without having to even take a breath. The cousins had been told the tale over and over as children and had been rapt in it.

"The Mackillops arrived as part of the exploration of the Fort Smith-Santa Fe Trail and settled in the Panhandle. Nobody knows where they came from, but there were likely some buffalo hunters among them. They dabbled in cattle, but that didn't work—not sure if they were any good as ranchers. But the women were good at prophesizing." She paused, giving him a chance to make a comment. He didn't. "They say it was the women who found Calamity Valley. Their Mackillop men claimed it."

"It must have been a tough life. What are we talking about? Eighteen eighties?"

She nodded. "They tried farming, but that didn't work either. Then the railroad came through Amarillo and life picked up."

"So they had an eye for business."

"Unfortunately, by the time our great-grandmothers were born in 1912, nothing was thriving. We've yoyoed throughout the years. Then our great-grandfathers turned up. They had an eye for business and didn't care who they crossed while making a grab for a good deal."

"Hold on. The Mackillops are only women now?"

"Three great-grandmothers, deceased. Our three grandmothers, with one daughter living—Marie—and we granddaughters. All husbandless."

Now, he smiled.

She returned it. She could practically see his writer's brain bubbling.

"In 1938 the great-grandfathers—we call them the GGs to show our lack of respect—built each of the great-grandmothers a house in their respective towns. Not with their money, with our great-grandmothers'. They more or less stole it, refusing to help everyone in the valley, only looking out for themselves. That's when our great-grandmothers got wise and began knocking them back in any way they could. There were lots of heated arguments. Lots of unrest in the valley. Then the GGs discovered their women were refusing to sell the land to the Palo Duro Canyon, which had become a state park a few years earlier."

Mark whistled. "Would have been a pretty price."

"It still would be, which is why Donaldson's want it."

"Go on."

She paused, but he didn't respond to her mention of the developers. "Our women dug in. It was *their* land. They kicked the GGs out of the valley, but their money had gone in brick, timber, and fancy furnishings. They never again set foot in the houses, just boarded them up."

"Strong women."

"The GGs never got over losing the money they could have made if they'd sold the land to the state park, so they cursed us and all descendants. We would remain husbandless and in fear of homelessness for eternity."

"But this is a story of survival—yes?"

She nodded. "Our women were good people. Still are. Generous to those who genuinely need assistance. Nobody in the valley went hungry for long. The great-grandmothers pulled everyone together and made do, until such time people could fend for themselves."

"It's pretty much what's happening now, isn't it? All this much-needed rejuvenation."

"I suppose it is. A few years back, our grandmothers decided the time was right to throw off the dust covers on each of the houses and make them useful. They were making noises about the valley being in danger. We didn't know why, but it turned out they were right—as always. Donaldson's came snooping around more than a year ago. We've held them at bay, until now."

"Were the Buckners working on the houses?"

Again, he'd disregarded her reference to Donaldson's. "Doc worked on this house. But, as with Molly's hacienda and the lodge belonging to Pepper and her grandmother, weird things started happening. Roofs collapsing. Falling masonry. Windows shattering. One guy working on Sage Springs almost got killed when the spike fell off the spire. If it weren't for Doc pushing the guy out of the way, he'd have been speared to the ground. Impaled."

"Ouch."

"Doc stayed in town, renting Mr. and Mrs. Fairmont's second house, and then he moved his brothers in too. The other builders kept coming back for a while, because of the cheap beer."

"So that's how my bar got its reputation. I was wondering how anybody had discovered it in the first place. This valley isn't exactly a tourist hot spot."

"But it will be," she reminded him.

"It makes for a cracking story." He leaned against the bannister, the solid one on the left-hand side.

Something in the air caught Lauren's attention. Not a noise, not a movement, nothing tangible, but her senses spiked.

"Be careful up there," she told him. "You said yourself it wasn't safe."

"I'm fine. How come these GGs of yours were capable of cursing?"

"It depends on belief. Cursing people is easy."

"It is?"

"You could curse me now and things might happen to me whereby it appears your curse is coming true, but in reality, it's just life. Eventually, if bad luck follows you for long enough, you appear cursed. Then everyone believes you are. And maybe fate gets stuck at that point, and even the universe believes you're cursed."

He looked doubtful but only for a moment. "There

could be something in that. I do think that if we believe we're doomed or cursed, then that's what we project and that's what we get."

She smiled to herself. Ava was going to like talking to this man.

"Still not sure it's possible for us to change our fate though," he mumbled, almost to himself. "Not in some instances. Like where anger and brutality are the keywords."

"Maybe passion beats anger," she said, and the moment the words were out, she found herself hoping it was true. Not only for herself and the faceoff with her great-grandfather and whatever else was heading her way, but for whatever it was Mark was thinking about with that sudden brooding expression.

Had Marie somehow been right with her offhand prediction about his family and the father he no longer spoke to? The need to get away and clear his head didn't ring true.

"So what's your business going to be?" he asked. "Or can I guess?"

His expression had cleared. He was back to Mark Sterrett at his most charming.

"Be my guest." He probably thought she was going to open that haunted house.

"I'm envisioning potted palms, fine china, and an indoor fountain. Wedding venue?"

She spluttered a laugh. Wouldn't that make the GGs livid? Love and romance all around. Except it wouldn't be sweetness and rose petals. It would be fraught nerves, bridezillas, arguing bridesmaids and demanding future mothers-in-law. "No wedding venue."

"Why not? I can see it working."

"I'm going to turn the house into a welcoming and educational enterprise for women."

He pursed his lips, not taking his eyes off her. "Open all year?"

The crease on his brow told her he was already mentally taking stock of how this would affect the saloon.

"We'll open each morning and afternoon for certain hours and activities. Maybe the odd evening. My intent for Sage Springs is to give women good company, great conversation, and a chance to learn and grow. Whatever it is they need, whether it be gardening tips, yoga, empowerment, or support."

"What do the guys get?"

"Your saloon."

He took a breath. "Which is where the problem arises. How is your spa thing going to blend in with my saloon?"

"It won't be a spa, and you mean, how is your saloon going to blend in with my enterprise and everything else I put in place for businesses in town?"

He smiled, looking genuinely amused. "You're a tough negotiator, Mackillop. Can we go back to flirting now?"

He pushed from the bannister and started to jog down the stairs. A step gave way and he tumbled, wood splintering behind him. Step after step broke, dust flying in the air as fractured wood exploded.

The plastic sheeting blew in, puffed out like it had a gale force wind behind it, its sealed edges straining against the brick of the open space.

It had happened in less than a second. Lauren's feet were still pinned to the floor.

"Whoa!" Mark righted himself and stared at the now buckled and broken wooden steps behind him. He laughed self-consciously and brushed the dust off his thighs. "Well, that put me in my place." He looked across at her with a sheepish smile. "No more flirting, I guess."

She stared at him, trying to contain the shock roaring inside her head. She didn't feel the ghostly drafts in the house. She didn't get a sense of being shadowed, but she knew now that there was something behind Mark. At his shoulder. Close to him, pushing him…

"Please come off the stairs!" She could hardly get her breath and her voice was raspy in her throat.

"I'm okay. Just my pride that got hurt."

She reached out her hand. "Don't go near the hole in the wall!"

"I'm fine, Lauren."

She wanted to move to him, to drag him physically off the staircase, but the light dimmed and her vision hazed.

The air in her ears cracked, and she had no choice but to let it happen. It took hold of her and the present moment was lost.

She was in the bar, with Mark.

He was surrounded by dozens of metal pails brimming with flowers, which were set up on an Old West wagon that had been renovated to look like a market stall. It sat just inside the front doors, against the wooden railing that delineated the bar from the dining area. Roses, chrysanthemums, daisies—all sorts of flowers. With little white flags with the price of each bouquet stuck in the pails. He was smiling at Lauren. He looked a little older, and Lauren, living in the skin of the woman in her vision, acknowledged she too was older.

"Which kind this week?" he was asking her.

The woman being offered the flowers was filled with love for the man, and the woman who was watching the scene was shaking almost uncontrollably.

"Your choice," the older Lauren told him.

"Good. Because I chose the dahlias."

He bought her a bunch of sunset-colored dahlias every week they were in bloom, and he'd been buying them for more than ten years.

"Lauren! *Lauren!*"

She came out of the vision with a cold, shivering start.

"What's wrong?" Mark demanded. "I thought you were going to faint on me." He was holding her up, his hands on her arms. "Lauren, you went deathly pale."

She looked into his eyes. He'd said he was going to write a novel about the town and turn the bar into a flower shop. Flippant comments. But her visions told her otherwise. She'd seen him in the attic, poring over his books as he wrote a novel about the Wild West and the valley. She'd seen him in Paris, buying her a cup of coffee. She'd seen their family running and laughing over a hillside outside of town. And now, she'd seen him in the saloon, buying flowers for his wife of many years.

"Hey," he said, his hands still on her arms as though expecting her to crumple to the floor any second. "Are you okay?"

No.

These visions weren't montages in a worried woman's overactive imagination. They weren't daydreams or wishes.

She was literally being shown the future.

Chapter Fourteen

MARK RAN AN eye around his establishment. He'd only been back an hour but word about tonight's meeting had already gotten around and everyone had pulled together, industrious as ever.

They'd cleared away the renovation equipment, dusted everything in and out of sight, and he and the Buckners had arranged all the chairs in rows and a head table for the committee.

The bar sparkled with a cleanliness and a freshness he'd never thought possible three days ago.

If his family wasn't in danger, he'd welcome the rush of adrenaline he got just thinking about how well tonight's first Rejuvenate Surrender meeting might go for all these good people. As though he were a genuine guy, buying a bar in an out of the way place and hoping for a tree change. One that might include a romantic interlude with a beguiling and fascinating woman.

Damn Donaldson! Damn Boomer! And damn his father forever for putting him in this position. If he'd met Lauren under any other circumstances, he'd have asked her to dinner within minutes of saying hello. He knew that now, after being with her, flirting with her, getting to know her and to like her.

Whatever had happened to her at the house earlier, he'd gotten the scare of his life, but she'd practically kicked him out the door, refusing to tell him what had made her so deathly pale.

It had to have been something physical. An illness. Would she see a doctor? Should he call one?

"Don't touch this urn, Mark!" Ingrid called out from the dining area. "There's a knack, and if you don't handle it like it was a little lost lamb, you'll get an electric shock."

Mark turned from the bar. "Do you think perhaps we ought not to use it?"

"And have no coffee to offer? Marie from Hopeless is bringing *cake*. We're already the poor relatives; we don't want to rub it in."

She went back to the kitchen and Mark pulled his phone from his pocket.

Perhaps he ought to call Marie.

"You were over at the house?" Marie said, interrupting him as he explained the reason for his call. "What did you feel?"

"Feel?"

"Think, I meant think."

"Uh…it's great. Great place. Have you heard from Lauren? She had a funny turn or something at the house. I was worried, but she wouldn't tell me what had happened and sent me packing. I thought she was going to faint."

"We Mackillops are always having turns. Tell me about

them! The turns I've had with all the strain I'm under right now would make a lesser woman gray. Imagine *that* happening with no decent hairdresser in sight."

"So, you've spoken to her and she's okay?"

"Such a sweet man to worry! How many cakes shall I bring tonight?"

"Um...whatever you think."

"Spoken like a diplomat. See you at seven o'clock."

Marie cut the call and Mark slid his phone into his pocket, somewhat relieved but not fully convinced. Marie hadn't been there. She hadn't seen her niece's features pale, her body still, and her eyes blank out, as though she'd been taken over by some force.

He ran both hands over his head, squeezing his fingertips into his skull. A force? He *was* going mad.

Hortense marched out of the kitchen. "Did you hear?" she asked. "Hopeless! They're getting a mobile coffee van! They're taking all the big ideas for themselves. They plan to tour the valley with their Hopeless cupcakes!"

"You mean the Hopeless sponge cake? Marie's bringing some for tonight's meeting."

"I mean the *cupcakes*!"

Ingrid ran up beside her and slapped her arm. "I was going to tell him! We've just heard," she said to Mark. "They've created a cupcake. It's likely to be as famous as the sponge."

Hortense shook Ingrid off, still glaring at Mark. "They're branching out and what are we doing? Offering electrocution with a thirty-year-old urn."

"That urn's seen us through many a wedding and a funeral," Ingrid stated, looking affronted.

Mark sighed. They were arguing and the meeting hadn't even begun.

His cell phone beeped with a message. Boomer. *"Hope you've gotten your act together, Sterrett. We'll be there tomorrow morning, nine a.m. Be ready for us."*

Mark squeezed the phone in his hand, wanting to crush it. He'd thought he had a couple of days before they got here. Now he had hours.

Nobody in this town would let the developers know their plans, but if all they did was argue tonight, nothing would be finalized. Not even a broad scope blueprint or a strategy. The wavering and stumbling would be noticeable. It wouldn't take Donaldson's long to learn there wasn't a single thing that had been agreed on, and that was when they'd leap in. They were bringing the press; they'd use them. Show the town and its people as a ridiculous oddity. Surrender would get tourists, all right—and they'd all be laughing.

"We need something grand," Hortense was saying. "Something shiny and new and ultimately profitable."

"Like what?" Ingrid asked, looking askance.

"Like *my* new coffee machine." Mark slid his phone into his pocket. "I just bought the saloon a brand-new stainless-steel, top-of-the-range espresso machine." He hadn't, but now he'd have to. How much would it cost? A couple of thousand? "It should be here the end of the week." Once he'd ordered it.

"See?" Ingrid said, looking smug. "Mark's got it all under control."

"One coffee machine isn't going to turn our fortunes around. What about that pink blog van they've got in Hopeless?"

"We don't need a blog van."

"So how are we going to deal with PR and marketing? From our kitchen tables?"

"We need ideas first, Hortense! Without them, we won't be PRing anything."

"So what's *your* idea, Ingrid Gerdin?"

"I haven't had time to think about it. Too busy arguing with *you*."

Ingrid marched back to the kitchen, Hortense grumbling as she followed. "What's the point of having a meeting if nobody brings ideas?"

Mark walked to the open door and stood in the doorway, inhaling air like a drowning man.

Donaldson's was arriving tomorrow. He no longer had days to work out what he was going to do. These people deserved their chance to make their town shine and thrive, and that meant he was going to have to go over Lauren's head tonight and push the meeting along and drive any suggestions he thought might work.

Then there was the other major issue. How would a saloon work alongside Lauren's idea for the house? There hadn't been time to discuss it before she'd kicked him out the door. Not that she need worry about it, because Mark wasn't staying, but she was going to hate him for taking over her meeting.

What option did he have? What damned option had he

ever had since this whole damn thing began? One little half a million-dollar embezzlement misdemeanor later and his father's actions had put more than his family in a vulnerable position. The playing field had widened. The involvement of innocent people spreading like wildfire to include Lauren and all the good people of Surrender. Perhaps the whole valley.

He hoped to God his father was firmly tied in chains wherever he was being held in Bermuda. Sweating it out. Because his son certainly was.

LAUREN HAD RUN so hard and fast up the hill to Ava's cabin, her chest was heaving and her hair sticking to the back of her neck by the time she got there.

"He was just at the house!" she said as she plonked herself in the Adirondack chair next to her grandmother, a hand on her chest to control her breathing. "Everything was fine—then suddenly he was on the stairs and they gave way! I didn't even move! It happened so fast—"

Ava took hold of her arm. "Take another breath, child."

Lauren hauled in more air. "I felt nothing while he was there, Ava, then a minute or so before it happened, I sensed something, like a change in the atmosphere."

"What was he talking about when this happened?"

"The house. He said he could see it as a wedding venue."

"What else was he talking about?"

Flirting.

Ava turned to Lauren when she didn't answer, her face a

mask of patience, but there was a smile in her eyes.

Lauren felt her face heat up. "Do you know about the visions I'm having?"

"I sensed."

"He's in them, Ava." Mark was around at a time of great turmoil for her and for everyone. But why wasn't she envisioning herself in ten years' time chatting with Mrs. Fairmont? Or Hortense? Or Molly and Pepper? Why him?

"This is the learning stage," Ava said. "Your gift isn't fully developed. There could be more than your visions."

"But am I seeing the *future*?" Lauren exclaimed, thumping the arm of the chair. "And why does it involve him?"

"Is there an attraction?" Ava asked.

Lauren threw herself back in the hard seat. "I want to like him, and I don't get any feeling he's a bad person. But he *is* lying, and I don't know anything about the real man." Yet uncannily, she knew almost everything about the man she saw in her visions.

"Don't get downhearted, child. You haven't got time."

"It's just that I don't know what's happening to me, and I don't know where it's going to lead."

"What did you think would happen in your life? We sisters let you granddaughters go your own ways. We respected your wishes and didn't push you to accept the skills we knew you had. There was a reason for that. You each had to learn the way. Your own way, in your own time."

Lauren drew a long breath. "Are you saying we were never likely to get away with being normal?"

"What good would normal be to a Mackillop?"

As in, a Mackillop *soothsayer*? Lauren hugged herself. "I don't think I'm cut out for this. I can't do what you do."

"You can't run from who you are. But you'd better get your skates on and prepare yourself for this meeting. There's cynicism and unrest coming."

"From where?"

"Have you got plans for the town?"

"I've come up with a few ideas now." Solutions that would help the whole town restructure their businesses and create new ones. "Our women have been held back. Giving them the chance to learn, the chance to broaden their outlook on life *and* business is going to benefit everyone in town. Especially now we're about to forge ahead. That's what I want from Sage Springs."

"Give them a chance and watch them fly." Ava smiled. "I liked your idea when you found it in Dallas, but it wasn't the place for you and it wasn't the time."

Lauren hugged herself harder. She'd stay in the valley forever now. It wasn't so daunting a thought these days. She'd changed. Life had changed her. She might get lonely sometimes, but who didn't?

"I wish you'd come to the meeting, Ava."

"Marie will be there."

And she'd be supportive, but she wasn't a soothsayer. She wouldn't read between the lines.

"Don't discount Marie's abilities," Ava said. "She's a special woman. She brought you and Pepper up after your mothers died like you were her own. You both were, in many ways. All three mothers were cousins, too, remember. And they were like you, Molly, and Pepper. More like sisters."

"Why didn't Marie get the Mackillop gift?" Her mother had it, as had Pepper's. They'd both embraced it from a young age—then they'd been lost in the prime of their lives and anything they might have taught their daughters lost with it. Until Marie took over. But Marie had taught in a different way, a nurturing, ordinary way.

Ava reached out and gently put a fingertip to Lauren's forehead. "Watch. Listen. Trust. Just don't be tricked by the words and actions around you. It's your heart that gives you the real understanding." She settled back in her chair. "Now scoot. I've got work of my own to do." She untied her bag of runes from the belt on her waist. "And Lauren," she said as Lauren stood. "Watch your back."

"The last time you said that, Mark crept up on me outside the gates to Sage Springs."

"Did you tell him to come see me?"

"Yes, but I don't think he will."

"Leave that problem to me."

Lauren kissed her grandmother's cheek but paused before heading off. "Do you think he's a good man?"

Ava met her eye. "Watch. Listen. Trust."

Still no indication that she *was* seeing the future and she wasn't going to force herself to like Mark more than she ought to, given she'd only recently met him. But a surge of fluttering butterflies rose in her chest at the thought of him being a decent man. He couldn't have portrayed Danton without throwing a little of Mark into the equation. No more than Lauren had been able to portray Scarlet without putting her real self into the balance.

Maybe she'd let him flirt tonight. Just to see where it headed.

Chapter Fifteen

MARK WAS AT the committee head table, taking a moment for himself. He checked his watch, then ran an eye around his establishment.

Everything was ready. Many of the thirty-odd people they'd expected had already arrived. The urn was on, hissing steam above a Warning Do Not Touch sign, and chatter filled the air as Marie sliced cake and handed it out.

She hadn't brought the famous cupcakes, so that was one argument he didn't have to worry about.

People wandered the bar with their plates and coffees, looking around, touching the furnishings and maybe reevaluating the place. It was likely the first time many of them had been inside.

This was what the bar would look like if someone got it up and running for real. Alive. Useful. Needed. A community hub, since it was the biggest building in town.

Regardless of what went down in the next few days, his treachery was bound to be discovered at some point. He didn't doubt it and he wasn't going to run from whatever backlash was thrown his way, but he'd grown fond of these people and it was going to hurt.

Someone opened both doors to the bar to let a group in and Mark glanced up.

Lauren was on the veranda, talking to old Gerdin.

She was wearing an alabaster-colored dress, not quite cream, not quite buttermilk, the hemline above her knees, and Mark couldn't take his eyes off her. She'd worn trousers every day he'd known her.

He strode to the door, almost in a daze. No woman had ever bewitched him like this one.

Out on the veranda the night air enveloped him, as did her perfume. Sage, lime, and the sweetness of orange.

"There's a lot of high expectation in there," Gerdin was saying. "Hope you're up for this."

"I am," she assured him in an even tone. "It's going to be a good meeting, Mr. Gerdin. I can promise you that."

"And the house?"

She winked at him, playfully. "I won't be forgiven if I tell you before I tell the others."

Something was changed about her tonight. Not just her clothing, something at the heart. She wasn't pretending to be cool and aloof, and she had poise, but it was from within.

And, by God, she looked good.

"So it's all going to work out?" Gerdin said. "The saloon and your business at Sage Springs?"

Mark stepped forward, making his presence known. "Lauren and I had discussions about that this afternoon, and we're on the same page."

She turned to him with a raised eyebrow.

"Although we need to iron out a few things," he finished.

"We certainly do," she muttered, but she said it with a smile.

Of all things he hadn't expected, it was to see her smile at him.

Gerdin must have felt he was in the way because he cleared his throat, mumbled something about his wife, and left Mark alone with Lauren, her light perfume, and her smile.

"Hi," he said. "How are you feeling?"

"Better. Sorry about before."

"What happened?"

"I guess I forgot to eat breakfast."

"I hope you've eaten now, because all I've got to offer is cake and beans with chili."

She laughed, her cheeks flushed with such a beautiful glow Mark reined himself in.

She was the one who was going to make the changes in the town. She was the one who was meant to lead—and he couldn't allow her to. Not tonight. Maybe not until this whole business was over and he'd gone. Too many lives depended on him getting this right.

"Are you coming in?" he asked, taking his eyes off her and stepping back to let her go inside before him.

She hesitated, no doubt taken aback with his sudden abruptness.

"How are *you* holding up?" she asked as she passed him.

"Don't worry about me."

LAUREN HEADED FOR the table that had been put out in front of the rows of chairs. She'd never seen the Surrender bar so clean, warm, and welcoming. Or full. Plenty of people had arrived for the meeting, including a few visitors from Hopeless. Davie was standing guard by the urn and pouring coffees. Winnie Johnson who worked in the salon and the takeout was fussing with plates and forks while Marie sliced cake.

Lauren put her tote bag onto the table, followed by her paperwork, and stepped away, waving to them. Davie beamed. Sweet little Winnie blew her a kiss—and Marie swung her cake knife in the air, indicating Lauren look behind her.

She spun around. "Find anything interesting?" she asked Mark, who was shuffling through her notes. She plucked them from his hands.

"Just wondering if we're on the same page."

"Difficult to tell, since you don't appear to have any paperwork of your own to compare notes."

"It's all up here," he said, tapping his forehead, then taking his frown and his focus to his bar.

Maybe she was looking at him through a changed viewfinder, but she didn't need her heart to tell her something was off with him tonight. He hadn't quite met her eye and when he did he didn't hold her gaze for too long.

"How far away is the lake and the waterfall?" he asked.

"How did you know about either?"

"There's a sign, on the brick archway."

A lopsided sign. She'd have to get one of the Buckners to

fix it.

"I'm planning on using the area, to bring Surrender and Hopeless together. Molly's photographers will love it, and if they also like hiking we can get a proper trail going between the hacienda and Sage Springs. Or if the photographers are men and they bring their wives and girlfriends, Surrender would have something to offer the women, while Hopeless catered to the men."

"That might take business off the bar."

"You'll have to fight for it. What are your ideas, anyway?"

"The good news is that the ladies in town are going to make sure there'll be no raucous brawls or gambling."

"You'll let them make decisions?"

"They're decent ones, so far."

"They don't interfere with your own plans?"

"Like I said to Marie, I've had a number of ideas, none of which fully appealed to me."

She wanted to like him, but it was as though she were being pulled between two different paths. One where she was comfortable in his company, the other where caution resided. Ava had said there was unrest on the way, and she had an ominous sense it was going to come from Mark.

She glanced at the paperwork in her hands, then back to him. "Are you here to snoop on me?" It was important to listen and watch and let her heart confirm the facts. But the trust issue was going to be difficult.

He paused for only a moment. "Are we back to that? Okay. Yes. I'm snooping on you. How am I doing?"

Her heart told her he was telling the truth, and although she had to suppress a shudder, there was still no sense of ill-will from him.

"You kick off the meeting by telling everyone your visions for Sage Springs," he said. "After that we'll play it by ear about how our businesses are going to be cojoined."

"Cojoined?"

"Isn't that what you want from me?"

"Are you sure cojoined is the right expression? It reminds me of till death do us part. Talking of which—what *are* your views on marriage?"

"I beg your pardon?"

"Children. Do you like them? What about longevity? What are your thoughts on that? Because it's what I'm going to be talking about tonight. Building on what we've got. Seeing it through no matter what. Trust."

"Lauren, I have no idea what you're trying to say but you've gone pale again. Are you okay?"

"Just dandy." She thrust her paperwork into her tote bag. "Excuse me." She walked off, heading for the coffee urn. *Idiot!* So much for her flirting skills. She hadn't gotten further than a smile and a blush out on the veranda.

She'd promised herself she'd never look for a man's good opinion again, and what had she done since he'd been in the house that afternoon? Fallen for his charm—all over again.

A few minutes later, she put her still-full coffee cup down. It was just a prop. An excuse to leave his side and give herself a few minutes alone.

Standing in the far corner of what had once been the

diner, she folded her arms across her chest.

Were she and Mark going to share their lives forevermore and bring up their children together? At this point she couldn't imagine it, but it was what she'd longed for when she was a child, dancing in the ballroom, imagining romantic interludes with her future husband. She'd been young, so there had been nothing more in her imagination than a few chaste kisses, but with Mark, a tall, confident male, she might let her mind wander to what they would get up to as adults.

There'd be nothing chaste about his lovemaking. His hands, for a start, were strong and capable. There was strength in his shoulders and his arms too, and there was that warm, tender look in his eyes when he was teasing her.

"Sugar, you can't keep your eyes off him," Marie said softly, suddenly at her side.

"That's because I might marry him."

"Somebody ought to," Marie murmured and made to leave.

Lauren caught hold of the sleeve on her cherry-colored cardigan. "You're not shocked by what I just said?"

"I told you, sweetie—stranger things. Why some woman hasn't already snapped him up and whisked him off on a honeymoon in Paris is beyond me."

She'd always known Marie's strengths, and since she'd been home she'd seen many more. But just how many talents did her aunt possess? "Did you know what I was going to do with Sage Springs?"

"It was obvious."

"Who told you? Ava?"

"Nobody told me! What else could you do with the place? It's exactly what our women need. A haven, that's what it's going to be. Now, let go of my sleeve. I need to have a word with Butch Buckner before Hortense eats him alive. I think she's got the hots for him."

Sage Springs Haven.

Could the name work? If her idea took off the way she believed it was going to, all the retail stores and businesses in town would benefit. The whole valley would benefit. Molly's photographic studio, Saul's hiking, and Momma Marie's blog wouldn't know what had hit it!

"Lauren!"

She turned to the sound of Mark's voice, excitement soaring and replacing her earlier dejection.

He beckoned her. "We're about to start."

No smile, no flirting tease in his eyes.

She'd spent a little time walking in and out of every room in Sage Springs after he'd left and before she ran up the hill to see Ava. She'd even sat on the staircase with the now broken treads. But nothing had swept over her. No coldness, no weird feelings, just—nothing.

What *was* his role in ending the curse and could she really see into the future?

Given his attitude so far tonight, all she'd be left with were memories of things that had never happened. But her future *was* full of what she'd have a hand in creating.

Sage Springs Haven.

She headed for the committee table, her heart light.

Chapter Sixteen

FIFTEEN MINUTES LATER, Lauren was finishing her speech where she'd enlightened everyone about her vision for Sage Springs Haven.

Mark had interrupted a number of times, but she'd kept a smile on her face because she didn't want their audience to notice any friction, although as far as she was concerned electric bolts were zapping between them.

"Finally," she said, "I'll be hiring people from town to help with renovations, redecoration, and for all the other small but important things I need for the cabin I'll be turning into an information hot spot. I think we can use the cabin to point our visitors to everything we have to offer, not just Sage Springs Haven."

She sat, pleased with the way her notion had been taken. Everyone had listened intently while she'd explained what Sage Springs would offer. The women nodding, a light of surprise and excitement in their eyes that made her insides warm and fuzzy.

Marie caught her eye from the back of the room and gave her a gleaming smile and a thumb-up approval. Davie was next to Marie, arms folded over his bodyguard chest, beaming at her.

"Congratulations, Lauren!" Mark said, standing, and applauding. "Wonderful concept!"

Everyone joined in the applause and Lauren ran her eye over the room and the townspeople she respected, some of whom she loved dearly.

"Now," Mark said, still on his feet and leaning his hands on the edge of the table as he looked out over their audience. "How can we use this brilliant business idea with what we've got in town and what we want to have in town?"

"I like the cabin idea," Ingrid said. "Hopeless has a tourist information board. Let's get ourselves a proper office and show them how it's done!"

"We need cake!" someone shouted.

"The Sage Springs cupcake!"

"The Surrender flapjack might bet better," Mr. Gerdin said. "All those oats are good for you."

"Hopeless has a parking lot, too, and a kid's play area. We'll need those."

"Wait!" Lauren said, raising her hand. She needed to put a halt to the arguing about what Hopeless had or didn't have. "We can certainly have specialized goods pertinent to Surrender, and of course we'll set out an area for parking and picnics. But let's leave the cupcakes to Hopeless while we do our thing in our own special way, because—"

"Lauren's right," Mark interrupted. "I haven't been here long enough to visit Hopeless or Reckless, but Surrender has historic elements that really stick out. Your town has an old-fashioned feel to it."

Their town. Not his.

"It's what I call yesteryear charm," Lauren interjected. "We're not going to be out of date or boring, but what we've got is quieter, more diverse than what they offer in Hopeless—and we'll still have all modern conveniences."

"You've got everything you need all around you," Mark said. "The outdoors. History. Charm. We just need to add *passion*!"

"Are you saying we're heading for success, Mark?" someone asked.

"Of course! What is it you've got that stands out? Let's think about that for a moment."

Lauren glanced up at him. They were supposed to be working *together* and it felt like he was taking over.

"Maybe you could tell us about your concepts for the bar?" she asked him.

"Oh—I think that's coming together nicely as it is."

If she could see into the future, why couldn't she see how Sage Springs Haven and the Scarlet Sage Saloon would or would not work alongside each other? Was it because nothing was going to happen with the bar?

"The whole town has genuine appeal," he told her. "Let's make use of it all." He looked out at everyone and gave the table a victory-thump. "Let's add that passion!"

"Fantastic ideas, Mark," someone shouted.

But he hadn't offered any ideas!

"Miss Flores wants to get her candle-making business up and running again," Ingrid said. "She's only fifty-three, so she's still got a heck of a lot of go in her."

Miss Flores sat at Ingrid's side, blushing the color of a ruby-red grapefruit.

"She's talented," Lauren advised Mark quietly. "She made the most heavenly candles, and offered candle-making packs to the public. They were popular." That was over a decade ago, when there'd still been a small turnover in town. But it went hand in hand with what the haven would offer. She was beginning to see a specific thread for the current and new businesses that would help reignite the atmospheric appeal of Surrender. Next, they needed a marketing plan.

She opened her mouth to speak, but Mark got in first.

"Miss Flores, this is great news. Having specialized talent and business in town is really going to help. It gives us a characteristic—and a place to start our marketing ideas."

That's exactly what Lauren had been about to say!

"Hopeless might have kick-started its many ventures," she said, determined to get her thoughts across, "but we've got something different. We've got the canyon on our doorstep for a start. The whole valley can make use of that. As an individual town, we don't have much to offer as we are now, but what we're going to offer in the future is going to be creative, eclectic, and worthy of curiosity."

"We're a no rush, no fuss kind of community," Hortense called out.

"That's it, Miss Lockwood!" Mark said with a grin. "We're going to use that slogan."

Hortense beamed. "I can think of more."

"You've got yourselves a pretty town," Mark said. "It just needs a bit of tidying up and sorting out."

"It's your town too," Lauren reminded him.

Thoughts and suggestions were coming thick and fast from the townspeople, and he was somehow twisting them around, making himself the instigator. He'd made a few wrong word choices too. *Our* town, then *your* town. *Our* marketing plan, then *your* needs. He was making this up as he went!

"We want visitors to the valley to come back, time and again," she told everyone. "We want them to know they've got a choice of three towns, each with a different appeal." She had a fleeting thought of Reckless—what on earth were they going to do with *that* town?

She shook the worry away. Best to concentrate on one town at a time. And anyway, there were more pressing things to think about, like—was she going to marry the man standing next to her? How the heck she might even *consider* saying yes to a marriage proposal from him was presently beyond her.

"What we'll have as a valley community is a welcoming vibe," she continued. "But we need to understand we're not going to get our town up and running fast." This was something she'd been considering all day. "However, we *can* show that we're citizen-driven."

"We're in the making," Hortense suggested, then turned to her neighbor. "That means we're demonstrating value. But first, we need to grasp the principle of our problems, and not head in trying to solve them with short-range projects."

Lauren had always known Hortense was a smart lady, and just a little on the odd side, but she'd never imagined her having such business acumen and insight. It seemed to be spilling out of her this evening.

"We can probably find all sorts of resources to help us," Ingrid said.

"I think we've got it all right here!" Mark told her. "Let's use what we've got and go with a free-spirited rhythm."

Everyone started congratulating each other and patting each other on the back or shaking hands.

Much as she was loath to admit it, Mark *was* creating passion. How did he do that? And he was more charged with each idea—which told her that before this meeting started, he hadn't had *any* ideas about what to do for the town.

"It's not like all of us will be operating businesses in town," Hortense said from the front row, craning her neck to peer at the people behind her. "But some of you can get jobs too. Diversity, that's what we need. Both for ourselves and for our tourists."

"Miss Lockwood," Mark said, "you took the words out of my mouth."

Lauren bet she had.

"Hopeless has all those signs around their town, too," Mr. Gerdin said. "We ought to have some."

"I'll make the signs," Butch said, and for a moment, everybody stilled, amazed that the quietest man in town had spoken up.

"I'll help you!" Hortense said, leaning forward to look at him at the end of her row.

"You can hurt yourself with a circular saw if you don't know how to use one. I won't allow that, Miss Lockwood."

Hortense's eyelashes fluttered. "How thoughtful, Butch. How about if I tell you what to write on the signs?"

Butch blushed harder than Miss Flores had, straightening on his seat, his big hands placed firmly on his knees, his focus on the wall directly in front of him. "If that's what you want."

"Oh, I think I want, Butch. I think I do."

Lauren coughed, attempting to dissipate the heat wave emanating off Hortense. It looked like she had a plan for Butch and if she wasn't mistaken, quiet solitary Butch might also be taken with the idea.

"The Buckners and Mr. Fairmont will be gainfully employed," she said, giving the gentlemen a thank-you smile. "But we'll need more help, and I've had a few ideas."

"We'll all pull together and do whatever we can!" Mark said.

Lauren ignored him. "Mr. Fairmont, you won't be doing any plastering and painting at the house until the brothers have built my wall. So I'd like to hire you to make some planter boxes for Main Street—like the ones you made for the entrance to the flower plot."

"You bet! I know where I can pinch some seedlings, too," Mr. Fairmont said with a conspiratorial wink at his wife.

"I'll happily supply seedlings and plant up the boxes!" she replied, beaming at him.

"We'll need to design and build the lady a proper flower shop," Doc Buckner said. "That would go down nicely if we get the candlemaker's up and running again. Would it help with your thoughts on creative, eclectic, and worthy of curiosity, Mark?"

"It sure will."

Lauren couldn't halt her frown. Hadn't eclectic and worthy of curiosity been her concept?

"I'll help," Kid said, smiling. "We can do stuff at night, too." He looked around. "I just can't believe we're getting all this work!"

Everyone returned his smile, murmuring approval for his willingness to step up and be useful.

"Don't forget Miss Lockwood's antique shop," Butch said, his voice barely audible. "That would add to the yesteryear charm you mentioned, wouldn't it, Mark?"

Yesteryear charm had also come from Lauren! Mark had called their town "old-fashioned."

"This is so exciting!" Mrs. Fairmont said, clapping her hands together. "In the meantime, Mark, could I use an area in the bar to sell my flowers? I've always wanted a proper flower stall, like an old wagon, if we can find one. It would look great in the saloon. So atmospheric!"

A shiver ran down Lauren's spine.

Mr. Gerdin nodded approval. "It would make the saloon a real friendly looking place."

"We can certainly discuss that further," Mark said with one of his engaging but noncommittal smiles.

Lauren could hardly believe it. She'd been shown he would have flowers for sale in his bar, in an Old West wagon, and here was the opportunity arising for the very scenario. Did that mean it was going to happen? That she *had* seen into the future?

"Talking of old wagons and the like," Mr. Fairmont said, "there's lots of memorabilia lying around the valley. I was always hoping to one day get the marketplace building opened as a museum."

"A museum?" Ingrid said. "That's *very* grand. I'm all for a museum. Hopeless doesn't have one."

They were back to seeing how Surrender could stack up against Hopeless. It wasn't that Lauren wanted it to be otherwise, but they had to regain a community feel, regardless of what they did with Surrender or what Hopeless did for Hopeless.

"We'll need financing for certain commercial needs," she told everyone, and flicked through her paperwork to find her notes on that issue.

"If me and my brothers are going to be engaged in building work at night," Doc said, "we'll need proper spotlights, we'll need scaffolding, and more power tools than we currently have on hand."

"And where will we get the money for the building materials for my flower shop?"

"I'll need some help with reopening my candle-making business," Miss Flores said, going red in the face again. "The shop's a mess. It's been closed for so long."

"There's more than that. Who's going to dig up the parking lot and build all the picnic tables for all our tourists?" someone asked.

"Or get one of the cabins ready for our information office?"

"I'm sure we'd get a grant for plenty of our needs," Lauren said, raising her voice to be heard. "Let me look into where we can appeal or apply for assistance. Although, I must warn everyone it won't be easy. We need to be prepared for the long haul, long-term."

"But the good thing is," Mark said, "you're not starting with nothing. You're regenerating what you once had and creating more from what you have now. I'm sure the bodies you appeal to for your grants will recognize that straight away. You'll be offering long-standing, viable, enduring options. You live here, so you'll want this to work and you'll commit for the rest of your lives. They'll understand that important factor. That's why I believe you can make this happen."

They could make it happen, not him.

"Smart man," someone said, which was followed by another round of applause.

"Hang on! We've forgotten the most important thing!" The room quieted as Mr. Gerdin stood.

"What are we going to do about these developers who are going to turn up any day now? Do we need to listen to them?"

"No!" Lauren said.

"Yes!" Mark said at the same time.

Lauren looked up at him.

"What I mean is, we make them think we're listening. If we don't appear to be professional, it'll make us look like mean-spirited, backwater bumpkins. Which we're not!"

There was silence after that. Not because of Mark's implication of backwater bumpkins, but because any day now

Donaldson's would arrive.

"I think we're done for the night," Mark said. "Lauren and I thank you for your amazing input. Everything discussed tonight is of real value. The Rejuvenate Surrender plan is a go, thanks to all of you."

There was a scraping of chairs as the meeting broke up, people returning their cake plates and coffee cups to the bar, chattering incessantly, giving the bar an excited vibe.

Lauren stood and packed her tote bag with her pen and paperwork.

"I thought that went well," Mark said, not looking at her.

"But we still haven't discovered how my haven will work alongside your saloon."

"We'll get there."

"It's a good job my townspeople helped you out with all *their* ideas otherwise you'd still be sitting in a closed, empty bar."

"I'll be forever grateful to them."

"I hope you mean that."

He looked at her.

She stared back.

"I imagine you're tired," he said at last. "It's been a long day."

He was brushing her off? She couldn't determine what thoughts were going through his head because his features were impassive. But there was something in his eyes. The same expressive look of regret—or remorse—she'd seen at the airport when he'd wished her *bon voyage*.

He took his focus off her. "Can I go now? Or do you have something else you want to say?"

If they *were* meant for each other, she could hardly say, "No! You can't go, because we're going to get married." She could hardly tell him they'd honeymoon in Paris and argue playfully over the price of a cup of coffee at the Arc de Triomphe.

He must have taken her silence for acceptance because he walked off, toward the doors where the Buckners and the Fairmonts were chatting as people filed out onto the street.

A split second later her ears cracked and the air got dense.

She was in the attic room at Sage Springs, but it was nothing like it had been in the vision where Mark was leaning over his books at the desk. It was still ramshackle and dusty. Nobody had been in this space for years.

She was looking through the opened window, at the road that led out of Surrender and watching Mark drive away, dust kicking up beneath the wheels of his rental car.

He was leaving. For good.

MARK SHOOK HANDS with people as they left, accepting their kind words of congratulations.

He was a heel.

Donaldson's were arriving first thing tomorrow and nobody knew but him. But at least the meeting had gone well, with some genuinely brilliant thoughts for the way forward. He was pleased for them. In many ways he was regretful he'd never see it all shape up.

He inhaled and readied himself as he waved off the last of the townspeople, knowing there was one more person in the bar.

He turned to her as she walked up to the doors, her tote bag in hand.

"Don't forget my grandmother wants to see you," she said, looping a lightweight scarf around her neck and shoulders.

He had forgotten. "I'll find time to visit. Where does she live?"

"I suggest you go tonight."

"It's almost ten o'clock."

"Frightened of the dark?" She glanced up, meeting his eye.

Oh, she was pissed. But he was hamstrung.

"Doesn't your writer's brain fire in all directions at the thought of coming face to face with a soothsayer who might be able to predict your future?" she asked.

The last thing he needed was somebody in the valley predicting *anything* about him.

"Can I walk you home?" he said, glancing out at the dark, quiet street.

"I've been walking the streets of this town all my life."

Yes, but there was still that scenario at the back of his mind where Mr. Donaldson in Bermuda might have her in mind for the dead body in Mark's crime scene.

"Hey," he said, touching her arm to halt her walking out the doors. "Watch your back, Lauren."

She gave a rueful laugh. "I can't tell you how many times I've been given the same warning in the last few days."

"I mean with this Donaldson's bunch. They're going to want to pull you down before anyone else."

Her eyes widened. "How would you have such insider information?"

"It's obvious. You're the go-to person in town. You're the one making changes."

She glanced at the committee table. "You could have fooled me."

"Look, I didn't mean to be overbearing during the meeting, but I felt it important to move things along. Even you put a stop to any would-be arguments about us being in competition with Hopeless."

"Now it's *us*?"

"I'm trying to watch everyone's backs here." More than she knew, but frustration was rising.

He hadn't wanted to hurt her feelings, and now that the meeting was over, he kept remembering her smile on the veranda. Had she been coming around to liking him? If so, he'd crushed whatever was blossoming between them with a damned heavy brick.

He watched her walk down Main Street toward the archway and out of sight. The moon was high; she'd have enough light to make her way home.

He closed the doors, locked them, switched off the main lights and moved to the bar where the overhead lights shone down on the glass bottles and the potted palm.

He gave the pot a shove, then slid his fingers over one of

the lush, green fronds.

Home. He'd never had one—apart from when he was a kid. He'd left at eighteen and set out on his own.

Being alone had never bothered him. Perhaps because it had never mattered before. There hadn't been anything at stake. But the emptiness and the silence in the bar was like a jury waiting to pronounce judgment. He might appear to be duping these people, but he was actually working for their good. He just couldn't tell them how, but if the real reason he was here ever got out, he'd be run out of town.

There wasn't time for remorse and regret. He had to ensure Donaldson's believed he was on the developer's side and not double-crossing them. When they were here in situ tomorrow morning, he might not get the chance to talk confidentially. People would be hanging around, listening to everything he said. He needed to put something into play now, tonight. But what?

Sage Springs.

He was certain they didn't know about the house; they'd never once mentioned it. If they understood how workable Lauren's idea was, how much enthusiasm it was going to muster, they'd want to squash it. They might even put a match to the house and burn it down. They might physically hurt her—and he couldn't have that. He couldn't have them hurting *anyone*.

What would they believe and yet discard as being viable to rebuild a whole town? The history of the Mackillops and the curse? Yeah, they'd have no choice because superstition abounded all over the valley and beyond.

He'd tell them the Sage Springs house was haunted and Lauren was opening it up as an attraction. He could throw in the wedding venue idea, too. That should put them off the scent of what she was really going to do, and it would make sense, since she'd run a boutique. They'd believe she was into ruffles and taffeta and bridal bouquets. He might add that the townspeople were arguing about the values of a boisterous saloon so close to the wedding venue. Make them think things were going badly, everybody confused about the best way forward.

He pulled out his cell phone and hit call for Boomer's number. As it rang, he pinched the bridge of his nose and turned his back to the mirror and the urge to look into it.

Chapter Se enteen

LAUREN SLAMMED THE front door to Sage Springs so hard, the remaining but now wobbly bannister shook.

She marched across the tiled hallway and up the stairs, skirting around the holes in the treads, not in the least bit concerned she'd stumble, fall, or even twist an ankle. That wasn't her lot. It wasn't her fate.

But it might be Mark's—and she wasn't referring to her great-grandfather and anything he might do to get rid of him from their lives. Right this moment she was inclined to invite him over so *she* could push him down the damned staircase!

She took a breath when she reached her bedroom, pulling off her scarf and throwing down her tote bag. It was useless getting riled. She needed to think this through. What the hell was he up to?

Would Marie know? Possibly—but she might not tell her niece.

Ava would certainly have a clue—but she'd talk in riddles, telling her to listen to her heart and not be tricked by words and actions.

But she *was* being tricked.

She fired up her laptop, plugged in the charge cord, and

hit Skype.

"You look gorgeous!" Molly said two minutes later, eyeing her dress. The one she'd bought from the original owner of the Manolo Blahnik boots. The one she'd worn because she thought it might make her feel a little more feminine than usual while she allowed the saloon owner to flirt with her.

"Did Mark notice how glam you look?" Pepper asked.

"He was too busy looking after himself and his own needs. There's something going on, and he's at the heart of it."

"Well of course he is! He's your man. The one fate dictated for you."

"Molly!" Lauren cried—then took another deep breath.

What *were* these dreams and visions? A pull between reality and what might be? Had she just been shown what could be but never would be? Was it some devilment from the great-grandfathers?

She looked at her cousins, waiting patiently for her to speak. They were so beautiful and she loved them to the ends of the earth and back. "Sorry for shouting. I'm at the end of my tether. I don't know what's going on!"

"Yeah," Pepper said. "But what can you do? You and this sexy Mark guy are going to share your lives and bring up your children together, no matter how much you're arguing now."

"How can that possibly be when I currently can't stand him?"

Pepper shrugged. "I don't know, but you're stuck in never-never land. I *told* you not to go home!"

Molly slapped a hand on the kitchen countertop in the hacienda. "Lauren—you have to keep him close and engaged. He's going to help end the curse on you and your town."

"But what about my suspicions? I *know* he's lying. If I'm a soothsayer, I must be correct!"

"I can't talk about what he's really up to. No!" Molly exclaimed before Lauren had a chance to interrupt. "It's not that I don't want to tell you, it's that I don't know. Alice told me to keep my nose out of it. I tried to pry into the otherworldliness that surrounds us, and she blocked me."

"Blocked you? The grandmothers can do that?"

"I wish they'd block me," Pepper mumbled. "Even I've been thinking about all this the last few days."

Lauren brought her focus back to the primary problem. Mark. Her blood boiled all over again. "Honestly, you should have seen him at the meeting tonight. Standing there in all his glory, raising enthusiasm and passion like he meant it."

"Passion, huh?"

"Could be he did mean it, once he got a taste of it," Molly said.

Was it possible? Was he being shown something too? Something of value to him? "Like what?"

"Think about it. What comes to your mind first?"

"Only my pathetic attempt at flirting with him and how I failed miserably!"

"You're just finding your courage with a man after misplacing it," Pepper said.

Both Molly and Lauren looked at her. It wasn't often Pepper came up with such prognostic declarations.

"What?" Pepper said. "It's nothing more than common sense. I'm like Marie. An ordinary woman with a lot of common sense."

"Says the woman who creates wonderful organic foodstuffs but prefers to eat junk food."

"Hey—it's not easy being a culinary genius! I need time off from all the healthy stuff. Just like Marie needs time out from all her hairdressing and beautification. That's probably why she started her blog."

Lauren caught Molly's eye. She knew about Marie's abilities now and so must Molly, but neither of them said anything. If this was Marie's preferred way of handling her gift, so be it. Pepper would find out for herself when the time was right.

"Okay," Lauren said. "What's your take on *this*? My latest vision told me he's going to leave me." As she stood in the attic watching him drive out of town, the Lauren in the vision had felt her heart plummet to her belly, as though she'd lost something precious—and that somehow, it had been her fault.

"I hope you have sex before he goes," Pepper said. "I'm looking forward to hearing about that part."

"Be serious!" Molly said.

"Come on. She was always an imaginative kid. Perhaps these visions are just a kind of regression, so she can walk into her future with more stamina."

"Perhaps I need psychotherapy."

Pepper chuckled.

"Without stamina, I wouldn't be here," Lauren told her. "I'd have taken up your offer to stay in your apartment in Arizona."

"Ah, but then you'd never have met the man of your dreams," Molly said.

"The man of my dreams is really annoying. And how can he possibly be *the* man?" There was no point falling in love with a guy who was going to leave.

"Never trust a man who says he can solve your problems," Pepper said, "unless he proves he can."

That's what Ava had said. How would Pepper know that?

She thought back to the Mark she'd begun to like. The man who'd teased her with a little seduction while she'd shown him around the house. The man who'd held out his hand and asked her to dance. He'd looked so handsome and earnest as he tried to ease the tension between them that her heart had gotten squished.

He was a fantastic kisser and probably knew how to hold a woman when he danced, but that wasn't love. That was fantasizing or hoping—or portending fate.

"What if I fall in love with him?" she asked, unbelieving of the possibility—but what did *she* know?

"More to the point," Molly said, "what if you don't?"

"Uh-oh. You've lost me now."

"It's her gift," Molly told Pepper. "It's not fully functional yet and won't be for a while, so we don't know for certain exactly what's going to happen. She's right. She might change his life by mistake."

Pepper rolled her eyes and picked up a tray of salsa 'n chips, ripping the top off the packaging.

"What if I do mess things up?" Lauren asked.

Perhaps there was already some Suzy Fletcher out there, waiting for him. What if he was meant for someone else and she channeled something and he changed his mind—or had his mind changed by forces she didn't understand—and fell in love with Lauren instead? That would be terrible. It wouldn't be real love or a real marriage. It would be entirely fake.

Pepper paused, a chip half way to her mouth. "You're falling for him, aren't you?" She threw the chip back into the tray. "He's not going to stay, you'll be heartbroken, and I'll hate him—even though I've never met him. I don't want to meet him. I hate him already—"

"Pepper—"

"Molly, stop interrupting."

"But you don't know what you're talking about."

"I know more than you think! This curse thing—I reckon there's some truth to it. As soon as I'm forced to come home, I'm not going to dither around like you two. I'm going to face it. I'll know it's there. I'll have the advantage."

"Wow," Molly said, almost in a whisper. "It's already happening for you and you're not even home yet."

Lauren leaned closer to her laptop screen. "You know that you're going to be forced to come home?"

"Don't be ridiculous," Pepper said. "Just because I think

there's a possibility I might be called home for some reason doesn't mean I'm predicting my future. I'm simply aware. I'm forewarned and forearmed, because let me tell you right now, if some man is out there and someone tells me he's meant for me, I'm going to find him before he even sets eyes on me."

"Then what are you going to do?"

"Punch him on the nose and make it bleed."

Molly blew out a hearty laugh.

"I'm not joking. I've tried several men in the last few years, and I've come to the conclusion they don't suit me or my intended lifestyle. I certainly won't accept one who's been *sent*. I'm going to remain unmarried and I'm going to be happy about it. The curse be damned. I'm going to beat it with its own intent." Pepper picked up a chip and dipped it into her tray of salsa.

"That's what I told myself," Lauren said. "Did you, Molly?"

Molly nodded. "Yep."

"You two," Pepper said, shaking her head. "You're so gullible."

"There's something else," Lauren said, running a hand over her eyes. Tiredness was creeping up, or maybe it was despair. "I had the strongest sensation earlier, about Mark. I think he's going to bring something bad down on our heads."

"I told you!" Molly said. "You have to stick by his side, and all you keep doing is pushing him away."

"He is suspect though," Pepper said. "I mean, he's got a

nerve, calling his saloon *Sage* when everything Sage in Surrender belongs to Lauren. Why would he do that except to piss her off? If he's the man of her dreams, why be so mean? I bet Donaldson's is using him in some way. They'll play you off him and vice versa, which means they'll be playing your business off his business. *That* could get nasty. You're going to have to keep on your toes, Lauren." She paused when she noticed her cousins staring at her. "What? It's common sense!"

"Right," Molly said, nodding. "Common sense."

Pepper yawned and put her salsa tray down. "Can we get some sleep now? What can possibly happen that you two soothsayers can't control?"

MARK WAS ABOUT to head upstairs to his private rooms when the roar of a motorbike out the back halted him.

His heart palpitated. Donaldson's men? Boomer? Had Lauren made it home safely? Damn! He should have walked her to Sage Springs whether she wanted his company or not.

Two seconds later, a wooden creak advised him he hadn't locked the rear door to the bar.

He glanced around, but there was nothing on hand to use as a weapon.

Then a woman walked through from the kitchen. "Ought to lock your back door," she said as she pulled off her helmet. "Never know who might walk in."

A whippoorwill gave a lonesome cry in the distance. Then an owl called out.

"King of the night sky around here, the great horned owl," she informed him. "You might want to listen out for the mateless mockingbird next. His cry says he's searching. It'll probably be a sound you recognize."

"Can I help you?" Mark asked, his throat thick.

She pierced him with a look from dark green eyes. "Lauren tells me you're a writer."

"Lauren?"

"My granddaughter. Don't tell me you haven't worked out who I am yet."

"You gave me a bit of a fright." He pushed out a shaky laugh. "I was supposed to come and see you…" He'd had no intention of visiting Wild Ava and hadn't for a second expected she'd turn up at his bar on a motorbike in the dead of night. "Would you like to sit?" he asked, pulling out a couple of chairs from a table close to the bar.

"I have a fancy to do a bit of writing myself," she said as she sat, using her boot to spin a third chair around so the seat was facing her. She lifted her feet and rested them on the chair edge.

"Really?" he asked, taking his own seat opposite her and attempting to control his breathing now that he knew who his midnight visitor was. "What would you write about?"

"How about I write your story? How about I put you in a position where you're under pressure? You have a family to protect, and for some reason that's why you've come to our valley."

Her eyes were olive green, and it was the all-knowing calmness in them that worried him.

"It's the reason behind it all that I'm concerned about," she continued. "People think you're worthy. I know different."

His features were stuck in a mask of incredulity and he thought perhaps even his heart had stopped beating.

"Spooked yet?" she asked, with a light in her eyes and a smile on her face.

He granted her a laugh. "Kind of."

"You're wondering how I know so much about you."

But she didn't. She couldn't possibly.

"I can do better," she said, and nodded at the rear side of the bar. "A mirror is like the surface of a lake. It can reflect what's next to it, but it also holds depth. What's behind or beneath the surface reflection—that's what you've got to ask yourself."

Okay, now he was freaked.

"What are you saying?"

"Perhaps I'm saying you're seeing things in the mirror because you need to see them."

A happy little girl, dancing her heart out? Why be shown that?

"Lauren was the one who told me my bar was cursed."

Ava smiled. "She was getting your hackles up."

"So there's no curse in here?"

"Only if you believe it."

It was what Lauren had said. People thought they were cursed, and eventually, if they believed it for long enough, it appeared to the rest of the world that they were. It still didn't explain how a rational man like himself saw those images.

"And the curse on her house? Is she safe in there?"

"What did you feel when you were in the house?"

He shrugged. "A little odd at times. Like there was someone at my back."

She nodded. "Gave you a taste of what it feels like when someone's at your back, snooping on you."

He straightened. Okay, that was scraping bone.

"What's precious to you?" Ava asked.

His mom. His sisters. They all still lived at home. His older sister was a bit of a loner, even at the age of thirty-seven, and he wished she'd found someone to share her life with. The middle sister was twenty-seven and shy to the point of painfulness. If she found a man to fall in love with, the guy would have to be equally reserved, although hopefully not as timid as she was, so that together they could drive the other forward. His twenty-year-old sister was a different kettle of fish. She'd never known their father—he'd left before she was born—and she thought the world was at her feet. Their mom worried she was too openhearted to see the bad in some people. The women in Mark's family were typical Dubois women. Shy, smart, a little sassy if pushed around by their brother, who was still and had always been the only male in their lives. But they were kind and generous. Just wanting to get on with their lives.

How come he wasn't made the same way? Why had he been given the genes of wanderlust, with no reason to look for a settled environment?

Was he just like his father?

"Are you in trouble?" Ava asked, breaking his reflection.

"No." He shrugged off her question with a smile.

"I think you are. Your father's in trouble and his issues are raining down on you."

He couldn't smile that one away. How could she know anything about his father?

She waited, watching him. Patience oozing off her.

He swallowed. Okay, he needed to maneuver this conversation. "I am here because of my father, in some ways." It was what he'd already told Marie, so he could open up a little now and stay as close to the truth as possible. "He got into trouble, and I'm trying to find a way to ensure my mother and my sisters aren't on the receiving end. He messed up." Big-time.

"He messed up the moment he left your mother."

Mark stared. It wasn't possible, even for a genuine soothsayer, to have this amount of accurate information.

"What would your father do," she asked, "if he were in a real bad position of his own making?"

"Run. He'd kick a puppy if it got in his way. His family means nothing to him."

"And what would you do?"

"I'd try to work it all out so it's fair for everyone. If I couldn't do that, I'd hand myself in."

"Which means you're not like him."

The sad fact was, he was becoming more like his father every second he was here in Surrender, and he'd better watch what he said or he'd end up giving her the entire sorry tale.

She pulled at a hessian bag tied to her belt, placed a white cloth on the table, and threw the bag's contents onto it.

"Runes?" he asked. The stones were crafted from crystal pieces in similar size and shape but were multicolored and multifaceted. Three jade-green stones had fallen slightly to one side.

"Those are yours," she told him.

"Aren't I supposed to ask a question of the universe before you throw the stones?"

"No need. I know what your question is. I know why you're here."

"Like I said, I'm here because I needed to get away for a while." The only question he had was *what the hell is going to happen next?* He nodded at the stones. "I hope you're going to give me some good news."

She chuckled. "There's no end until you've gotten yourself through the start and the middle. I reckon you're at the middle."

So how was it going to end?

"You're at cross purposes," she told him.

She was right. His purpose was *double*-crossing.

"Are you playing us, Mark Sterrett? Or do you want to be genuine?"

He wanted a lot of things, probably her granddaughter included, but she didn't know about his situation. She couldn't possibly. Was it guesswork? Did she know of a way to peel back layers, pinch relevant bits of information from all around her, then use it to taunt a guy?

"Are you going to write about all this one day?" she asked.

"No."

"I think you will."

He didn't move; he didn't even blink. Was that a prediction? He hadn't intended to write again, ever. "What do those stones tell you I'm going to do?"

"I already know what you're going to do. I'm helping you find your way. That one," she said, pointing to the left jade-green stone, "is an element of the past. People are doing you a favor. You're wondering about having to respond in kind." She glanced at him, then down. "The middle stone refers to your dawning. Your understanding. You'll feel energized like never before. The stone on the right is your future. Providence. Karma. Fruitfulness."

"Sounds like it's good news."

"Depends how you decide to plant your crops." She gave him a look that made his spine tingle. "That which has been sown will then be reaped," she said quietly.

Again, she was right. He'd lose the friendship and camaraderie he'd built up with the people in this valley. He'd lose face due to having stabbed them in the back. He'd probably never be the same man.

"That middle stone says you're going to go down before you come up again. This cycle is eternal, and it started when you were a child. You ran from what you experienced as a young boy. Lack of paternal love and your parents' difficult marriage. You won't find love again—a man's love for a woman—until you look for it. And you're going to have a tough ride."

"Thanks," he said, unable to halt the wry tone.

"Be careful about your feelings and what you believe. Especially around Lauren."

"Why?"

"You'll be given an option, and it'll tear you in two. You won't believe it possible. You'll run from it."

"And that's a mistake?"

"It depends which path you take."

"Which one do you think I'll take?"

"Can't say."

"Take a bet."

The air got serious all of a sudden.

"You're the one to make the decisions about what you believe, Mark Sterrett. I'm trusting you."

Somehow, this woman knew he was playing everyone around him, but she wasn't sentencing him. "Can you write a person's fate and it plays out?" Was she showing him an exit route from the mess he was in?

"No. Neither can Lauren."

"What has she got to do with my future or my fate?" There was no way Lauren could help him, and no way he wanted her involved in the current seedy side of his life. For all he knew, he'd end up branded a criminal.

Ava rose. "I'll throw the lock on the door after me," she said, picking up her helmet from the bar and making her way to the kitchen without looking back. "And remember—change is up to you. Listen out for that call from the mockingbird."

Did she think he was lonely and wanted a mate? Or was it a play on words and she was *mocking* him?

As for change, his future was set, thanks to his father. He'd be on his own for years to come, forever recalling how badly he'd behaved—or appeared to have behaved—during his short stint as a bar owner.

He scrubbed his face with his hands as the back door closed, the click of a lock falling into place. Whatever she'd wanted him to hear or feel during that extraordinary meeting, it was up to him to make sense of it all.

He'd spoken about passion at the meeting. Passion and value. He had to make an impact with more than words. With more than nods of agreement and suggestions of how *they* could change the fate of *their* town.

He'd been working alone all the time he'd been here, without realizing what he had around him—value and passion. From the townspeople themselves.

For a second, part of him longed to be one of them. Their slow way of life was about to change, and the only way he could at least attempt to make things right before he left was to become actively involved.

One day he might look around for a place like Surrender. Somewhere to put down roots. Unless he was in prison…

He pulled out his cell phone and sent his mom a text. *"Hey, Mom. How are you?"*

A few minutes later she replied.

"Darling! What are you doing texting this late?"

Time hadn't been on his mind.

"Sorry. Been writing hard. Forget what day it is!"

She sent him a kiss-kiss. *"All well here. Take care of yourself. And don't forget to EAT!"*

He found a smile. She was okay. Nobody had gotten to

her or frightened her with strange phone calls or threats.

Next, he sent a text to Boomer. *"I'm ready for you tomorrow. Everything in place. They had a town meeting tonight—and they don't know what they're doing."*

Then, he dialed the Buckners. "Doc," he said when the middle brother picked up the landline phone. "I've just discovered Donaldson's will be here first thing in the morning. I need everyone's help. I've got a plan."

Chapter Eighteen

A LOUD, PERSISTENT banging brought Lauren around from her dreamless sleep. She pulled the pillow over her head but the noise continued.

Someone was at the front door.

She pushed the coverlets back as a breeze ruffled the heavy curtains against the window she'd left open last night, revealing a patch of dark sky and a spattering of stars. It wasn't even dawn!

She got out of bed and padded to the armchair reaching out for her dressing gown. It couldn't be bad news. If anything had happened to her cousins, or Marie, or any of the grandmothers, they wouldn't spend time knocking on the door. Davie would likely punch his way right through it.

"Coming!" she called when she was halfway down the stairs, picking her way around the damaged steps. "Where's the fire?"

She undid the heavy bolt, turned the key in the lock, and pulled the door open.

"I let you sleep as long as I could," Mark said. "But now you have to come with me."

She *must* be dreaming. Or was she envisioning things in

her sleep now? She pinched her wrist to check if she was awake—*ouch*!

"Get dressed," Mark said.

"Where are we going? A costume party?" He was wearing jeans with a silver buckled leather belt, a button-down black shirt open at the collar, a high-point black Stetson with the brim pulled low enough that a shadow banded his eyes—and a silver star on his breast pocket that said Sheriff.

"You look ridiculous!"

"I'll explain as we walk. Can you please get dressed?"

She pinched the skin on her wrist again. Surely she was dreaming.

"Lauren," he said in a tone that suggested he was holding onto his patience. "Donaldson's will be here at nine a.m."

That was like a slap in the face with a cold, wet fish. "We're not ready for them!"

"Yes, we are. I'm opening up the saloon so we can put our own campaign on show."

"We're what?"

"Don't worry, everything's under control."

"*What* everything? Why didn't you wake me up earlier? And if you're in that get-up, what the hell am I supposed to wear?"

"Dress for the press. Donaldson's is bringing reporters. By the way—I met your grandmother. She popped in late last night."

That couldn't be right. "Ava never visits anyone. People go to her. It's a rule all the grandmothers have."

"Looks like I'm special."

"What did she tell you?"

"I have no idea. But I was inspired when she left. I'm changing the play. The Buckners, Hortense, the Fairmonts, the Gerdins, and a few others have been in the bar all night. I'll explain as we walk. Oh, and don't worry about breakfast. I got you pretzels. White fudge. They're your favorite, aren't they? I also picked up my coffee machine a few hours ago. I couldn't get through this day without decent coffee. None of us could."

She momentarily lost track of everything else he'd been saying. "Coffee machine? In the middle of the night?"

"Anything's possible when you wave the right amount of moolah under people's noses."

Lauren stared.

"Fate, Lauren. We're going to beat it, but we can't do it without you, so would you please put your skates on and get dressed?"

He was going to challenge fate? What on earth had Ava said to him?

"HOW COME YOU'RE so amenable today?" Lauren asked as she walked-skipped to keep up with him.

He ducked his head beneath a low hanging vine of coral honeysuckle on the redbrick archway and came to a halt. "I've been up all night, don't push your luck."

She'd been firing questions at him for the last ten minutes, trying to get her head around what was going on and his role in it. Along with the surprise of his having a plan to deter the developers today, she wasn't able to stop the niggling sensation he was bringing trouble to town.

"So we're going to make Donaldson's believe we're making a mess of it all?" she asked, still disbelieving of the value of this plan.

"They're going to laugh us off. We're all going to be arguing about ideas for growth. They won't know that what we put into place at the meeting last night is actually going to work because we're designing that growth around what we've already got."

She narrowed her eyes. "Are you sure this is wise? We've had an awful lot of laughter pointed at us in the past."

He checked his watch. "They'll be here in two hours. What's your alternative plan?"

"If you'd woken me earlier, I might have had a chance to come up with one!"

"They won't know that your business plan for the haven is going to be the maidenhead. The pillar. The matriarch. The business that joins not only any new retail in town but also the entire valley. Think about it—your haven is going to be like your cousin's photography studio. It's going to open up opportunity for everyone in Calamity Valley."

"I know that!" She couldn't help but think he was solving her problems without having been asked, and without any real thought for the consequences. "What about your saloon? What role is that going to play in today's charade?"

He smiled, the freshness of the light in his eyes contradicting the fact he hadn't slept. The creases around his dark brown eyes and the slight shadow beneath suggested a little weariness, but she'd only noticed because she was so close to him.

She was about to step back when he took her hand.

"I'm feeling good, Lauren. About everything."

"What everything?"

"We're going to win."

"Against the developers?"

"Against them and everything else against us. There's just one thing." His tone was lowered, his smile gone. "I'll let you do the front man thing today. You can handle the press and the PR stuff. I'll stay in the bar. If I stick close to the developers, I'll overhear things that could help us, and I can also put them off the scent of what we're really doing for this town. You be the front man. You can talk truthfully to reporters about our plans. You're our anchor man."

"You mean woman."

He ran his eyes over her body, right down to her pale green pumps, then back to her face. "I certainly do."

She'd pulled her own clothes out of her wardrobe. Nothing designer, just off the rack. She felt presentable in her silk top the color of a string of pearls and her fawn-colored pants. She ought not to be so pleased he'd noticed.

He squeezed her hand, his eyes warming with the tease she was used to seeing. The tease she'd missed last night when he'd been so abrupt with her and had taken over the meeting.

"Let's get you some breakfast. Kid's been cooking eggs since four a.m. And Mrs. Fairmont's setting up her flowers. I'll buy you a bunch."

Her heart skipped a beat.

"What kind would you like? Or can I choose?"

Was he being considerate, hoodwinking her, or falling for her? Something had changed him, and it might have been something *she'd* done, even though whatever gifts she possessed were jumbled and new and baffling.

His seductiveness and romanticism at the house had been real—or she'd thought it had—and there *was* a pull of attraction between them, there had been from the start, but he'd also been cagey from the beginning, never telling the truth about his reason for being here.

Now he was talking about buying her flowers and he wanted to choose them. Would he decide on the dahlias? The big orangey-yellow flowers that looked as though someone had painstakingly stuck a thousand petals together to create the perfectly balled flower head. They weren't her favorite, she hardly gave them a glance—but she'd been shown the future when they would be her preferred flower because the love of her life had chosen them.

"This is all so confusing," she muttered. He was going to attempt to alter fate, but did he have any understanding of what fate had in store for him? Was he supposed to change it? Was she supposed to stop him?

"Why *are* you dressed like a sheriff?"

"It'll all make sense in thirty seconds," he said, pulling her along, his hand still around hers. "Come on. I'll show you."

A minute later Lauren stood in front of the bar, mouth open, eyes wide, as she read the new signage painted in curling gold and moss-green script.

Desert Sage Saloon

Wholesome food and quality entertainment for the whole family

Come on in! Bring the kids.

(Free lunch for under-fives and octogenarians)

"Kids?" She looked around, half expecting to see some.

Mark led her forward then released her hand as he bounded up the steps to the veranda, pushing through swing doors and holding them open.

"Where did you get those?" They were proper Old West-style saloon doors.

"Hortense found them at the back of her shop. Butch put them up. What do you think?"

She glanced up at the sign again. "Entertainment for the whole family?"

"It's going to be a place for tourists to take a break, grab some lunch or just coffee and a slice of the famous Surrender flapjack. No hard liquor, but I'm thinking wine and fancy beers would be acceptable, plus soft drinks, and milkshakes for the kids."

"You're doing this for real?" she asked as she made her way up the steps.

"Why not? It's a great idea."

"And the sheriff outfit?"

"I was coerced into it. But I am the proprietor and we're a family-orientated saloon with our own law enforcement. Any kid who doesn't eat his or her greens is going to have to talk to me about it." He adjusted his hat and rocked on his booted heels as though in arrest mode.

She spluttered a laugh.

"Still think I look ridiculous?"

Her eyes skimmed the breadth of his shoulders He was too self-possessed, had too much confidence to be anything but handsome and engaging. And he wore the Stetson like he'd been born in it.

But she wasn't about to say any of that. She wiped the remainder of her smile away. "Okay, Sheriff Mark, show me inside."

Hammering, chatter, some laughter, and a few barked orders met her when she walked through the doors.

Hortense, Ingrid, and Miss Flores were over at the coffee machine, handling various parts as steam rose and the frothing spout hissed.

"I set the machine up," Mark said, following her gaze, "but I couldn't figure out how to make it work, so the ladies took charge."

"We've got it going!" Ingrid called. "First proper coffee of the day coming up!"

"Good work!" Mark called back. "Everyone take five." He turned to Lauren. "Marie's on her way and Davie was here earlier. He helped me collect the coffee machine."

"Want some eggs, Lauren?" Ingrid called. "Kid's cooking."

She shook her head. Her stomach was too knotted to eat. There was so much to take in.

The walls above the wood paneling and in all the recesses had been painted a fresh, pleasing light green. The railing cordoning off the bar and what had been the dining area was still in place. All the tables and chairs behind it had been polished and set with white china vases filled with sage.

"Where did you get the sage?"

"Your place. I figured you wouldn't mind—and I am currently the law around here, so I took advantage and pinched some."

The bar was too large and cavernous for the aroma of the herb to take precedence, but the hint of its perfume reminded her of Sage Springs house and the overgrown gardens.

"No *Scarlet*?" she asked him softly.

He bowed his head and met her eye. "Desert Sage Saloon is perfect, if you're okay with me using the word *sage*."

It was a fine name, and it drew Sage Springs and the town together.

There were signs everywhere.

Adventurers Gaming Corner had a selection of Scrabble and Monopoly boards, a pile of puzzle books, and kids' drawing equipment.

She walked toward the sign Rough and Tumble Corner by a side door and looked out the window to the rear gardens and a bounce house.

"Where did you get *that*?"

"Old Gerdin went over to Reckless and borrowed his great-grandson's. Took us nearly all night to inflate it. He cranked the hand pump like there was no tomorrow. We had to make him lie down once it was up."

"Is he all right?"

"Said it gave him a new lease on life, seeing his old bar

take a turn like this."

She took her focus for a ride around the room again. Her heart beat a little faster when she saw Mrs. Fairmont setting up her buckets and pails filled with her homegrown flowers.

The Flowerpot Corner, the sign said.

Her focus got stuck on the dahlias. They *were* attractive, now she gave them a proper look.

"Was this all your idea?" she asked, turning to Mark.

"I had the notion about how to put the developers off the scent, and everyone took it from there. They're behind this, Lauren, and I think they're up for it."

"I can't tell you how annoyed I am you didn't wake me up along with everyone else."

"You're going to have your hands full today. I wanted you to get as much rest as possible."

"But still, I could have—"

"You'll need your wits about you. You're our anchor person, remember."

The plan was she tell the truth to the press and everyone else fool Donaldson's with tall tales of ideas they felt would rejuvenate the town. Donaldson's would be thrilled, thinking it was going to be an easy deal after all, because no way would the nonsensical plans be viable. Mark said the developers would be rubbing their hands, believing Surrender was about to fall apart, and thinking they could swoop in within a month and grab the land for much less than already offered due to the town failing and the residents being utterly despondent.

"But if the press knows the truth, Donaldson's will find

out as soon as they leave town."

"Yes, but we need to hoodwink them just for today. We want to make a good impression with the press and any outsiders who turn up. If we're arguing with the developers, that's going to be the main story, making us all look like we really *don't* know what we're doing."

Lauren bit her inner cheek. "You're not making us a laughingstock on purpose, are you? Because all this," she said, indicating the incredible transformation in the bar, "looks plausible." Everything about the newly named Desert Sage Saloon and its sudden attractions for families not only worked on a commercial level, it also went hand in hand with their town's ambience and with what she was going to offer at the haven.

"That's why our double play is so brilliant. The developers will think me a nut job, but we know it's all going to work."

"How are we going to keep the developers away from the reporters?"

"That's my role."

"What if the press wants to talk to you?"

"I'm hoping you'll keep them away from me." He drew her to one side, away from Mr. Fairmont, who was moving his painting gear and stepladder. "I've mentioned this to Marie, and also now to Ava, but I haven't told you. There's a problem with my father. He hasn't been in our lives for twenty years, but he's done something wrong and I'm trying to clear up his mess. I need to keep out of the way of the press because I have a mom and three sisters. If it all blows up, they might be caught up in it."

"What has he done?"

He shook his head, his eyes closed for a moment. "I don't want to drag you into it. You've got enough to handle."

Listen. Watch. Trust.

Her heart was telling her he was embroiled in more misfortune than he was letting on. "I'm sorry for your troubles."

"Nothing I can't handle."

This was certainly a changed man. Had he been given something of value by coming to the valley, like her cousins had said? Whatever his problems were, had he found a means of dealing with them while here?

"Like I told you, Lauren, it was Ava who instigated everything that happened overnight. Not directly, but she inspired me, although I still don't know why she was talking about my future path, or how I was the one to make decisions."

So that was what she'd said. But what decisions would he have to make?

"You inspire me, too," he said with a smile. "Ever since I was in Sage Springs house, something I can't put the right word to is different. I feel more in control."

"Of what?"

He shrugged. "Destiny?"

This was the problem. What was his destiny?

"You just concentrate on pulling the press aside," he told her. "Talk about your vision for not only the town but the valley. They'll believe you."

"Why would they?"

"Because you're smart. Because you're poised. Because you can talk the talk. You've got guts and everyone in your presence knows that within minutes of meeting you."

She was no longer the woman who'd portrayed sleek aloofness in California to gain entry to her ultra-wealthy customers' playground. She wasn't sure she could pull off the real Lauren, although the rise of adrenaline flushing through her said she didn't have to pretend, she just had to be.

"All right," she said, nodding acceptance. It might work. Anyway, there was no time to come up with a different plan.

Chapter Nineteen

GRACE. THE WORD came to Mark so quickly as he watched Lauren walk down the veranda steps and make her way to one of the cabins where the Buckners had begun clearing it out, that he paused to let the deduction sink in.

It was the right word for Sage Springs, too. An effective and evocative adjective that implied emotion, not just a visual depiction. The house, and its owner, was graceful and elegant. Poised. Soft of limb, strong of heart.

He raised a hand to block the sun when its rays fell on Lauren, cloaking her slim frame, lighting up the tips of her chestnut hair, and making her look like a lifeforce, a guiding light.

What facets of the Mackillop gift did she possess? Were they visible or hidden beneath a cloak of secrecy?

He'd probably never find out, but if he were to write about this town, like Ava had said he would, he'd show that graceful elegance in Lauren. That meant he'd also have to marry her off to some guy who wandered into town one day, because there was no chance a woman like Lauren wouldn't get a marriage proposal—or a dozen. But what sort of guy would he write for her? What sort of man would capture her heart?

He was sure she was more than slightly attracted to him and their attraction to each other was an unusually heightened thing. Something bigger than both of them, regardless of the deceit on his part and the need to fight it out on her part.

How could his relationship with her possibly end well? He'd teased and flirted from the start, but it had been an involuntary need to reach out to her, to communicate with her, although he could only now see the truth of that. Now that he knew her, he respected and admired her, and he also thought her the loveliest woman he'd ever met, inside and out. His desert sage.

Wow, he'd wanted to say when she stood on the street earlier, looking at the new sign on the bar, her hair cascading around her shoulders and her face a picture of surprise. His heart had billowed, and he'd felt as though he'd been brushed with the wispy trails of a bewitching spell.

He was his own man and had always been proud of that, of never having to rely on others. Never begging for a loan or sleazing his way in or out of a situation. This morning, he was a changed man. He was ready for anything, and he was going to write his own story—and, by God, he'd make sure it was a good one. A happy, fulfilling story of real life.

The early morning clouds moved and the sun's rays streaked across the rooftops of his town.

His—again, he was making pronouncement out of nowhere. *His* town. *His* girl.

He didn't know what it meant, but he wasn't going to question it. He liked her. He more than liked her; he practically adored her. Suddenly, as though out of nowhere, certainly since he'd been in her ballroom, his heart had gotten involved with the town and with the town's beautiful daughter.

He thumped the veranda railing with a fist.

Donaldson's be damned. Whatever he had to do, he was going to do it. "Bring it on," he murmured.

His cell phone rang.

Boomer.

Hell. What now?

LAUREN CHECKED HER watch. They had less than half an hour until Donaldson's arrived.

"Sure you don't want breakfast?" Ingrid asked. "Kid and Butch are going to do chef duty for us all day."

Lauren shook her head. The flutter in her belly was nerves and she couldn't have forced down even a white-fudge pretzel. She'd have to put on the professional persona soon. The woman who knew exactly what was happening in her town—and she'd only just discovered most of it two hours ago.

She'd left the cabin in the capable hands of Doc and Butch, after making a few suggestions for her initial needs. They'd cleared the cobwebs, brushed and washed the tiny veranda, and Mr. Fairmont had given the interior a swift coat of calm, cream paint.

She'd returned to the bar to check with Mark about what else was needed, but he wasn't around.

She glanced up the stairs to his private rooms where she'd been told he'd gone. What was he doing?

"So we're selling food?" she asked Ingrid, bringing her attention back to the goings on in the Desert Sage Saloon.

"Only staples, like burgers, fries, chili—and our famous flapjacks. Turns out Kid Buckner's got a baker's hand. He's the one who made the flapjacks. Three hundred of them!"

Three hundred? The flutters got worse. How many members of the press would turn up? A handful of half-hearted reporters? Or a dozen keen, perceptive journalists looking for a real story? One they could get their teeth into.

"How's the cabin?" Hortense asked. "Need any ornaments? Old swivel chairs? Books? Maps of the world?"

"Thanks, no. I've got a desk and a noticeboard. Miss Flores is printing off leaflets for me at Duggan's General Store and I've got vases of sage and honeysuckle." It helped take away the smell of fresh, still-wet paint.

She glanced at the staircase again. Was Mark up there, alone, worrying about his father, or his mother and three sisters?

Knowing he had all those females in his life gave her one more decent perspective of him. What unpleasantness could he bring down on them? He wouldn't have been up all night, working so hard, spending his money on expensive coffee machines if he was conning them. Although if her visions were true, he was leaving. Even Ava said he was going to leave. Why would he, after sinking so much into the saloon and the regrowth for Surrender? How would she feel if he did leave?

Lost. Sad. And somehow—responsible.

People survived decades of marriage because they shared things. Secrets, wishes, desires. What did she and Mark share? Lies. They were opposites and a terrible match.

She had to step back from him and not allow him to flirt or behave in a romantic way until she was sure she *wasn't* capable of changing his future. Because it looked like her crush was back.

Why couldn't she have been an ordinary woman who hoped the man of her dreams might one day turn up, but who didn't really expect him to? Hope was a much better emotion than guilt. If she was changing Mark's future, there was a lot to feel guilty about.

"Uh-oh!" Hortense called out. "Here comes trouble!"

Lauren spun to the windows as the blogmobile ground to a screeching halt outside.

Marie got out, a vision in Chanel-style silks and tweeds. She slammed the driver's door, marched up the steps to the veranda and through the open saloon doors, waving a newspaper above her head.

"Sweetie! Don't panic. I can control this."

MARK GRITTED HIS teeth as he answered Boomer's call. He'd jogged up the stairs to his rooms for privacy but could still hear the activity and voices from the bar below.

"Your father's gone missing," Boomer said without preamble.

"He's *what?*"

"A little mishap our end. You need to find him."

"How the hell can I do that?" He hadn't even spoken to him for twenty years, let alone seen him. He didn't have a clue what the man was like or the way he thought. "I can't leave town. Your men are turning up any moment. I need to be around."

"You're going to fix this little problem for us, Sterrett."

He'd guessed that Donaldson had his father imprisoned somewhere in Bermuda, waiting to be flown to California and the crime scene the hit guys had set up if Mark didn't come up with the intelligence about what the Mackillops were planning to do with Surrender. But maybe there was a chance to get out of this mess now. Own up to his own deceit, take the consequences, but be assured his family and the people of Surrender—and Lauren—were safe.

"How about I just call the cops?"

"You do that and maybe someone you know will turn up dead at the crime scene."

"You touch *anyone* and I'll find you. If it takes me the rest of my life, I'll find you."

Boomer laughed, deep and rumbling. The sound now so familiar it made Mark's teeth hurt.

"You're not in control though, are you, Sterrett?"

Neither was Boomer, since he was *requesting* Mark's assistance. "Where were you holding my father?"

"It doesn't matter. He's on the run."

"I need a place to start. You have to give me more. Does

he have money? Does he have access to his bank accounts?"

Boomer didn't answer for a few seconds. "He spent the cash he had on an airfare. We closed his accounts when we discovered his crime against Mr. Donaldson."

Then opened a new bank account for him—with a fake charitable name. But this intel gave him something to start on. Johnson Sterrett was out there, with nothing in his pockets and nobody to turn to.

"Where did he fly to?"

"California," Boomer said, his voice hard.

Mark felt like he'd been kicked in the chest. "Where in California?"

"We don't know."

"How did he get away from you?" His father's escape indicated they'd either been soft on him or his father had genuinely given them the slip. Was he that smart?

"Stop with the questions! Just find him."

Boomer cut the call.

Where would a criminally intent, broke, ageing playboy go in California? Unfortunately for Mark's heart, the one person Johnson might think still cared enough about him to help him or hide him was the wife he'd left high and dry two decades ago.

He punched in his mom's number on the cell phone.

"Darling! How lovely to hear from you again so soon. Still working hard?"

"I sure am." He made himself smile so he didn't sound like he was clenching his back teeth. "Mom, there's something I want to ask you, and it's going to be a bit of a shock.

Do you know where Dad is?"

The silence pinned him to the spot. His mom's brain would be ticking as she attempted to figure out why he was asking. "I just wondered, because I'm working on this story for some guy, and the plot is turning out to be a little like our family's. You know—a mom left with four kids, Dad does a runner…" He didn't need to remind her of what that particular plotline entailed.

"Bermuda," she answered, sounding cautious. "You know that."

"I don't suppose you've heard from him recently?"

More silence, then an intake of breath. "Mark, if you suddenly feel the need to get in touch with your father, I will not stand in your way."

"No! It's nothing like that." He didn't want to get in touch with the man. He certainly didn't want to meet up with him. He'd likely kill him and end up doing time for it.

"You've gotten me a little worried recently, darling. You fly into LA unexpectedly, then you disappear. I haven't called you because I don't want to interfere, but I hear nothing for over a week, then I get a text message and now a phone call the next morning."

His mom was a loveable, engaging woman, but when it came to her children, she was a bear. The weekly call was a ritual. Just a few words to let her know he was fine, he was working, and usually to also let her know that he hadn't met a nice woman he was planning on settling down with. But the last few days he'd been remiss, with a lot more on his mind.

"Been a little busy," he explained. "This script is a difficult one. Lots of twists and I haven't quite nailed it. I've been holed up."

"Are you at your apartment?"

"I'm at a friend's place. So—you haven't heard from him? No phone call out of the blue? A letter? A note? Anything?"

"Mark, what's going on?"

"I told you. It's this storyline. It's the first time I've had such a block." His mom was already involved in this thing more than he would like. Worst of all, she didn't know it and he couldn't tell her. Not while he was still in the game and had some means to maneuver Donaldson.

But he'd worried her.

"Actually, Mom, you're dead right. My mind's all over the place. I *have* met someone. She's getting under my skin."

"Oh, Mark!"

"It's nothing yet. You know how these things are. I like her. I think she likes me…"

"Who is she?"

"Someone I met at LAX."

"Does she live in Laredo too?"

"No. I'm—I'm at her place. Look, I've got to go. Let me know if you hear from Dad, would you?"

"Darling," his mom said, sounding guarded suddenly. "It's odd that you ask about your father, because Mrs. Rosemont—she's the one whose second cousin burned down the video rental store ten years ago because his DVD kept jamming—well, she knocked on my door yesterday, totally surprising me, and told me her cousin had seen your father."

Mark's heart palpitated.

"I said it wasn't possible," his mom said. "But it's a coincidence that you've now asked me about him."

"Must have been someone who looked like him. He's in Bermuda, like you say. There's a lot to keep him there." Or there had been, like lonely, wealthy widows looking for holiday romance and a man to spend their money on. Like a great job as a property manager, before he embezzled half a million dollars.

"I expect you're right," his mom said, sounding relieved. "Although Mrs. Rosemont said he'd told her cousin he was going to Venice Beach."

He could get lost and stay lost in that area. But only if he had enough cash. Unless he was intending to worm his way into the affections of some wealthy widow or divorcee. "Did this man who looked like Dad ask Mrs. Rosemont's cousin for money? Did the cousin say anything else?"

"Not a thing."

It was all he was going to get, but it was a start. "Okay, Mom—gotta go. Love you."

"Wait! What's your lady's name?"

"Um—Lauren."

"Am I about to gain another daughter, darling?"

"Mom, please. You're getting way ahead of me here."

"But, Mark—"

"How are the girls?" He wasn't going to get off this phone call until he'd gone through all the rituals and conversations, but while he listened to the account of what his sisters were up to, he had a brain wave.

"Mom, I've got a friend, Big Sam, who's in your area. Thought I'd send him over to meet you. He's heard all about your fried chicken."

"Your friends are always welcome. And really, my fried chicken isn't any better than anyone else's."

"It's the best in LA. Mom, look, Big Sam is—" How did he describe him? "Pretty rough looking. But he's a lamb. I promise."

"Darling, I don't care what people look like, so long as their heart's in the right place."

Big Sam's heart filled his chest. But no matter how much of a softie, he looked like a biker—and was acquainted with a few of them.

"I'll give him your number and your address. You'll like him." He'd look out for her, and Mark's sisters. Big Sam would do anything for him since Mark had listened to his sorrows one night in the local bar in Laredo. Sam had been going through a breakup in his relationship which had hurt him badly, so Mark had taken him back to his place, where they'd drank coffee until three a.m. while putting the world to rights.

"He sounds lovely, darling."

Maybe some woman might see him that way. He had a tendency to cry if he watched a sad movie, his blubbering so loud on occasions that he had to be removed from the entire cinema complex. He rented a room in LA now, and shared his takeout meals with the homeless. He'd likely get on well with the Buckners.

A couple of minutes later, he managed to end the call to his mom on a reasonably cheerful note.

Next, he punched in Big Sam's number.

"Buddy, how are you?" Sam answered in his softly spoken, gravelly voice.

"I need a favor."

There was a pause and Mark could practically see the big guy squaring his shoulders.

"Name it."

"I've got a job for you. Two jobs. My mom's in trouble, and I need to find a guy in Venice Beach."

It only took a few minutes to explain the basic facts. Big Sam had already begun packing his gear for the drive to Venice Beach where he'd try to find Johnson Sterrett before heading to Mark's mom's place and checking on her.

Mark pocketed his phone when he ended the call.

At some point he'd have to tell his mom what was happening. Maybe she and the girls could go to Granny Dubois's place in Idaho and ride out the shame in relative privacy and safety until this was all over.

The unexpected developments put him in a real tight spot. But he'd managed it, as best he could. Now, it was up to fate.

All he had to do was get through today without being discovered.

Chapter Twenty

Lauren Mackillop in ring of underworld crime

"IT'S ALL SUPPOSITION, sugar."

Lauren slapped the *Texas Portal* with the back of her hand. "Where did they get this?"

"Keep your voice down." Marie led her farther into the dining area, away from Ingrid and Hortense who had gone very quiet behind the coffee machine and were staring.

Lauren studied the rag and the article, which was on the front page and immediately noticeable, along with a photo of her, smiling in a debonair manner, wearing very expensive clothing that she'd bought for next to nothing. But they'd doctored the photo, putting children into the image who she appeared to be ignoring, making her look like a bitch with attitude. She knew that photo—she'd been delivering scarves and cardigans to the local nursing home. Something she'd done with excess stock every month. There hadn't been a child in sight. Only the elderly lady who'd taken the photo as she waved her off, and later sent it to Lauren.

We have reliable information Miss Mackillop was working alongside some of Santa Ynez's shadier residents when she ran her second-hand clothes shop,

In Need of Loving.
Criminals and gamblers were undoubtedly part of her everyday life.
But it looks like she got in deeper than she could cope with.
She lost her business in a poker game.

"They've twisted everything!"

Now, she's opening another business in Surrender, Calamity Valley.
But do the vulnerable townspeople know who she really is and what she's capable of?

"This is terrible! What if the *Amarillo Globe* gets it?" They were a bona fide newspaper, with proper journalists and huge distribution.

"We'll play on it," Marie said as she snatched the rag off her. "Leave it to me."

Lauren took the newspaper back. "I think I'd best if I deal with it myself."

"But you can't proclaim yourself extravagant, intemperate, and wanton. I can."

"Wanton?"

"In the best possible sense."

How could there possibly be a best sense?

"They're muckraking," Marie said. "Nothing more."

"What do you mean *wanton*?"

"Are we reckless and extravagant just because we want something and go for it? No, we're not. And I'm going to prove *you're* not."

Lauren's heart raced. "This is sounding worse than what they've written about me. You haven't already said this to anyone, have you?"

"Not yet but it's going to come up."

"How?"

"Don't worry about that. There's a very nice reporter at the *Globe* I spoke to when the developers spread those nasty rumors about Molly. He's got too many body piercings for my liking, but he's a good boy. He'll do as I say."

"Marie! What have you told him to do?"

"So much panic! You haven't got time."

She was right. They had about twenty minutes before Donaldson's arrived and set up their campaign table. They were undoubtedly the perpetrators of these vicious rumors but how had they stumbled upon the facts in the first place? It was going to be hard to keep the panic hidden. Her stomach was churning into knots.

She hauled in a breath and turned to the bar where Ingrid and Hortense were stock still, staring.

"It's fine!" she called, managing a smile. "But there's a little something I didn't tell you. About what happened to my business. I need to explain."

"Remember, sugar," Marie said. "Everything has an end."

"Thanks for the advice, but I'm not happy with the journey." She paused as something Pepper had said came into her head.

I bet Donaldson's is using him in some way. They'll play you off him and vice versa, which means they'll be playing your business off his business.

"You don't think..." She almost couldn't voice it after giving him so many of her good thoughts this morning. "Do you think *he's* done this? Mark."

"I refuse to believe that poor man, under the kind of pressures you and I can only imagine, would do anything so outrageously cruel to you—the loveliest women he's ever met. But..."

Lauren held her breath.

Marie pulled her iPhone out of her jacket pocket and tapped on it furiously. "I found this on the updated online *Portal* as I was driving over here."

"When you're driving, driving is the main thing you're supposed to concentrate on, Marie!"

"Oh, hush. I've got Bluetooth and voice control, and when did we last see the police out here?" She handed over her phone.

The gorgeous brunette is about to open a wedding venue with a difference. The difference being—the place is haunted.

Fancy a honeymoon in spooky old Surrender with a ghost spying on your bedroom antics?

Lauren Mackillop, the woman who lost her business through her gambling addiction, is giving you the opportunity. But be prepared to pay through the nose for it.

The lady likes her money.

Her chest felt like it had caved in. "They're making me look like a criminal—and a joke!"

"I know," Marie said, taking her phone back. "I told you they were shifty."

"You think it's Donaldson's?"

"Who else?"

"But how did they know about Sage Springs house?"

"One of their underdogs, probably. Someone they've sent to snoop."

That only made Lauren think about Mark again. Could he have done this to her? Had she been duped once more? "Mark was the one who suggested a wedding venue when I showed him around the house. He knows it's haunted too—I told him."

"Mere coincidence," Marie said in a tone that suggested the subject was closed and Mark was innocent.

There had been too many supposed coincidences recently, but there wasn't time for evaluation. Neither was there time for self-pity. Before she faced the press, she had to face her townspeople.

"I'll have a quick word with everyone in the bar." She checked her watch. "We've got ten minutes." Not enough time to gather the whole community together to tell them her sorry story. "I'll ask everyone here to let the others know."

"Sugar," Marie said softly. "I think they've already gotten wind."

Lauren turned to the people she'd known all her life who were now gathered in the bar. Hortense, Miss Flores, the

Gerdins, the Fairmonts, and the Buckners. Each face held concern. They were all staring at her.

"Lauren." Marie took her arm, halting her. "Let Mark help solve your problems. That way, he'll also solve his own."

He had problems and they were somehow burdensome, but there was something not right about his behavior. She didn't want to attack him verbally over this new issue that had arisen, because she was beginning to have real feelings about him. But neither could she get too cozy with him. Not until she'd gotten through the middle of her journey and reached the end.

"I think it's best if I look after myself." At this stage, "the end" was looking like a far-flung horizon, the road paved with landslides and avalanches.

She steadied herself as she took her place in front of the people she loved and respected, her heartbeat rising.

"I have to be brief, and I can answer any questions you may have later. There's an article in the *Texas Portal* this morning, and I can tell some of you have already read it online." Only Marie had all the daily newspapers delivered. She drove every morning to the fork in the road that led to the highway and collected them from the drop-off point she'd arranged with a local delivery service.

"It's got to be a nasty rumor!" Ingrid exclaimed, slapping the bar.

Everyone murmured agreement.

"It is. But I'm afraid I did lose my business, and I lost it in an unsavory way."

The door at the top of the stairs opened and Mark

stepped out.

Lauren looked up and met his gaze. "You need to hear this."

He frowned, more than a little weariness showing in the creases around his eyes.

"There's a trashy rumor about our Lauren in the *Portal*," Ingrid told him. "Saying she was involved with underworld crime lords and shifty poker players."

"Saying, basically," Hortense supplied, "that she's a bad investment, a bad businesswoman, and possibly a crook."

"Thank you, Miss Lockwood," Lauren said and shifted her stance.

Mark stepped down the stairs until he reached the bottom step, his eyes on her.

She spoke quickly, mostly because there wasn't time to dawdle but also because she wanted to get the words out and done with. She told them about her partner, the forging of her signature, and how he lost the business. She told them about the police involvement and how she hadn't been able to produce evidence of her partner's crime and therefore had been legally stumped.

"So I came home." She glanced around the shocked faces. "If you can forgive me my stupidity over the whole affair, I can promise my heart and every fiber of my being is involved with our town and its regrowth. For good or worse."

"Well, that sure is a terrible tale," Ingrid said. "You poor girl."

Mark hadn't moved a muscle, but his hand had clenched

on the brim of the Stetson he held. His knuckles were white and Lauren's heart was pounding. *Listen. Watch. Trust.* It was still the last issue she couldn't come to terms with.

She cleared the thickness in her throat by swallowing hard. "The other thing they're saying, about the haunted house and the wedding venue—you know that's not right."

"But it puts us in a pickle," Mr. Gerdin said. "We weren't supposed to mention the house to the developers; now they must know all about it. What do you suggest we do, Mark?"

Aware of Mark's intense stare, Lauren glanced at him. His features were set, his mouth a grim line, but a look of remorse, or regret, was in his eyes.

It almost crushed her. Had he done this?

"I suggest we stick to our plan," he said, taking his focus off her. "I'll keep Donaldson's at the saloon, we all do everything as arranged to make them think we're arguing and making silly decisions about proposed businesses…like the haunted house."

Had his voice broken, just slightly?

"And Lauren is going to face the press. With my help. I'll let them interview me, too. Lauren and I will give them the truth about our plans."

He was going to step up and face them after telling her he didn't want anything to do with them? It had to be a sign of guilt, but was it also an indication of a strong man who was willing to right his wrongs?

Her heart was now bouncing in her chest. Up, down. He was decent and could be trusted, he was unscrupulous and she ought not to forget it. For some unfathomable reason, she wanted to protect him until she knew for sure. But how?

"Honey!" Marie said to Mark, stepping to Lauren's side. "That's a noble gesture, but you leave the press to me."

"I want to help," he said, his voice firm.

"I think you've helped enough for now," she told him with a smile, although she'd lowered her voice and aimed her words directly at him.

He reddened a little.

"Here they come!" Ingrid said, pointing at the window.

Everyone rushed to the front of the bar as a fleet of vehicles headed into town from the northern end, slowing and parking on the side of the road or in the old, never-used parking lot which was full of pot holes and cracked concrete.

"There's a TV crew," Hortense said. "We hadn't expected that."

"There's also what looks like a dozen family cars, and a busload of tourists!" Mr. Gerdin added. "A *bus*load."

Everyone stilled, concern prickling the air now that everything they'd put into place was about to unfold.

"Think about our town sign," Lauren said. "Welcome to the Serenity of Surrender. We need to remember that."

"I reckon the whole of Texas is going to be watching us," Hortense said.

Lauren trembled. So much for having the gift of vision. Why hadn't it turned up at six a.m. when Mark woke her by banging on her front door?

"Real tourists!" Ingrid clapped her hands and turned to the group. "Everyone get into place. Smile a lot, and remember we're making Donaldson's think we don't know what we're doing while letting the press know we're on track for success."

Butch Buckner scratched his head. "It's beginning to sound complicated."

"I bet the tourists are only here because they're hoping to smell a rat," Hortense said.

"They're not going to find one!" Lauren said firmly. Although by all accounts from the *Texas Portal*, she was the rat.

"We can do this!" Mark said, stepping forward. "Time to make our stand, folks. Lauren's right—we act professionally and politely to the developers if they approach us and give them contraindications of what we're planning. But I'll do my best to keep them occupied and out of your hair."

"Whoop!" Ingrid said, rubbing her hands together. "Let's go. Everyone remember your roles and what we discussed. It's going to be a great day."

"It's certainly going to be different," her husband mumbled.

They all moved fast, some wandering outside, totally ignoring the developers who'd already started unpacking their car, pulling out boxes full of posters, flags, and banners. Those who were going to help run the bar rushed to the kitchen or the dining area. Kid was at the coffee machine being given last-minute instructions from Hortense on how to use it. A pile of warm flapjacks were stacked beneath a glass dome and the aroma of burgers and chili wafted from the kitchen.

Lauren walked to the saloon doors where Marie was

holding up a small mirror, reapplying her lipstick.

"Why did you step in to save Mark from meeting the press?"

Marie smacked her lips together and put the lid on her lipstick tube. "Because he'll get in my way. He also needs to keep focused on the developers and if he comes out of that role to protect you, it could get messy."

Protect her? It was more likely he was covering his tracks. "I think Butch was right. This is getting too complicated."

"It's the only way through to the end."

"Marie—I think I should speak to the press and only me. I got myself into the mess in Santa Ynez, I ought to get myself out of it."

Marie stuck her lipstick and the mirror into her purse, slinging the gold chain over her shoulder. "You say you want to look after yourself. You say you *can* look after yourself and, sugar, I know you're capable. But why put a halt to a little backup from the people who love you?"

"Because I feel responsible."

"Pfft! You didn't forge a signature. You didn't get crazy drunk with your success one night and lose a successful business in a poker game with criminal vermin!"

"But I let it happen." She'd been home less than a week and her life had turned upside down. Yesterday, she'd been on a road to some sort of happiness, and now this rumor could damage her work and the rest of her life. She didn't want others to get hurt in the wake of her bad reputation.

"Today is your chance to put things to right," Marie said. "It won't be long before the reporters at the *Amarillo*

Globe cotton on to what's really happened—and they're smart. Are you going to let them tell your story and make up the bits they don't know about?"

"Are you admitting reporters tell lies?"

Marie gasped as though stung by a bee. "We don't *lie*—we fill in the gaps as honestly as we can. Then wait for the truth to come out. But I'm not waiting now, not when you're in trouble. Any journalists arriving in town today are going to be glad to see me. They know they'll get an honest word from me."

"Even those who don't know you?"

"I make it my business to ensure *everyone* knows me. Heck, most of the Texas press corps is following my blog. Sugar, no matter what I do—I'm irresistible to other reporters!"

Lauren hugged her quickly. "Thank you. Just don't go overboard with whatever it is you're going to tell the press. Try to be rational."

Marie straightened her jacket and stepped outside. "D'Pee! Slick!" she said to the developers with one of her dazzling smiles. "Don't you both look ravishing? My heart's all a pitter-patter."

The men paused in their setting up and stared at her.

"If this is some form of manipulation," Leonard D'Prichia—whatever his name was said. "It's not working."

"Then I shall have to try harder," Marie responded. She flounced off, waving to the TV crew that was still in their van, cruising down Main Street. "Park behind my blogmobile, sugars, you'll get the best reception for your satellites and antennas. It's all to do with the dip in the canyon behind town and those waves bouncing off whatever they bounce off. Believe me, I know what I'm talking about."

The guy driving the van gave her a smile. "Are you Momma's Hopeless Blog dot com?"

"That's me, honey! Come on over and let's have a good old natter about what's going on here."

Lauren blinked as a sensation she'd never experienced before crept up on her. It was as though she were in tune with Marie. Was it the bond of Mackillop soothsayers? Had Molly felt this tingling of the skin, this raw energy?

The sensation was broken when Mark stepped up at her side.

"Are you going to be okay?" he asked quietly.

She nodded, unable to meet his eye.

He took hold of her hand and gave it a squeeze. Was it for support? Or was it an apology?

"I'd best get on with it," she said, pulling her hand from the warmth of his. "Good luck," she added.

He hesitated, as though he expected her to say more. "You too."

He moved to a window and watched the developers set up their campaign table and all their paraphernalia, his shoulders tense and his eyes narrowed.

She didn't know why she'd wished him luck, but she had a feeling he was going to need it as much as she was.

She pulled herself together, settled her expression to one of relaxed and welcoming, and walked outside into the fray.

Chapter Twenty-One

MARK WOULD NEED to head outside any moment and do the welcoming act for Donaldson's. But for now, he was attempting to observe their behavior so he could gauge their temperaments.

It wasn't working.

His head was filled with thoughts of Lauren and what he'd been responsible for by giving Boomer the fake intelligence. He hadn't known how she'd lost her business, and it made his blood boil that she'd been so badly abused. She'd lost everything she'd worked hard for, but had she crumbled and fallen apart? No. She'd come home to help those in need.

Shame filled him. How the hell was he going to correct his wrongs, and how could he ever make her believe he hadn't meant this to happen? He'd given the intel because it had seemed like the softest option—but he hadn't expected them to rake through her past and use her in this manner.

He straightened when Gerdin came up, thumbs tucked into the belt loops of his baggy jeans.

"You haven't met them before?" the old man asked, clicking his dentures as he stared through the window.

"Why would I have?"

"That tall one, he's D'Pee, head man. The big, sly looking fella is known as Slick. He does the running around, fetching whatever D'Pee asks for. There's a third developer in their office, but none of us have met him. He's probably not important enough to be slithering around, tricking us out of house and home."

"They haven't got your land yet," Mark reminded him.

"Don't mind telling you, son, they came pretty close a while back. We had a few households wanting to take the money they offered and move on. If they'd done that, we'd have been shackled to my way of thinking. Once you start chipping at the concrete foundation, the brick posts are eventually going to crumble."

"I've never met anyone in town who didn't want to stay."

"That's because of what Molly did in Hopeless. They all wanted to sell until she put her ideas into practice. Then we heard Lauren was coming home, and it gave us all heart. This is our home. Most of us were born here, as were our children and our children's children. We want to win. We want to show, once and for all, that we can do things for ourselves."

"You're blessed people. All of you."

"We had help," Gerdin said. "The Mackillops always look out for their own, and they consider every one of us a part of their extended family. But I reckon none of us in Surrender could have done all this without you."

He didn't want this praise. He didn't deserve it. "You're

the ones who have come up with all the brilliant ideas. I've done hardly anything." Except behind their backs.

"Maybe so," Gerdin said. "But I still reckon you were meant to be here."

"And I'd better get on with my job." He hadn't felt tired or drained from his sleepless night until twenty minutes ago when he listened to Lauren speak. He'd been wired, given what he'd had to put into place with his father's disappearance, but this additional burden of responsibility squeezed his heart.

He pulled at the brim of his Stetson and headed onto the veranda.

Donaldson's reps had already put up a table and a whiteboard and were opening their briefcases, which were piled with leaflets.

The guy, Slick, noticed Mark first. He nudged D'Pee. "Cops."

D'Pee frowned when he saw Mark. "Morning, Officer. Can we help you?"

Mark paused, then remembered he was wearing a sheriff's badge. "Mark Sterrett."

D'Pee grinned, visibly relaxed. "What are you in that getup for?"

"Idiot," Slick said, and went back to stacking leaflets on the table.

"Part of the charm of the Desert Sage Saloon," Mark told them.

D'Pee looked up at the sign above the doorway and shook his head. "Charm? You're making a fool of yourself."

Which served him right. It had been Ingrid's idea he wear the getup, backed by Hortense, who'd found the badge, and he'd gone along with it. But the humor behind the intent had vanished. He no longer felt able to show the friendly family-bar-owner demeanor.

Except he had to.

"Can I get you guys coffee?"

They ignored him and Mark clenched his jaw. They were showing their force, and no matter how much he'd enjoy a dustup, it wasn't going to happen. What did interest him was why they'd appeared so wary of seeing a cop in town.

"Is that her?" D'Pee said, nodding down the street to where Lauren was standing outside the new information cabin. She was surrounded by some of the press and Mark's heart summersaulted. He wanted to leap the veranda railing and run to her.

"That's Lauren Mackillop," he confirmed.

"Good-looking piece of ass but a lousy businesswoman. I'm doubting she could create anything of lasting value in this dump. If a family saloon and a haunted house are all she's come up with in the last week, our job's going to be easy."

"If I were you, I wouldn't underestimate anyone around here."

"Well, you're not *us*, are you?" D'Pee hissed. "You're nothing but the son of a loser."

"How come you didn't tell us about this Sage Springs house until late last night?" Slick asked.

"I didn't realize you didn't know about it."

D'Pee handed Slick some posters and told him to hang them on the railings. "We can pull all the romantic stuff down pretty easily," he said to Mark. "Who'd want to get married in this eyesore of a town? But what else is planned?"

Mark inhaled. "Like I told your compatriot, the Texan with the deep voice, they're making things up as they go. I helped them come up with the idea of the family saloon, Lauren came up with the haunted house concept, and the rest of them are winging it. "You'll no doubt hear all about their ideas throughout the morning."

"Good. Because we need to talk to them face to face. We've got sweeteners, plus we reckon they won't be too gung ho about following the sexy brunette now that they know her background."

"Who was responsible for the leak to the press?"

D'Pee glanced at Slick, then grinned at Mark. "You were."

His heart rate rose. "Why wasn't I told about what had happened to her in Santa Ynez?"

"Because it was none of your business," Slick said, stepping up to the table and shoving his hands into the pockets of his suit trousers. "Now, how about that coffee?"

Mark nodded. "Sugar?" He hoped to God they said yes, because there was rat poison in the shed out the back and he was tempted to open the packet.

"You've given us good intel," D'Pee said in a conceding tone. "But if you're holding out on anything else, you'll pay for it. Or your mommy will."

Mark managed to stop himself from throwing a punch.

"Well, howdy, gentlemen! Isn't it a glorious day? Ingrid Gerdin." Ingrid thrust her hand out and D'Pee took it, looking slightly dazed as she pumped it. "I was a 1935 synchronized swimming champion—and I've still got all the moves. Wanna see some?"

D'Pee pulled his hand out of Ingrid's, picked up a leaflet, and handed it to her, a shark's smile in place. "Great to meet you, Ingrid. I'd like to chat about some incredible luck coming your way."

"I'm ninety-three, fellas. I reckoned my luck had just about run out until we suddenly came up with ideas for our town's rejuvenation. You haven't told them already, have you, Mark?"

He shook his head. "Haven't said a word."

Hortense came storming up the steps to the veranda. "Ingrid Gerdin! I hope you're not flirting with these scumbags!"

"This here's Hortense," Ingrid said. "She's thirty-three and a quarter and runs the antique shop, although it's currently full of junk. And we've got Miss Flores, who's only fifty-two. She's gonna be turning her candlemaker shop into a dog beauty parlor. We're also thinking of opening up a cattle ranch just outside town. Not that any of us know a darn thing about cows, except how to eat 'em, and we haven't got the dollars to splash on anything grand, but we figure if we don't start somewhere we'll end up nowhere." She beamed at the bemused faces of D'Pee and Slick.

"Yeah," Hortense added with a scowl. "So shove your propaganda where the sun don't shine."

"Oh, come on!" Ingrid said. "Let's be welcoming." She moved to the veranda railings and lifted her back leg. "How about that synchronized swimming display? I'm limbered up and ready."

Mark's heart was so full, he was getting choked up. As arranged, Ingrid was good cop, Hortense bad. Confusing the hell out of the suckers with the leaflets and the ingratiating smiles.

"I'll grab those coffees," he said, and moved into the saloon.

Taking a seat at the bar, he pulled off the Stetson, set it on the counter, and swiped his brow.

"Need something, Mark?" Kid asked.

He nodded. "Two extra-strong, extra-sweet espressos. Hold the rat poison."

Kid frowned, and Mark found a smile. "Just two coffees, buddy. Thank you."

"You seem to be getting on well with those shady bastards," Gerdin said from his barstool where he was reading the *Texas Portal*. "I'm mighty proud of you, son. I couldn't face them."

The back of Mark's neck heated up. "Gotta do what you gotta do."

LAUREN CAME OUT of the information cabin with a handful of leaflets about Sage Springs Haven and found herself face to face with reporters. All had cameras and notebooks.

"Do you have any comment on your dealings with crime

lords in California, Miss Mackillop?"

"Is it true you lost your business in a poker game?"

"Have the police been involved?"

She put the leaflets onto the table, nerve ends firing. She hadn't prepared for such a barrage.

"Thank you all for coming," she said with a smile she hoped didn't look as shaky as it felt. "It's wonderful to see such positive interest in our town."

"Wouldn't say it was positive just yet," a man said in a cynical tone.

"Do you have a comment about your dealings in Santa Ynez?" another asked.

"I have nothing to say about the comments made in the *Texas Portal* this morning, except that the accusations are false. I'll be preparing a statement." She'd have to. She had to fight this. "I do have a lot to say about Surrender though and how we intend to progress."

"Can you at least give us some background on your communications with criminals?"

Marie's words came to mind, about filling the gaps until the truth came out. She didn't want them spreading lies so she'd have to speak up, with or without a lawyer and a statement. Today's intent was supposed to be all about the town and the only way to get the focus back was to give the press some of the truths.

"I knew only one criminal, my business partner."

"A source tells us he was shot in the back. Is that true?"

Where on earth had they gotten that? She'd made it up at some point, but when? Who had she said it to?

"Are you selling out to Donaldson's?"

"Never."

Laughter erupted at the other end of the street, and the reporters turned to see what was going on, giving Lauren a chance to find her breath.

The TV crew was setting up, and Marie looked like she had them in her spell. Their van and the blogmobile were now parked in such a way that it obliterated Donaldson's view of the cabin.

"Who's that?" a reporter asked.

"My aunt."

"Is she one of the fortune-tellers?"

"Soothsayers," Lauren corrected quickly. "The Mackillops are ordinary women with special gifts. There's nothing odd about them."

"Quirky story though."

"Yeah, but not the one we want right now," a bespectacled reporter said. "What are your thoughts about Donaldson's Property Development, Miss Mackillop?"

"Not ones that should be published."

That brought a little laughter. She was gaining their attention. Now she needed their trust. "But they are pressuring and harassing us."

The reporters scribbled in their notebooks.

"Looks like they charged in and set themselves up, regardless of what the town wants," a female reporter said. "Didn't they try to do that in Hopeless too?"

"They did. And just like Hopeless, we've got plans in place to deal with them—but don't tell them I told you."

It gained her a few smiles.

The same reporter picked up one of the Sage Spring Haven leaflets. "What's this all about?"

"The house isn't open yet. Neither are some of our proposed new businesses. But our intent is to regenerate by keeping Surrender's historic and peaceful ambience, and Sage Springs Haven will be a place for women to arrive tired and leave inspired." That got the reporter's attention along with her female colleague's. "We'll be offering business classes, life skills, empowerment, and anything women of today need to make their lives more rewarding or just more enjoyable. Time out from the pressures of everyday life."

"Is this the house with the ghosts?"

"We said that to deter Donaldson's—and don't tell them I told you that, either!"

The amenable expressions of her audience were growing, and the tenseness in her shoulders lessening.

"We'll be keeping everyone up to date with regular newsletters. If you really want to help, would you suggest that people sign up?"

"You want to use us as a promo opportunity?"

"Why not? You're here, aren't you? You want a story, and I want to give you the best one I can."

"What's with the saloon? What's the score there? Who runs it?"

She wasn't going to mention Mark; it was part of the deal she kept the press away from him. "Have you been in there yet? It's a great family environment. It's going to turn this town around."

As she said it, she knew it was the truth. Mark's family saloon would be just as big a drawing card as the haven. Their two businesses could survive, side by side.

If he stayed.

MARK UNDERSTOOD WHAT Marie had done by parking the vans in front of the developer's table, but it cut his vision of the cabin and the reporters surrounding Lauren.

Nervous energy rumbled around his system. He still wanted to leap the railing and go to her. But that wasn't the arrangement.

She'll handle it. She was smart and she had her heart in this venture, but knowing her capabilities didn't help with the building anxiety.

In a quiet moment, after Ingrid had finished her synchronized swimming display that had fazed D'Pee and Slick so much their coffees had gone cold, he'd tried to pry information out of them regarding Boomer.

"Don't know the man," D'Pee had said, not meeting Mark's eye. "Wouldn't want to know a man like that."

Something about D'Pee's demeanor sparked a concern. He knew more about the man who had sole contact with Mark than he was letting on.

"You!" a female said behind him in a hushed tone. "I want a word."

He turned to find Marie standing inside the bar. She must have come in from the back, and she looked like she meant business. Had she discovered his role in the article about Lauren's business past?

He checked on the developers. They were chatting to the Fairmonts, who were giving them some absurd spiel about their plans to open an enclave in their flower plot and turn a corner of Surrender into a 1960s annual hippie festival.

He followed Marie inside and to the far end of the bar, nodding to Doc, who was barman today, currently serving soft drinks to a group of people who'd wandered in ten minutes ago. If the Buckners wanted a change in career, they had one here as far as Mark was concerned. Doc would make a brilliant manager, and Kid was a whiz in the kitchen. Butch was going to be tied up in a romance with Hortense, although it wouldn't stop him working in the bar in between renovating the antique shop, if that was what he wanted.

But none of them would be able to afford the purchase price of the lease.

What the hell would happen to the place once his real reason for being here got out?

How many more of the thirty people who resided in Surrender would find new ways to build their income and change their current status from static to excitingly opportunistic? They'd all turned up today, and every one of them was out there on the street, doing their bit. They'd left the most challenging tasks up to the people Mark had the most contact with, like the Gerdins, Hortense, and the Fairmonts. But each one of them knew the plans and was acting on them. Engaging the tourists with smiles and a big welcome. Distracting Donaldson's by appearing interested in their leaflets and posters, advocating a possibility they might be up for selling their land.

Marie grabbed him by the sleeve when he reached her side. "Sit," she said, slapping her purse onto the counter as she sat on a stool. "You're in trouble."

Didn't he know it. He sat, preparing himself for the onslaught. He wasn't going to lie this one out. He also had to tell Lauren what he'd done as soon as he got the chance.

"How's Lauren getting on with the press?"

"Holding her own."

The sunrise had found him looking out over the town and referring to it as his, believing it possible he was heading into a decent future. He'd admitted his feelings for Lauren and had hoped to one day call her his girl. He'd thought he was making things happen, and what man didn't want to create a solid, familiar, and stable environment for himself? He'd been ready for anything—and prepared for nothing. He'd played right into Boomer's hands.

So much for thinking he could write his own story.

"You've done some good for the townspeople," Marie said. "Giving them jobs. Giving them a chance to shine. The Buckners, for example. Thank you for that."

"It takes more than schooling to make a good man."

"They're the hope we've kept going all these years. They didn't run off. They stayed with us and made a home here."

Good men. Reliable men.

He pulled his hat off and set it on the bar. "It was me," he confessed. "I did it. I told Donaldson's about the haunted house and the wedding venue."

"Which was a lie you put in place to look after her real

interests."

He glanced at her, surprised by the unruffled tone. "You're not angry?"

"You did what you thought was best. But like a fool man who already has enough on his plate, you step up to protect Lauren when there's no need. What were you *thinking*, offering yourself up to the press?"

She didn't know what was going on in his life outside of Surrender, but Lauren must have spoken to her about his reasons for not wanting to front the press.

"I intend to tell Lauren as soon as I can." And take the consequences. The thought sank his heart to his stomach. "I've fallen for her, Marie."

She patted his hand. "Just try to think rationally when it all goes wrong."

"It already has, hasn't it?" It had been wrong before it started. He should have thought of some other way out instead of accepting the job to snoop on these good people.

"I'm talking about the rest of your life, Mark. Consider this—only you have the power to decide where your thoughts lead you."

He had no idea what she was referring to, but Ava had said something similar. *Be careful about your feelings and what you believe.*

"You worry about yourself, Mark. We've got Lauren's back."

"You mean the townspeople?"

"I mean the Mackillops."

His cell phone rang.

"You need to get that," she said, slipping off her stool and picking up her purse. "It's important."

"It'll be my mom," he said with a forced smile, which was undoubtedly crooked because he'd just seen the caller ID. Boomer.

"Tell that to your granny from Idaho," she said with an ironic grin. "She's watching you, too—along with a few others. You're not as alone as you think you are."

He paused as she left. After experiencing visions in the mirror, weirdness at Sage Springs, and the midnight visit from Wild Ava, the Mackillops were beginning to give him the heebie-jeebies.

He picked up his hat and took the stairs to his private rooms two at a time, slamming the door closed behind him.

"What is it now?" he asked as he answered the call. He was over giving this man his patience.

"Have you found your father?"

"For God's sake, I've had a few hours!" Who was this guy, and where was he based? "You damned well know I haven't seen or heard from him in twenty years. I have no idea where he is or where he'd go."

"You've got a problem, then. There was a bank heist in California late last night. Pretty close to where you mom lives. The cops have put out an APB for him."

"You're saying my father robbed a bank?"

"Don't be stupid. He only steals from the easy sources—like the property management account in Bermuda he was given control of."

"So why are the cops after him?"

"A source close to us advised them he was the perpetrator who had gotten away with thirty thousand."

Mark began storing information the way he would when plotting for a book. Donaldson knew his father was in California, but not where and that meant they weren't only relying on Mark for information on his whereabouts; they had their henchmen looking for him too. Was it their men who pulled off the bank heist? Were they capable of such things? How many operatives did this Donaldson have and how did their underground crime ring work? Because that was surely what it was. An enormously wealthy philanthropist whose reputation was squeaky clean on the outside but who wouldn't hesitate to have someone murdered to justify his own revenge.

"I'll find my father, but you have to give me today. I can't leave town today."

"We don't want you to leave—you're too much use to us where you are. But we don't want you getting soft and forgetting about Daddy. Mr. Donaldson has plans for him, and don't forget, if the cops find him before you do, they might turn up at your mother's place. It won't be long before they discover how she won that brand-new vehicle."

Boomer cut the call and Mark gripped his cell phone. For once, he'd like to be the one to hang up first. To cut the call and show his disdain.

It rang again.

"Found him," Big Sam said without preamble. "What now?"

"You found him? *Already?*"

"It was easy. He was sleeping rough with a few homeless people I know. He didn't give me any trouble. I just yanked him up, carried him to my vehicle, and dumped him in the trunk."

"Where are you now?"

"My aunt Maisie's place. She left me the house. First time I've been in it. It's got two bedrooms and a little porch. I might stay. It's real pretty out here."

"Is the house secure?" If it was on a suburban street, neighbors would start to ask questions about Big Sam's sudden arrival.

"Out in the country," Big Sam said. "Closest neighbor is five miles away."

This was incredible. Things were looking better—suddenly, as though he had a guardian angel on his shoulder.

"Want him roughed up?" Big Sam asked. "I don't want to do it myself though. Don't like hurting folk, even if they deserve it."

"No need for that. I just want him out of sight."

"Shall I feed him?"

How about rat poison? "Maybe something simple on the gut. Mashed potatoes and cabbage."

"You got it."

"Sam, if you can get out of the house in the daytime, would you check on my mom?"

"It's covered. Got a friend looking out for her. He's ex-army. Recently made homeless, so I gave him enough cash to feed himself for the week, and he put up his sleeping bag in the park opposite your mom's house. She's already found him and offered to help him get a job. He opened up a conversation and my name came up, so she's thrilled because she thinks she's helping someone who knows you through me. My friend is right inside the house, Mark. She and your sisters are safe."

Mark covered his eyes with his hand. How lucky could an unlucky guy get? "I owe you, Sam."

"No. After what you did for me when I was down, we're even."

Sam cut the call and Mark fitted his Stetson back on his head, evaluating the situation's new twists and turns.

If Donaldson tried to pull off the crime scene murder—God forbid they kill anyone—Johnson Sterrett would have an alibi, since he'd have been in Big Sam's company the entire time. His mother was being watched over twenty-four seven whether she realized it or not, and if the police bothered her Mark could explain how everything had happened and personally hand over his father to the cops. For the moment, only he knew where his father was, which gave him time to put his focus back on Surrender and the safety of people here. Lauren's safety. He needed as much intel on Boomer and the scum out on his veranda as he could get, and today was his only chance.

The warbling of a bird distracted him. A whistle then a chirp, loud and persistent.

He went to the window and scraped aside the curtain. The leaves of the plains cottonwoods lining the street were barely rustling. There was nothing in the sky except silky white clouds. But down on the street, a group of reporters were standing in front of the bar, notebooks in hand—and Donaldson's had their full attention.

The bird trilled again. Was it mocking him? He was tired, he hadn't slept in more than twenty-four hours, and it was possible he was hearing things, but, nevertheless, his thoughts went to Lauren.

What were Donaldson's saying about her now? Trite lies, vicious falsehoods. Big or small, all of them would be damaging and he couldn't let them hurt her a second time.

It was time to put his best foot forward. Regardless of what happened.

Chapter Twenty-Two

"WHAT'S GOING ON now?" Ingrid asked.

"Marie's trying to take the focus off Donaldson's."

Lauren stood at the rear of a group of tourists and some of the townspeople, who'd been on the street since this began, doing whatever they could do for their town.

The press was huddled up front, having left the developers when they saw a crowd gather around the now-famous Momma Marie.

She'd been assisted onto a large pine table by Doc and Butch and stood on it as though on a stage. Lauren could almost see the spotlight shining down on her.

The TV crew was in place, camera rolling.

Marie raised her perfectly manicured hands and the chatter and whispering stopped.

Lauren held her breath.

"Those shameless people at the *Texas Portal*—none of whom had the guts to come here today—are spreading rumors, and I'd like the opportunity to put those rumors to bed."

"Are they involved with the developers who want to buy

your land?" a reporter asked.

"Why do you think I parked my blogmobile in front of Donaldson's campaign table—to hide the shameful liars, that's why! I just thank the good Lord you decent journalists managed to find the time to visit us today. I know you're going to report justly and fairly."

"We need something to go on, first."

"And I've got it for you, honey."

"Donaldson's told us—"

"Pffft! Do you want lies or do you want the truth?"

"I'd listen to anything you say!" one smiling young man called out.

"Well, listen up. That rag is reporting that my niece is an extravagant prodigal—and it's the truth!"

"You're saying she *has* been wasteful?"

"I'm saying she came home having lost everything, but is she riddled with greed like the *Portal* says? Is she taking advantage of her family and neighbors? You bet your butt she isn't. She's a prodigal, all right—and if you think that means she spends money recklessly, you've only been reporters since this morning!"

"Some at the *Portal* probably have!" the smiling young reporter said.

"But not you fine people. The best of us know the word 'prodigal' also means having or giving something on a lavish scale, and that's what Lauren is doing for us. That word sure can be a tricky one if not handled correctly. Getting it right is what we experienced reporters call a journalistic conundrum!"

A few laughed good-heartedly.

"Her shop *was* lost in a shady poker game. Underworld crime did play a part."

"Marie's really good at this reporting thing," Ingrid said. "I'm hanging on to her every word."

"Perhaps I ought to step in and take over," Lauren said, unsure where Marie was heading.

"Don't you dare. You've gotta trust her; she loves you. And those reporters love her! Look at them. They're bug-eyed."

"But it was her business partner's doings. *He* was the criminal. *He* was the one with pockets full of greed, and he stole from her. He was the one who dealt with nefarious crime lords, and that shameless man wasn't shot in the back, so don't go glorifying him. The sucker choked on a chunk of pineapple!"

"Better story than the one in the *Portal*!" a chuckling reporter from the *Globe* called out.

"You can swing a story any which way, honey, but you and I know we rely on a tip-off and then we dig deeper. Being a reporter can be downright dull," she said to the tourists and the town residents. "So we juice our story up a little, but we pepper it with facts. Facts prove the truth. I should know—just look at my blog numbers."

The reporters tucked their notebooks and microphones under their arms and gave Marie a healthy and somewhat amused round of applause.

"We're in a fight with some despicable troublemakers," she said. "My niece is up for the challenge of Surrender. Will you support her? Will you dig deeper for the true story?"

The reporters whistled and cheered approval, some clapping—all of them smiling.

The cameraman gave her a thumbs-up. "Got it, Marie! No need for a second take."

"I'm a one-take kinda woman. Just don't forget to advertise Momma's Hopeless Blog dot com. I've got fifty-nine thousand followers hanging onto my every word. They'll want to know what I've said here today."

"Hey, Marie!" one of the reporters called out. "What are you wearing?"

"Why, honey, I just flung on the first thing to hand—a Chanel-inspired tweed jacket and skirt and a pure silk blouse. I'm toned in shades between cerise and rose, and my shoes are kitten-heeled raspberry pink."

"Got it! Thanks."

"You're good, honey—these things are important. My followers will want to know. They come from all over the world and possibly beyond."

That brought more good-humored laughter and whoops of acknowledgement.

Marie bowed her head, acknowledging her accolade graciously.

Pride made Lauren's eyes smart. When it counted, there was nothing like family to help a person out. Even though it wasn't exactly the rational response she'd asked for, it was brilliant nonetheless.

She'd still need to make that statement and get a lawyer, but Marie had taken the intense focus off her and challenged the reporters. They'd undoubtedly be contacting their colleagues in California.

The gathering dispersed, and she headed for the cabin, checking over her shoulder to see what was going on at the saloon.

The developers were trying to grab the attention of a few reporters, waving at them and calling out that they'd like their say in this debate.

Debate? They'd started it, and now that it had gone against them, they were showing their true colors, like all bad losers.

Mark wasn't there. He'd be inside, since the press was on his front veranda.

She bumped into someone as she turned. A group had congregated in front of the bus that was parked down a side alley between Duggan's General Store and the rundown candlemaker's. "Excuse me," she said to the driver as he crossed in front of her. "Who arranged for the bus?"

"I've done a few tours out to Hopeless," he said affably. "Heard about this open day and thought some folks might enjoy seeing this place too." He patted his pocket. "Looks like I was right! I had to refuse nearly twenty people. Now, if I were to get myself a second bus…"

Lauren shook his hand and wished him a pleasant day.

He wandered off, but people from the bus had followed him and she was suddenly surrounded.

"Is there a map of the town?"

"Is everything open? What shops have you got?"

"Every shop in town is due for renovation and rejuvenation," she told them. "The shop owners will be happy to let you know their plans. We're all very excited. And thank you for coming. Please sign up for our newsletter at the information cabin, and there are free flapjacks at the family saloon. There's plenty to keep the kids occupied there too."

"Great. Thanks."

"Hey! I know you!"

Lauren did a double take as a little man with a shiny bald head pushed his way through others who were heading off.

"What a coincidence!" he said with a beaming smile.

She shook his hand. "Lovely to see you again..."

"Frankie," he supplied. "Frankie Caruso."

"Of course!" How could she have forgotten the little man from LAX? This *was* a coincidence!

Frankie pulled out his cell phone. "Can I get a shot of you, Miss Barrett-Bernard?"

She laughed. "I'm afraid I wasn't having a very good day when we met, and I made up that name."

"That's right!" he said, clicking his fingers. "Your lover was shot in the back by crime lords."

"My business partner. It was a professional relationship." She frowned as a memory jarred. This was the man she'd told the lie to about how her partner died—and now the *Portal* had been spouting rumors about crime lords and criminals.

"You look important," Frankie said. "I reckon you know what's going to be happening with the town. Wouldn't give me the scoop, would you?"

"Why would you want it?"

"I heard the place is up for sale and the valley residents are arguing. If there's going to be a fight, I want to capture it on video. Then I'm going to sell it to the guys at the *Texas Portal*."

Why mention only the *Portal*—none of whom were here—when he was surrounded by press from Amarillo and Lubbock, including a television news crew?

"What are you doing here, Frankie?" And why had he been at LAX at the same time as Lauren? Had he always been in the queue in front of her or had he pushed in? She vaguely recalled some scuffle over queue jumping but hadn't been in the mood to register why.

"I'm taking in the sights and hoping to make a buck or two…" He shrugged, hands spread, wide smile in place.

She'd gotten used to any number of strange coincidences since she'd been home, but this one worried her more than any of them.

"Everything all right, sugar?"

Lauren moved aside as Marie joined them, staring at Frankie as though she was looking at an apparition.

"Hi," Frankie said, holding out his hand.

Marie kept her hands firmly at her side.

"Okay. Be like that." He turned from Marie, who was now frowning so hard she might be cursing him.

"What?" Lauren asked when he moved off, snapping photos of everything around him as he went.

"Who is he?"

"Frankie Caruso. I met him at LAX. Marie—he's the one I lied to. I told him about my partner being shot in the back."

"Well, this is a turn up," Marie said, her focus on the street, mouth pursed.

"What are you sensing?"

"Not sure, but my momma's intuition is taking a hit."

Lauren followed her gaze down Main Street, trying to pinpoint why she, too, felt on edge.

Then she saw Mark.

He was out on the veranda with Donaldson's, in full view.

"Look," she said, putting a hand on Marie's arm.

"He's been fetching and carrying for them all morning," Marie said. "I heard D'Pee bark at him, and he didn't bat an eye. Just did as he was instructed. He's not who he says he is, Lauren."

Lauren's stomach churned. "Then who is he?"

"A better man than the one he's being forced to portray."

Lauren lowered her voice. "Why is he so attentive to Donaldson's? It's like they've got him tied around their little fingers."

Marie led her off the street to the redbrick archway where it was quiet, with no listening ears. "Blackmail, I'd say. Isn't that usually what happens to young men with brilliant futures who are forced to protect and defend their family?"

Not usually. But this was Calamity Valley, anything could happen. "Is it something to do with his father?"

"Must be."

"You think he's double-crossing us?"

"Undoubtedly. I might do some snooping of my own."

Marie waved across the street, and the bespectacled reporter from the *Globe* waved back. "After all, it's not what you know, it's who you get information out of."

"Is it wise to involve the press?"

"I'm not going to mention Mark, sugar. It's that little bald-headed guy I want information on."

"Frankie? You think he's got something to do with all this?"

"Don't you?"

She nodded. "I think we need to find out if Mark knows Frankie. That might give us a clue as to what's going on. Can we get them to meet up somehow?"

"Frankie," Marie said reflectively. "He doesn't look like a Frankie."

"That's what I thought. He looks more like a plain old Bob Smith."

Marie stumbled, as though zapped with a cattle prod, and Lauren grabbed her arm to steady her.

"I didn't see it!" Marie exclaimed. "Bob Smith—he's the third developer! The one we've never met. *That's* why I got such an intuitive hit when I saw him!"

The sudden sting in the air goose-bumped Lauren's skin.

"Sugar, I think when you thought him a plain old Bob Smith it was a sign. I told you there was one of them back in the office. No photos of him on the corporate website. Nothing except his name—Bob Smith."

"But if he's one of Donaldson's, why hasn't he been near the campaign table?"

"He's undercover. Shady little maggot…" Marie grimaced. "Sometimes, there are things we Mackillops don't see. Signs that aren't obvious. Signs we need to remember until they hit us in the gut and make sense."

"Let's not tell Mark what we've discovered," Lauren said. "We'll try to engineer a meet up with him and Frankie, but we don't know what's really going on for Mark, and if we do something wrong, people might get hurt. He said he was worried about his mom and sisters and that's why he wanted to stay out of the press's way."

"You need to let him know he's not alone. Show him support without telling him what we suspect."

"I need to get to the saloon." The agreement was that she stayed away, but she had to see him.

"No need, the man of your dreams is heading this way."

He was what?

She turned quickly and there he was, shaking hands with people and chatting as though he hadn't a care in the world. He indicated the saloon, and a few headed toward it. But reporters had noticed the group and were heading toward him.

"I have to get to him."

Marie halted her. "Let him do what he's doing. He'll have a reason."

Lauren could hardly believe it. He *was* double-crossing them—but also trying to help them. What the hell was the man going through? "Once our people know why he's really here, they might not wait for explanations." They might lynch him!

"You have to let them do what they need to do, too."

It didn't seem fair, to have information and then withhold it and let things play out.

"Can't we influence them before something bad happens?" She didn't know what he'd done, but she wanted to shield him.

"Lauren Mackillop. I told Molly, now I'm telling you—don't go looking for things to fix. You girls have got decades of learning ahead of you. You won't be in a position like your grandmothers until you're close to my age. And even then, it's going to be different for each of you."

"Like it is for you?" Lauren asked, peering at her questioningly.

Marie's smile blossomed. "I admit to having a momma's intuition whenever it comes to any of you girls. And I have been surrounded by soothsayers all my life, and a good woman like me picks up on things. To be honest, sugar, sometimes my astuteness astounds me."

Astuteness be damned. Marie simply didn't want to discuss her gift or how she used it or even that she had it. Neither did Lauren want to talk about her own growing gifts or abilities, but at some point, she was going to have to tell Mark.

She glanced at him. He'd gotten away from the reporters and was walking toward them, then he was held up by visitors from the bus.

"Marie, I keep having visions of our future together, but one of the visions was of him leaving town. Leaving everyone."

"Leaving *you*?"

She nodded, holding back the smarting tears in her eyes. "I've fallen for him. I couldn't help it."

Marie's gaze softened. "Sweetness, the knots of your problem will either tighten or loosen—depending on both of your reactions."

"To what?"

"Can't say. But chin up, here he comes. I'll leave you in those strong, capable hands. I have to think. There's more than one something about to happen." She squeezed Lauren's hand reassuringly then left, heading for the bespectacled reporter with her butter-wouldn't-melt smile.

"What are you doing out here?" Lauren said as Mark joined her.

Without looking at her and without faltering his step, he put a hand to her lower back and moved her through the archway to the rear, where they were sheltered by the brick walls and the honeysuckle, away from prying eyes.

"Mark, the press is everywhere. You stand out. The uniform," she said, nodding at his sheriff's badge.

He pulled her into him, and suddenly she was embraced, his arms firmly around her. "I'm sorry," he said, his voice gravelly. "I'd never willingly do anything to hurt you."

"Mark!" His chest was warm, the strength in his arms almost undoing her. It was like being folded in security.

"I told them, Lauren. It was me. I told Donaldson's about the haunted house venture. I did it to protect you, and I promise, I had no idea what had happened to you or how they'd use this information."

His hold strengthened, and her cheek was pressed against

his shoulder and throat.

He smelled of his bomber jacket. Bergamot, mint, spring grass, and mountain air. A strong, earthy aroma that was steadying and inviting.

"I understand." Her voice was barely a whisper. When he'd kiss[illegible] VIP lounge there had been only the contact of mouth [illegible] mouth. Now, she was buried against him, his warmth saturating her, and it was more exhilarating than a kiss.

Her brain must have fried, because she was imagining how it would feel to wind her arms around his body, tilt her head, lift her mouth to his…

"Let me go."

He released her instantly.

"We're Mackillops," she told him, attempting to show impatience with his apparent contrition, while also regaining her breath. "We're wacky enough as it is—a wedding venue? Do I look the sort of woman who wants to run around fixing ruffles and flounces and soothing frayed nerves?"

He winced. "I thought you'd be angrier about the haunted house aspect."

"That happens to be true!" Not that she'd wanted the press to know.

"Lauren, I'm responsible for the press hounding you today. I spoke to a few of them just now and advised them it was me, and that it was a ploy to put the developers off the real scent—which is you opening Sage Springs Haven."

"That works," she said, nodding. "It's what I've done too."

"But they're still going to pursue you."

"Hopefully, they'll help. If there's some way I can reopen the case, maybe the truth will come out."

"Can we find another way? I don't want your reputation damaged any further while they pry into your life. I'll do anything in my power to prevent that."

All day she'd had the sense he was going to bring something bad down on them, but she hadn't expected to bear the brunt of it. She hadn't even had time to properly explain to everyone what had gone on in Santa Ynez. "I can handle it myself, Mark."

"But, Lauren—"

"Did you get any information from Donaldson's we can use against them?"

"Thanks to Marie, the press is already onto them. But that D'Pee guy, he's not the boss."

Lauren had guessed as much over the last hour. "So who's the main man?"

Mark hesitated. "I don't know."

Trust.

He wasn't telling the truth, but she thought perhaps it was because he didn't know enough. Were they pressuring him so badly? *Was* it blackmail? What could they possibly hold over him?

"Hey! There you are. Been looking for you. What are you doing hiding around here?"

Lauren turned quickly to Frankie, who must have snuck up on them, perhaps even eavesdropped.

"What's with the sheriff outfit?" he asked Mark, staring

at his badge. "You impersonating a cop? That's against the law." He snapped a photo of him on his phone. "Boy!" he said, eyes wide when he looked up. "It's the pretzel guy!"

"You know each other?" Lauren's heartbeat rose in an instant.

"We shared some time at LAX," Mark explained, his expression showing nothing but genuine surprise.

Things fell into place like a strike of lightning. Not enough to logically explain who Frankie was but enough to send her senses zinging.

"Me too," she said to Mark, giving him a pointed look. She was standing slightly behind Frankie. She was nearly a head taller than him, Mark even taller, so it was easy to warn him.

He caught her eye, understanding dawning as he cleared his frown, and placed a smile on his face.

"Good to see you again. Frankie, is it? What are you doing in Surrender? It's a helluva coincidence."

Wasn't it? But Mark didn't know him except from the coincidental meet up—so what game was Frankie playing?

A horn tooted, and the bus driver edged his vehicle out of the alleyway and onto the main street. "Time's up, folks!" he called out the open window. "We're leaving in five minutes."

"Hey—got to grab my ride," Frankie said. "See you guys another time. I didn't get my video," he said to Lauren. "But I'll be back. You can bet on it."

He walked off, saying something to the bus driver as he passed. It looked like he was indicating he'd be a couple of minutes and was asking the driver to wait.

I'll be back. What did he mean?

"What do you think is going on?" she asked Mark.

He shook his head. "I don't know."

Frankie was now heading toward the saloon.

Mark stepped beneath the archway and onto the street, his focus on the bald-headed man.

"He's working for Donaldson's," she told him. He needed this information now. "Marie thinks he's Bob Smith, the third, seemingly office-bound developer."

Mark glanced at her. "The airport…he was tailing us. Both of us."

Listen.

"I can understand why he'd tail me, since I was the one heading home to defend my town. But why you, Mark?"

Watch.

"I don't know. I suppose…" He broke eye contact. "It must be because I'd bought the lease on the bar."

Frankie was talking to D'Pee and Slick, who seemed to be hanging onto his every word, mouths pinched, brows furrowed.

Frankie beckoned D'Pee closer and said something in his ear.

Even from this distance, it was obvious D'Pee had balked. Slick was hovering by the table, chewing his bottom lip.

"They look terrified," Lauren said.

Frankie moved off, laughing heartily, and for a second, his laughter rippled from the high-pitched jokester's warble to a deep, nerve-grating tremor.

"Oh, my God. It's Boomer…"

Mark said it so softly she hardly heard him, but his features had slackened from intense scrutiny to shock.

"He's been around you all this time! All damn morning, while I'm sucking it up to Donaldson's. That's it." He pulled his cell phone out of his pocket and punched at the keypad. "I'm calling the cops."

"Mark, wait! What is it? Who's Boomer?"

"I am *not* having you in this much danger."

"What danger?"

"Yes," he said, attention on the phone. "This is Mark Sterrett of Surrender in Calamity Valley. We need immediate police presence." He pocketed the phone. "Stay here," he told her.

No way was she staying put. "Mark!" she cried, following him onto Main Street. "Why do we need the police? Nothing's happened!"

"No," he said as he marched toward the saloon. "But it's about to."

Chapter Twenty-Three

MARK STORMED THE steps to the veranda, his heartbeat steady, his intent clear, but he couldn't halt the sweet fantasy of letting his anger boil over until he crushed these jerks.

"Ingrid, would you kindly take everyone into the saloon while I have a word with these men?"

"Something up?" Ingrid asked.

"Mark."

"Lauren—you go inside too."

She stepped to his side.

"Lauren," he said quietly. "Let me just have a few minutes with them."

She pulled her mouth to one side, worry in her eyes. He was putting himself in a difficult situation, because she might begin to think he was on Donaldson's side, but he had to know more about Boomer.

"All right," she said. "I trust you," she added.

He couldn't have wished for better words, although he didn't deserve her trust.

"Come on," she said, turning and holding her arms out to shepherd the townspeople who were gathered on the veranda. "Let's step back and give Mark a moment. He has a few questions for the developers."

There were grumblings and murmurs, but they did as she asked.

Mark walked to the table, glad that everyone had been moved away. He'd still have to keep his voice down, and once he opened this conversation, so would these men.

"And your problem is?" D'Pee asked, throwing down a pile of leaflets.

"That bald-headed guy who had you pinned to the table a few minutes ago. Who is he?"

"Some idiot," Slick said.

"Would you like me to tell him you said that?"

Slick pulled his mouth into a tight line.

"It's the guy who set me up, isn't it? The guy you said you didn't want to be associated with, yet here he is. Who is he?"

"What can you possibly need that information for?"

"Perhaps because I intend to call the cops."

D'Pee thumped the table with a fist, then glanced at the far end of the veranda. "Don't forget *Daddy*," he said, voice lowered, jaw clenched. "And the bank heist."

Mark met his eyes. "Don't forget my father is missing. Don't forget I know all about your crime scene setup. How would Mr. Donaldson like it if he heard you'd messed up?"

"And how am I going to mess up?"

"You just did. You admitted you know about the guy called Frankie—or is it Bob Smith? It won't take the police long to put two and two together, and then Mr. Donaldson himself will be involved, perhaps implicated."

"You leave the police out of this."

"Why? What have you got to hide?" Mark curled his mouth. "Oh, yeah—your involvement."

"That's it!" Slick stepped forward, but D'Pee put an arm out to halt him.

"This man," D'Pee called out, pointing at Mark, "is threatening me!"

Lauren, Marie, and others broke from their huddle.

"I'm being accosted!"

The press moved down Main Street, pushing their way through a group who were heading for the bus.

"Mark?"

"Lauren. Please go into the saloon." He wasn't about to start anything physical, but if it happened, he wanted her out of the way. There was no way a guy like D'Pee, with his slack jaw and ill-fitting suit, would know how to throw a punch, but a flailing arm might hurt someone.

Slick, on the other hand, looked like he was raring to go.

Marie pulled Lauren back to the safety of the doorway and put an arm around her shoulders.

"You stay put," Mark told Slick, a warning in his eye.

Everyone stilled, and even though it was for a nanosecond, Mark felt it go on for eternity. Then Slick lunged.

Someone screamed.

Mark's breath was knocked from his lungs as the big guy tackled him. He stumbled backward into the railing, aware of panic taking hold all around him.

Reporters' phones were clicking, cameras flashing—and

the wail of a siren sliced through the air.

He kept his eyes on Slick as he grappled with him, but was aware the Gerdins and Fairmonts were ushering anyone left on the veranda into the bar.

He rolled Slick over, so the man's back was pinned to the veranda railing. That was when he saw the bus.

The driver was closing the door and within two seconds, the bus was heading out of town.

Boomer was in full view in a window seat at the rear. He sent a smile and a salute Mark's way.

Damn it!

His concentration momentarily lost, Mark took a blow to the jaw from Slick's elbow as he tried to free himself.

It hurt. Time to end this.

He turned Slick so his back was up against him and grabbed his torso with both arms. With one swift wrench, he performed the Heimlich maneuver.

Slick choked and spluttered on his own spit.

Mark pushed him off, but Slick turned, his face puce and his eyes enraged.

Fine. If he wanted more, Mark was happy to oblige.

He kicked at Slick's leg, his foot hooking the back of his knee, and Slick stumbled, but righted himself and threw himself at Mark, getting a punch in where he could.

Then the weight of Slick's body was lifted off him.

"Deputy Carl Lewis, Randall County Sheriff's Office. What's going on?"

Slick was sitting on the floor, legs spread, the deputy holding him by the scruff of his suit jacket.

"Wayne," he said to his officer. "Grab this guy while I have a little chat with these people."

Officer Wayne stepped forward, pulled Slick to stand, and forced his hands behind his back. Slick struggled, obviously pissed at being manhandled. "Might need to restrain him, Carl."

"Do it."

Officer Wayne cuffed him.

"Right," Deputy Lewis said, legs astride, hands on hips. "Who wants to speak first?"

"Mark was just standing there minding his own business," Ingrid said, "when that lumbering lout charged him."

"Got him in a stranglehold," Hortense added.

"In front of all these families! Good thing the children left on the bus!"

Mark wiped his mouth with the back of his hand. He couldn't taste blood, but his jaw was tender, along with a few ribs.

Lauren ran to his side and hunched down. "Are you all right?"

"Didn't mean for all that to happen." Once again, he hadn't thought, just strode in, ready to fix wrongs, and to beat it all, he'd been involved in a dustup. The very thing he'd wanted to avoid.

"You were brilliant!" she told him, eyes shining. "I could kiss you."

Well, that made up for the jaw ache.

"Who are you?" Deputy Lewis asked him.

Lauren snatched the sheriff's badge off his shirt. "Don't

want you charged for impersonating a police officer," she whispered.

"Well?" the deputy asked.

He hauled himself to stand, helping Lauren up too. There was an APB out for a Johnson Sterrett, but that was in California. There was no reason these deputies would recognize the surname and start asking him questions about his father. "Mark Sterrett. I own and run the saloon."

"You the guy who called it in? Looks like this fracas only just happened. Why did you call before it occurred?"

"I was concerned about a man who was in town. I believe him to be dangerous and had reason to think he was going to cause trouble."

"*Was* in town?"

The press were focused, cell phones and cameras in hand, and D'Pee was visibly sweating.

"Deputy, I'm Leonard D'Prichiatori. Donaldson's Property Development." He pointed to Mark. "This man accused me of unreasonable behavior. My assistant had every right to be angry."

"I'll decide what rights you might or might not have." The deputy turned to Mark. "Why were you fighting?"

"He charged me. I held him off, then he started choking, so I helped him out."

"Yeah, of course you did. Pretty good move, that Heimlich one. The pressure can wind a person who's not actually choking."

Time to move the story along. "The man I was concerned about skipped town on the bus. You would have passed it on the way in."

"What's his name?"

"Bob Smith. Frankie Caruso—and God knows how many more pseudonyms he goes by."

The deputies glanced at each other. "Caruso?" Deputy Lewis asked.

"I don't know the man," D'Pee said quickly.

"Don't you have a Bob Smith back at the office?" Lauren said.

"He retired."

"When?"

It was a moment before D'Pee spoke. "Recently. I believe he's traveling in Europe."

"How easily they lie! Like syrup dripping on a hot summer day." Marie stepped up, smiling at the deputy. "How *are* you, Deputy Lewis?"

"Oh—you. I'm still happily married, thanks."

Marie blushed. "There was a little misunderstanding when we met in Hopeless," she explained to everyone. "Donaldson's people were spreading rumors about Molly, and like a fool, I flirted with the deputy, hoping to get into his good books. And what good woman wouldn't? So strong and commanding. But I was wrong! Deputy Lewis is an officer who can't be blindsided by one little woman batting her eyelashes."

Deputy Lewis cleared his throat. "So, what are you doing in Surrender?"

"Helping out in whatever small way I can. Dissipating the rumors in the *Texas Portal* about this good person, my niece, Lauren Mackillop. Rumors spread by this bunch, I must add."

"You haven't got any proof of that!" Slick said.

"I'm a reporter and a Mackillop. Believe me, if the proof is there, I'll find it."

"Hey," Officer Wayne said. "Are you the Hopeless blog woman?"

"Sugar, I can't deny it. I can't wait to tell my readers all about our wonderful Randall County officers. Now, Deputy Lewis, what you need to understand is we're being pressured and deceived by Donaldson's. We need to know who this Frankie Caruso is so we can prepare ourselves for more trouble. I just hope it's not the vicious, murdering kind..."

Deputy Lewis pulled off his cap and scratched his head. He glanced at his fellow officer, then sighed. "Okay, you've got my attention. There's a Caruso on the national database. He goes by a number of names. He's wanted all over America and he's the trickiest player the cops have ever known. Some say he doesn't exist, others say it's not one man but half a dozen."

Mark heaved a sigh of relief that Boomer hadn't had time to hurt Lauren. He hadn't expected the brawl with Slick, but he had time to let this play out now that the cops had been updated on Frankie's recent appearance.

"Miss Mackillop believes the man was tailing her," he told the deputy. "I think he was also tailing me."

"Why would he do that?"

The TV camera was rolling, the clicking from the reporters' phones and cameras still going off.

The press would get the true story about Lauren and how she was abused by her business partner and he couldn't stop that, but now, hopefully, they'd start looking into Bob Smith, which would implicate the developers.

"I presume because he's associated with Donaldson's in some way," he said, nodding at D'Pee and Slick. "It's certainly an odd coincidence he's in town the same time they are. That vicious rumors were spread about Lauren and that Donaldson's played on them." He spread his hands. "Hey, look. I thought trouble was on its way, so I called the cops. Turned out I was right, although I hadn't expected to be set upon by these guys."

The more information that came to the surface from other sources, the better placed he was to protect his mom. He'd have to concoct some story about why he'd hidden his father, but hell—he was a writer. If he couldn't manage that, he didn't deserve to ever write again, even if he wanted to.

"Are you saying you've been lying to us the entire time we've been here?" D'Pee said, turning to the townspeople who were grouped in the doorway to the bar.

"You could say that," old Gerdin advised.

"The press knows our intentions for our town," Mark said to Deputy Lewis. "We've been truthful."

"Wayne," Deputy Lewis said. "Call it in. Get another unit to intercept the bus."

Officer Wayne dragged Slick to the cop car and picked up the radio mic.

"This is ridiculous!" D'Pee said, stepping in front of the table. "We came here today in good faith. What do you

think the local sheriff's office can do? Nothing—they haven't got the manpower. They haven't got the experience."

"Right," Deputy Lewis said. "That kind of annoyed me. I'm taking you in for questioning. Wayne, get that bozo in the car."

"You can't do this!" D'Pee said. "We have rights!"

Deputy Lewis stepped back. "You can walk to the vehicle unassisted or I can give you a helping hand."

"Am I being arrested?"

"If you don't put one foot in front of the other in the next five seconds, you're going to find out."

D'Pee looked like he was about to explode. "This is humiliating."

"Serves you right," Ingrid said.

"As soon as I've spoken to my lawyer, I'll be laying charges."

"Against who?" Hortense asked. "And what are you going to use for backup? The press has it all on film!"

"I'm not saying anything else!"

Deputy Lewis took D'Pee by the arm. "That's a shame. I've got a number of experienced colleagues in many states who'd like to ask you questions about this Frankie Caruso, Bob Smith guy. Let's go."

"What about our belongings?"

"We'll send them on," Gerdin said.

Mark turned away and texted Big Sam. *"Everything all right?"*

"All good. I'm back with your father and I've now got two of my buddies with your mom and sisters."

"Sterrett!"

He slipped the phone into his pocket. "Deputy?"

"Don't leave town."

Mark met the deputy's stern eye and nodded. "I'm not going anywhere."

As Donaldson's men were escorted to the cop car, the townspeople lined up on either side of them.

"Sure hope those handcuffs don't hurt," someone called.

"Hope the Calamity curse doesn't get you on the way out!" another offered.

"That's enough, people!" Deputy Lewis said, slamming the rear doors of the vehicle. "Stand back, please."

The deputies and their charges were out of town in a cloud of dust within a minute.

Mark hauled in a breath and put a hand to his rib cage when it snagged a little.

"That was quite dramatic, honey," Marie said behind him.

"Sorry."

"Don't be. The press has got it now. It won't be long before the truth of it all comes out."

Along with his role.

He looked down Main Street, taking his focus off Marie who was peering at him like she might be reading his mind.

The townspeople were now ushering visitors into their cars and waving to the press as they packed up their gear.

"Did you see him?" he asked Lauren when she joined them. "Frankie. He got away on the bus."

She nodded. "The police will stop it."

"No—he'll be gone. He'll have had an escape plan."

Lauren sighed. "So he's lived to tell another tale."

"Oh, boy," Marie said. "And we've still got Reckless to get under control."

"He wouldn't dare!"

"Let's hope you're right, sugar."

"They'll be back to question all of us," Mark told them.

"We'll worry about that when we need to," Marie said. "This day hasn't ended yet."

He'd gotten used to the unusual tingle in the air when he was around Marie, and Ava too, but he felt the heaviness of bad luck descend around them. Or maybe it just blanketed him. What had Ava said to him? He was in for a tough ride and he had to make his own decisions. Well, he was doing that. He was on the brink of handing over his father to the police and giving them the full story, including the crime scene setup. Although he had no idea where Donaldson had set the scene, and he'd have to be careful in case some unsuspecting person got hurt.

All he had to do now was tell Lauren the real story. She'd be upset, and probably angry, and he wouldn't blame her. But if he could persuade her to see reason once he explained himself, surely fate would send sunshine down on him? After all, he'd found the place where he wanted to put down roots. Perhaps the woman he wanted to share his life with. He still wasn't sure about that, but she *had* bewitched him, and he was content with his feelings. Things happened for a reason and he was beginning to see the truth in it. He was almost through his tough ride and there was light at the end of his tunnel.

He shook off the bad vibes.

"Couldn't put a curse on all that before I send it on to them, could you?" he asked Marie, trying to lift the mood as he nodded at the campaign table which was scattered with leaflets, posters, and empty coffee cups.

She shivered and Mark's forced humor disappeared as fast as it had arrived.

Suddenly, the silence in town seemed oppressive. People stood around, looking at the road out of town and no doubt discussing the goings on. Some dispersed to their businesses or homes, and a few headed for the bar, probably to collect any belongings they'd left there.

"I'll leave you both to it," Marie said. "I have to go."

The finality in her tone got him even more uneasy. Leave them to what?

She took Lauren by the shoulders. "All I can do is what I'm capable of doing. The rest is in your precious hands."

Lauren didn't question her, but her words made little sense to Mark.

A look crossed between the two women, one of intense love, perhaps harmony.

Lauren nodded, her eyes clear but there was a little frown on her forehead.

"You won't be alone, child," Marie said, backing away, her focus still intent on Lauren, as though bestowing a wish on her. "You stand firm. And you," she said to Mark, "remember what you've been told about your options."

She left them, walking to her van, back straight. For the first time since he'd known her, she wasn't smiling.

"Something going on?" he asked, looking down at Lauren.

Their gazes met, and held.

A tremor ran up his spine.

LAUREN COULDN'T HAVE shaken her focus off Mark if an earthquake rocked the town and cracked the street in two.

Something was going to happen. Something astonishing and it was going to result in sadness.

"Do you have any idea what she was talking about?" Mark asked, his brow furrowed. "I got the shivers there for a moment." He gave her a boyishly crooked smile. "I mean, there's always something in the air when I'm around you Mackillops, but that one..."

Marie never called her "child" it was a term only the grandmothers used. Often when forewarning.

Apprehension filled her. She hadn't had a single vision of her and Mark together in the future all day. The last memory she had was of him leaving, and if he had to do that, she couldn't hold him back.

He hadn't told her or Marie who this Boomer was—he'd made no mention of it—but she wasn't going to interrogate him. Not anymore.

"Hey, you two!"

Mark looked over her shoulder at the sound of Ingrid's voice, but Lauren kept her eyes on his face. The tanned, handsome face of a good man.

Let's make memories he'd said in the ballroom. But she

already had many memories. Of things they'd done together. Of things they'd shared together. And none of them had happened yet.

"How about celebrating?" Ingrid said. "We won. For today, at least."

"Break out the apple juice and the wine," Mark told her. "It's on the house." He returned his attention to Lauren, took her hand and held her fingers. "Let's celebrate, while we can. Let's take the moment."

Perhaps she wasn't meant to resolve anything for him. Perhaps whatever was going to occur for either of them had to happen in order for both to walk forward into their futures. Separate or together.

"I have to go home. Tell everyone I'll see them tomorrow."

"You can't! They want you to be part of this. They want to be with you." He put the slightest pressure on her fingers. "*I* want to be with you."

She pulled her hand out of his. "I'm tired."

She had to get back to Sage Springs and she had to keep Mark away. It wasn't safe for him and she needed time alone in the house to figure out what his role was in ending the curse. Because that's what he was meant to do. That's what Marie had silently been telling her.

"Lauren, wait!"

Without turning back, she walked along the veranda and down the steps to the street.

Chapter Twenty-Four

MARK WAS UPSTAIRS in his living quarters while the gang downstairs swung into party mode.

He called Big Sam to double-check the situation in California was still secure. Thankfully, it was.

"It won't be long now, Sam." The police would be back to question him and others, but the longer Mark could draw this out, the more the press would discover. He wanted time to ensure everyone's safety, and there was something else making him hesitate to call the police and confess everything he knew.

Lauren.

There was trouble on her heels. Why else had that strange, harmony-filled yet eerie moment have passed between her and Marie?

He needed to keep time on his side, just for a little while longer.

He texted Boomer in case he needed another ruse. He doubted the man was still around; he'd be long gone, but just in case...

"I've found my father. Text me a time and place to hand him over."

He waited a few minutes, but there was no answer.

Boomer might already have become someone else. Gone.

The police wouldn't hold D'Pee and Slick for long. They'd have their lies in place for their supposed lack of knowledge of previous employee, Bob Smith.

He grabbed the saloon keys and made his way to the stairs. On a whim, he left his cell phone behind. He wanted to give Lauren his undivided attention tonight.

He paused as once again, Ava's words came to him. *You'll be given an option, and it'll tear you in two. You won't believe it possible. You'll run from it.*

What were these Mackillop women telling him?

He guessed he'd find out.

Ten minutes later, he was knocking on Lauren's front door. "It's me!" he called when he heard footsteps from inside.

The door opened a crack. "What are you doing here?"

"I didn't want to celebrate without you. I brought wine." He held up a bottle of champagne. "And since you're reluctant to share in the good fortune going on around town, I've brought the party to you."

She glanced over his shoulder, surprise registering when she saw the gang standing on the pathway. Her friends and her townspeople.

"Don't lock us out, Lauren," he said quietly. "We care for you."

"You shouldn't have come. The house is not safe."

"In that case, I'm getting you out of there." He slipped a foot between the door and the frame in case she closed him out.

"That's not what I mean, Mark. There are things you don't understand."

"All I understand is that we need to talk. For a start, what was going on between you and Marie? Why did you run away?"

"You wouldn't believe me if I told you."

"Try me."

"Hey, can we come in now?"

He raised an eyebrow. "You're going to look mean-spirited if you don't let them in."

She blew out a breath and opened the door wider.

He smiled as he handed her the champagne and beckoned everyone in.

The Buckners, Hortense, and the Gerdins trooped up the path and onto the porch.

"This is right good of you, Lauren," Ingrid said as she walked into the hallway, eyes on everything around her. "Mark told us you'd invited us over."

Lauren shot him a withering look.

He gave her a smile, then stepped back as her friends gave her welcoming hugs and made their way into the kitchen with a picnic basket and more bottles of champagne.

She shot a look at the still broken staircase. Was she thinking about the time she'd showed him around the house? That had been the day it all changed for him. His feelings for the town, and for her. As soon as this party was over, he was going to come clean and tell her who he was, why he was here, and why she *could* trust him.

LAUREN OUGHT TO be angry with Mark, but she couldn't bring herself to it.

She probably had been thoughtless, leaving town the way she had. There was nothing bad in the house after all. It was exactly as it always had been, full of the aroma of sage, warmed from the day's sun, and quietly resplendent.

"Come off there," she told him. He was teasing her by standing halfway up the staircase.

He grinned, and a second later, pretended to trip.

Regardless of the pretense, she ran forward.

"Ouch," he said, holding up a finger. "Think I got a splinter."

"Stop it!"

He smiled. "I wanted to get your attention. Everyone else has had it for the last half hour. It's my turn."

She looked over her shoulder.

"This is some house!" Hortense said, fingering the push-button light switches and turning the chandelier on and off, making it twinkle as the light faded then sparkle again.

"Always wanted to see inside," Ingrid said. "I didn't get the chance when the renovations were started."

Nobody mentioned the fact that they'd stopped—due to the curse.

"Everyone should use the downstairs bathrooms," Lauren told them. "Until I get the staircase fixed."

"Oh, we wouldn't invade your privacy by taking a peek upstairs without your permission," Ingrid said, expectancy in her eyes.

"When the bannister's back on and the stairs are safe,"

Lauren told her. "I promise, you'll be the first to see the house as soon as it's renovated."

"It won't take much," Hortense said to Ingrid. "It's spectacular."

"Why are you so worried about me being on the stairs?" Mark asked when the others continued their perusal of her home.

She pulled a frown. All right, she'd give him a little insight—after he'd given her some. "Didn't you get bad vibes when you were last on them? When you fell?"

"I tripped."

"Pull the other one."

He pursed his mouth. "Okay. I did feel something…odd."

"Like what?"

"It was—hell, I don't know. I thought for a second I'd been pushed, that's all. I felt a hand on my shoulder…" He trailed off, then smiled and jogged down the stairs. "Come on, let's not spoil the party."

"Mark, wait. Did you pretend just now? Or did you trip?"

"I bruised a finger." He held it up again. "Want to kiss it better?"

He was flirting with her and she wasn't supposed to let him. A cacophony of emotions rose, scrambling her mind. "This is so dangerous," she told him, then took his face in her hands and kissed him on the mouth.

His hands came to her waist as he accepted her kiss, his mouth strong against hers.

When they broke, his eyes had darkened. "You've really given the town something to talk about now."

She didn't know why she'd done it. Some wild streak inside her, after all, maybe. But she wanted to do it again. To feel his mouth on hers, as though that might protect him in some way.

She'd promised herself not to sway him in any way whatsoever. Now what had she done by kissing him? Changed fate? Again?

"Love is in the air!" Ingrid said. "Gerdin, open that next bottle of champagne. This could be your lucky night."

The party was in full swing, everyone enjoying a hearty debate on what the developers might try next. But Lauren couldn't bring herself to move far from the staircase.

Ever since Mark had amused himself by pretending to trip, there'd been a chill around her shoulders.

She hadn't felt any chills in her house before now, nor had she been given any indication that there was something bad in the air, not even when she came home earlier and searched for it, waited for it. But the chill now bit into her.

She looked up at the staircase.

Something was wrong. Very wrong.

All of a sudden, her ears cracked, but when the sounds around her disappeared, she wasn't carried to the future. She was in the here and now.

Something passed her vision. A wafting. Not smoke, but a vaporous thing, and in a moment, she was at the base of the stairs without being aware she'd moved.

"Lauren?"

It was Mark's voice, but she was unable to turn to him. She was unable to speak. She was tied to another. It was like a heavy chain, dragging her up.

"Lauren!"

There were other voices now too. Her townspeople. They sounded shocked, shaken. But she was powerless.

Someone or something had built a wall between her and her people, her family. It was trapping her. A staleness, full of resentment was behind her, pushing her—and in front of her, an invitation to step forward. To greet it. To accept it.

Her fingers curled into her palms. She wasn't supposed to reach out. She wasn't supposed to go.

"Lauren!"

It was Mark's voice again, easily distinguishable, but there was another voice in her head. A voice she hardly remembered, although it crawled from the depths of her recollection, making its way to her heart. Her mother.

"Don't go." The voice was ethereal and rich in appeal. And the inviting hand—intimidating. Was this her great-grandfather, come to show her his power?

She clenched her hands tightly.

"Lauren, stand firm."

Ava's voice.

She drew on all her courage until it buoyed her.

Maybe passion beats anger. It was what she'd said to Mark when she showed him the house and told him about the great-grandfathers and how her brave Mackillop ancestors had beaten them. She'd hoped it was true. She'd been thinking it might help should her great-grandfather ever try to do harm.

She'd been giving herself her own forewarning. She *was* a true Mackillop.

"Damn it—*Lauren*!"

Mark again.

But she was so deeply in this trance, it felt like her feet weren't touching the ground. Her heartbeat resounded in her ears. She was floating, the love in her heart brimming, like a cup overflowing, like the waterfall that fell from the clifftop and met the lake in a pounding rush.

THE LIGHT BULBS in the chandelier and in the wall sconces had all gone out. It was dark, with only the stars and moon sending shadowy light through the thick plastic sheeting attached to the gap in the wall.

Mark's focus was on the staircase. On Lauren. The denseness of the air was so thick he could practically see it.

"Lauren!" He couldn't get to her. He couldn't reach her.

She was halfway up the steps, just before the staircase curved, and she was suspended, literally hovering above a step.

He was pushing against some invisible barrier. The Buckners were next to him, also trying to break through. He put his shoulder to it, but whatever it was, it was an intangible wall of steel.

KID WAS PUNCHING the barrier, his face red from the effort.

Gerdin's mouth was pinched, eyes scrunched, as he, too, used all the strength in his body to drive through the blockade.

Ava! Do something.

THE FEMININE POWER was overwhelming, and it was protecting her, but Lauren's inner strength was being tested, and she'd need to use all her determination, all her willpower, and all her beliefs in what was good and what was right.

As the energies around her heightened, the balance of power swung, rocking her, as though the air had been knocked out of her. A second later, a moment later—she had no idea of time—the denseness melted and calmness prodded the atmosphere, chipping away at the bad until good reigned supreme.

Her arms dropped to her sides, as though weighted. Her breath was still high in her chest—but she was free.

She'd done it! She'd been challenged in the most daunting manner and she'd come through.

She turned, not yet fully aware of her surroundings or of the time that had passed, and met the stunned expressions of her houseguests.

Reality sank in fast. What had they seen? What had they felt? "Is everyone all right?"

After an inordinate silence, Mr. Gerdin spoke, "Well. That's not something you see every day."

Everyone laughed in a relieved but befuddled way.

"Do you know what just happened?" Mark asked as he

stared up at her.

She couldn't hold onto her joy or her smile. "I did it, Mark. I *did* it!"

"Did what?"

She was freed from a bond she'd never known had bound her. "My great-grandfather. The curse," she explained, "it was real." And she'd just gotten rid of it, much the same way Molly must have done at her hacienda.

No wonder her cousin hadn't wanted to talk about it!

The emotions and sensations that had overcome her had been strong, and yet she'd had a miraculous command streaming through her. How could she ever explain it to another person?

"I think I need another drink," Ingrid said.

"We might have had too much!" Hortense exclaimed. "Did we just see what we just saw?"

"I doubt anyone would believe us," Doc said.

"I thought it was amazing," Kid said. "Whatever it was."

"It happened." Ingrid took a step forward. "Unbelievable or not, we saw it—or what we were allowed to see." She glanced up at Lauren again, her baffled expression still in place.

"How do you feel?" Butch asked softly. He was holding Hortense's hand—gripping it, and no doubt thankful his woman wasn't capable of such things.

"I feel wonderful." In some small way, she'd just met her great-grandmother and had been reunited, for the briefest, heavenliest moment, with her mother.

How could she ever thank the powers that be?

"It was certainly not something I could explain away," Hortense said.

Ingrid raised her hands, meeting each person's eye. "What we've seen tonight is what we saw, and not one of us can deny it. But we're not going to talk about it. To anyone. This stays with us."

Everyone agreed, but with a deeply embedded instinct that was new to her, Lauren already knew the story wouldn't stay buried. But it wasn't going to be a viciously spread rumor, it was going to help her cousin, Pepper, in some way. She just didn't know how.

"Sweetheart," Ingrid said, "you're one of a kind."

"No," Lauren said, pride overcoming her. "I'm a Mackillop."

Chapter Twenty-Five

LAUREN PICKED UP a dish towel and began to dry the plates she and Hortense had washed while Ingrid and Kid packed the remains of the party food into the picnic hamper.

She'd just said her goodbyes to everyone. They'd only stayed long enough to help clear up. Mark was seeing them to the door.

She looked up at the kitchen's pressed-tin ceiling, then around the space, at the wooden countertops and cupboards, the dressers, the china serving plates on the walls. What would this house be like in ten years' time? What would it be like to live in it for the rest of her life?

She'd never thought the house would mean so much to her, not even as a child, when she'd snuck in and made wishes as she twirled with her string of fake pearls.

She was proud to own this gift, even though she wasn't sure what her abilities were or what she'd be left with once she and her gift had gotten to know each other. Not that the gift felt like an instantly accessible thing, more a mental astuteness, a perception, waiting to settle.

Unless it had left her. The thought startled her so soon

after experiencing the real Mackillop ability, but she hadn't had any more visions of the future. Had her gift been given to her fleetingly, so she could release her family and her town from the curse?

"Hey, you. Spooky woman."

She turned on a laugh.

Mark smiled, then took the dishcloth off her and flung it onto the counter.

"Are you all right?" she asked him.

"This has been one crazy night." He took her hands in his.

"Do you think they'll be okay?" she asked, indicating the hallway and the front door behind him.

"They worked all last night and all today for the benefit of the town. They're bound to be a little weary."

"And they got a surprise this evening."

"Want to talk about that?"

In the last half hour while they regrouped and cleared up, Mark's gaze had settled on her repeatedly, as though he was ensuring her presence was a reality.

"It's difficult to explain. I don't think I understand it all yet." She paused, remembering the coldness of the hand that beckoned her. "Some force was pulling me. I think it was my great-grandfather. But there were beautiful forces holding me." Her skin tingled. "I think one of them was my mother."

He paled slightly and caution nipped her. She'd thought it little wonder Molly hadn't wanted to talk about this, and here she was, giving her thoughts to a man who would probably never understand.

"Do I scare you, Mark?" she asked quietly.

"Hell, yes."

How come he had the power to make her smile at the most serious of moments?

"Nothing will happen to you now," she told him. "You're safe here."

"I honestly never thought I wasn't."

"But you wondered. You felt things because the great-grandfathers didn't want you here."

"Why not?"

"You're a man. And you were associated with me."

"Were? Are we not friends anymore?"

She smiled again. "When did we become friends, Danton Alexandre Dubois?"

He paused, then lifted her hand and gently kissed her fingers. "Almost from the start, Scarlet Juliette. Despite everything."

Yes, they had, in many ways. Despite everything...

"Come with me. I want to test a theory." He led her out of the kitchen, into the hallway and to the doors to the ballroom.

"What draws you to this room?" she asked.

"You."

He opened both doors, flinging them wide, then hit all the light switches. The chandeliers came to life, flickering, as though unused to being lit. The wall sconces spluttered, like real candles would in a draught.

"I thought I saw you. In the mirror at the bar. You were

a little girl, twirling in this room."

My God. He'd been shown his own kind of visions? It was a wonder he was still in town. "Oh, Mark. I'm sorry. There is no curse on your bar. I said it to annoy you."

"Maybe it was real, maybe not. I don't know, but to me, this room means you."

He led her into the middle of the room and spun her until she was facing him.

"Dance with me."

She paused, looking up into his eyes. "There's no music."

"Let's pretend there is." He pulled her into him, curling his arm around her back, taking her hand in his, and danced her around the room.

They were living in the moment. Dancing in an old house, the whoosh of the curtains as they flew past and the spluttering and sparking of the light bulbs their music. They were making a real memory, and there was a new energy around him. His focus was on her, but beneath that, she felt what he was feeling as his heartbeat dashed against hers. Exhilaration.

In some ways, they were reenacting the last time they'd been in here. But she'd refused to dance that time. Tonight, it was a different story and there would be a different ending.

He brought them to a halt by a window, where the moon and the stars played outside.

All she could hear was his breath, her breath.

When he kissed her wonder encompassed her, along with his male energy, his aroma—peppermint, fresh air, and adventure—and the pure strength of his desire.

"I wanted to kiss you from the start," he said. "Wanted you to kiss me back the way you just did."

He held her firmly, as though he thought she might disappear. He held her as though determined no force would take her from him.

Expectancy wound its way through her. Her senses had never been so full. Body sensations, not mental. She didn't care where her mind was going, because it was in his hands.

"Take me to bed, Mark."

"I thought you'd never ask."

Her hand was in his all the way up the stairs, starlight following them until they reached her bedroom where the dusky evening light came from the moon outside the open window.

"Are you sure about this?" he asked.

She nodded. How could he think she wanted anything else?

"It's not just the moment?"

"It *is* the moment." The right moment. The right time. And it was real. It was happening.

But he had more questions; she could see it in his eyes.

She pulled his shirt from the waistband of his jeans and started to undo the buttons. "Does this make you think I don't want you?" She slid her hands up his broad chest, and around his torso, then reached up on tiptoes until her mouth was almost on his.

"Are we making memories, Lauren? Like in Paris, in the VIP lounge?"

"Yes."

"What happens after?"

After they made love, or after—but there was no *afterward.* Everything she'd experienced with him in the future had been hers alone.

For a second, she faltered.

Then Mark's mouth was on hers, prying her lips apart, and every memory they hadn't shared together faded.

"I'm not proud of a few things I've done," he told her, his hand warm on the curve of her spine. "And I've never been surer about this. But I wonder if we should tell each other a little something about ourselves first?"

"If you need us to."

Did he want them to tell their secrets now? It momentarily frightened her—she had every intention of telling him about her visions, and he'd probably laugh. After what he'd seen tonight, it surely wouldn't come as a surprise.

He took her face in his hands. "I think I was meant to meet you."

Happiness spread throughout her in a rush of warm, blanketed heat.

They *were* meant to have met. How else would all of this come about?

"Now you," he said.

She had no hesitation. There was only one question she wanted an answer to.

"Did you like Scarlet more than you liked me?"

"I never saw Scarlet. I only saw you."

Whatever it was she possessed with her gift, she promised herself, there and then, to stay grounded in reality. Because

Mark was real, and she was in his arms.

"And you?" he said. "You said you liked Danton. Does that mean you'd prefer him to be here, in your bedroom, desperate to make love to you?"

"I said I liked the pretzels better."

He scooped her up, his smile wide and his eyes dancing. "Then let's take our moment."

Lauren sank into him, and let the magic happen.

Chapter Twenty-Six

MARK OPENED HIS eyes and blinked as his senses awoke with him. The pale dawn light filtered through the opened curtains on the windows, making the bed he was lying in look like it was backlit on a movie set.

Memories rushed to the fore. Memories of him and Lauren and what they'd shared together in the night.

It was real, everything around him, including the naked woman resting her head on his chest, their hands lightly clasped, fingers intertwined. It was the most romantic moment he'd ever experienced. Waking up with his woman, the warmth of their bodies intimate.

Lauren roused and moved so she was looking up at him.

Her moss-green eyes were so dark and inviting, so perfect. How could he ever have thought he didn't like potted plants and china teacups?

He bent to kiss her. Her lips tasted sweet as her hands slid up his chest. But the invitation made him think of everything he had to finalize.

They'd been together, were together, and he couldn't believe how much luck had shined on him. And although he'd have liked to tease her into another lovemaking bout, there were important issues to discuss.

"Lauren, there's something I've got to tell you."

After a beat, she sat up. "Me too."

It couldn't be as big as his. "You go first."

She settled herself, the sheet beneath her arms. "I know this will sound incredulous, but my gift is partly an ability to see into the future. Even more astonishing—I've been given insights into *our* future."

"Our future?" Maybe he hadn't heard her correctly.

"Our relationship. I've had visions of us and our life together." She pushed to her knees. "I don't want you be scared of any of this."

"How can I be scared? I don't understand what you're saying."

"What I've seen in the future is that we're going to get married, and we'll have children, and you'll write books—"

"We'll what?"

She pushed her hair back from her face, concern in her expression.

"You're telling me you can see into my future?"

"Yes. Well—and mine. Our future. And our children's."

"Are you kidding?"

He went cold. Dead cold.

He pushed from the bed. Foresight. Divination. Destiny. Chance, providence, insight, fate, luck—doom. The words were scrambling in his brain. All this time he'd been thinking he was in charge of himself—and he hadn't been.

"You're angry," she said, getting out of bed, holding the sheet up against her to cover herself.

How futile was that? Covering herself up when he'd seen and touched every part of her!

He was standing, hands on his hips, when he realized *he* was still naked.

He grabbed his pants from the chair where he'd flung them and pulled them on. Suddenly, the dawn's light wasn't cozy and it was chilly in the room. The room where he'd given his all to the woman he was falling for.

"I need to clarify a few points." Had his attraction to her all been an illusion? A potent spell after all? "When you first met me, did you like me, or did you say that because it was a ploy?"

"At first, I thought you were trying to pick me up."

"And after the VIP lounge?"

"During, not after. I started to see the gentleman in you when you slowed down for me. I was wearing boots that were too tight—secondhand. Then I became enchanted by you. You didn't laugh when I ordered white-fudge pretzels. I think I saw the real you. That's the man I had a crush on."

"When did you fall in love with me?"

"I didn't say I've fallen in love with you."

"But isn't that what this is all about? This attraction between us, leading to marriage and happy families?"

She took a breath. "Attraction isn't love. I'm very attracted to you and always was, even though I thought you were up to no good."

"Why didn't you *know* who I was?" She didn't know now; he hadn't had a chance to tell her. But that wasn't the point. They were currently arguing about their future. The one he'd had no idea he was going to be a part of on a full-time basis.

"How many kids are we going to have?"

She bit her bottom lip. "Three."

She could see their whole future together, and she hadn't thought to mention it!

"Lauren. Do you have any idea how all this sounds?"

"I'm not explaining properly—but I can only believe what I've been shown and that it's going to happen."

He slammed his hand against his thigh. "Last night we agreed this was real. It was our moment. Now you're telling me you knew all along I'd take you to bed."

"It wasn't your decision. I had a say in it too—but yes, I wanted us to share the moment."

Her eyes brimmed with worry, but he had to ignore it. "This is utterly preposterous."

"I know it must sound that way…"

He'd accepted the impossible when he'd seen her hover above the steps on the staircase. What guy would hang around after that? *He* had. He'd been open-minded. Incredulous, yes—but supportive. And now this…

Had his supposedly peaceful sleep been the result of a trick? "Last night. It wasn't a real moment, was it?"

"Yes, it was. It was our moment."

"How could it be when you knew the outcome and I didn't have a damn clue?" It didn't seem possible she'd engineered this, but what else was he to think?

Or had it been her relatives? What if Ava had put everything into place—with his father stealing half a million dollars to get the ball rolling? Had she known what might happen next, or had she initiated the start and ignored the repercussions? The consequences of which happened to hit Mark and his family damned hard. Donaldson on his back and blackmail. Fear. Worry. Not to mention a possible dead body.

"So when am I going to fall in love with you?" he demanded.

"I don't know…"

"And when are you going to fall in love with me?"

She bit her bottom lip so hard, it paled. "Perhaps when you leave."

Mark threw his hands in the air. "This is *ludicrous*! What's the point in falling in love with me the moment I leave? How could I possibly forgive you and come running back, a bunch of flowers in my hands, asking you to marry me?"

"I haven't been shown—"

"Lauren, listen to yourself! We're not even in love. We're not even *close* to being in love."

"We are—a bit," she said fast, shooting her focus up to his.

He hardly heard her; his mind on a fast track to a sad future. "You'll fall in love when I leave, which will break your heart. I won't even know it because I'll be gone. But now, I'll always *think* about it. Because you've told me!" He swung away from her. "You've made me a heel, and I haven't even broken your heart yet!" It was damned unfair.

"I didn't tell you you'd break my heart," she said, in such

a reasonable tone that he looked over his shoulder and scowled at her.

"It's the obvious conclusion, isn't it?"

"Maybe I'll break *your* heart!" she said, glowering at him.

"Hah!" he flung at her, but his heart did a double-jump. "Is that because you can see me in the future? Bent over my desk, bereft at losing you, unable to write a damned word because I'm heartbroken that the beautiful woman I was beginning to like a lot, the woman who made love with me so passionately, with such heartfelt joy, is laughing at me, waiting for me to see the error of my ways and come crawling back to her?" He couldn't think straight a moment longer. "You'll be waiting a lifetime," he informed her as he made for the door, yanked it open, stepped outside and slammed it closed behind him.

LAUREN WAS PINNED to the spot, her heart beating fast, her pulses electrified and the slam of the door ringing in her ears.

If being in love with someone meant she felt destroyed and deserted when they denied her a chance—not even a right, just a chance—to explain something slightly unusual, then she was *already* in love with him.

She'd even predicted it. *Perhaps when you leave…*

And he'd certainly left.

Shouldn't he be grateful she'd told him about her gift and not hidden it from him? She couldn't possibly have fallen in love with him right this second. Look at the attitude on the man!

She dressed quickly in jeans and a tee. So much for her rosy future. He'd called it ridiculous. He'd called their whole future life together ridiculous!

Worst of all, she couldn't see the ending. She was on her own, left wondering, left heartbroken. Why hadn't she seen *that* in a vision? The sorry conclusion of Lauren Mackillop's momentary happiness—a one-night stand with a handsome man who'd loved her and left her.

Perhaps the great-grandfathers' curse was too strong to break after all.

Suddenly, she had a compulsion to close her eyes. As if something was drawing her in, like a sensory tunnel. But it wasn't like when she was about to be hit with a vision. This was different. Something real was about to happen. Something she knew about—and yet standing here alone in her bedroom, she didn't know. What sort of soothsayer was she?

Her grandmother's voice reached inside her mind.

"Come and see me."

"I'll work this out for myself."

"You know what's going to happen next. But you won't trust yourself."

"I'm spinning in circles. I don't know what to think—and don't forget I had a busy night."

"You did well. I'm proud of you."

Lauren squeezed her eyes tighter. *"I felt my mom, Ava."*

"I know, child. I felt her too, through you. Thank you."

She opened her eyes, self-pity gone in an instant.

If she was going to work this out for herself, she'd better make a start.

The stone she'd taken from Ava's cauldron winked when the sun shone on her dressing table, and the chill that shivered over her skin had nothing to do with the great-grandfathers.

She flew out of her bedroom and raced up the stairs to the attic, the only place where she could see the road heading out of Surrender.

The door opened with a creak and a flurry of dust, then banged against the wall as she ran to the window, heart racing.

It was exactly as it had been in the vision. But this time, it was real and in the moment.

She was in the dusty, ramshackle attic that nobody had been in for years, except when she'd shown it to Mark and when she'd been here, in her vision, watching him leave.

And he was leaving now. The dust kicked up from the speed he was driving indicated he couldn't wait to get far away. He couldn't have had time to even pack his bags. He'd just made an instant decision. No thought for the people he was leaving behind.

She was in love with him. For real in love. She should have told him about her visions before they dashed upstairs to her bedroom. She should have given him the chance to ask his questions last night, before they'd given themselves to each other. They'd gotten closer to each other, physically and mentally, and she'd messed everything up by being truthful.

But he'd gone, and she only had herself to blame.

She wanted to fall to her knees, where her heart was spilling her hopes and dreams all over the wooden floor.

Chapter Twenty-Se en

“IT’S OUT,” MARIE said, slamming the door on the blogmobile and marching up the steps to Sage Springs house, her raspberry heels tapping like gunshot in what had been a painful but reflective day of silence.

Lauren rose from the wicker chair by her front door.

“You sure had an interesting night, sugar.”

Her cheeks heated.

“I meant the great-grandfathers!” Marie said, eyebrows raised.

“Oh, that.” Not the night she’d spent in Mark’s arms. “It was unworldly.”

She didn’t bother wondering how Marie knew about the faceoff on the staircase. Even if Marie had felt something eerie or spiritual, she wouldn’t admit to it.

On the back of that thought, she choked on a sob. “He’s gone,” she managed, and was instantly buried in her adoptive mother’s hug.

“It wasn’t you and your Mackillop capabilities that scared him off, sugar. He rushed to his mother’s side.”

Lauren pulled herself together, sniffled, and pulled out a tissue to wipe her eyes. “What do you mean? What’s happened?"

Marie leaned against the veranda railing as though it was an ordinary day and she was settling in for a chat. The wandering ivy trailing up a post and along a beam surrounded her like a picture frame.

"It's all out about Mark. Although the stories in the *Texas Portal* and the *Globe* differ considerably, but I was right! The man of your dreams was being blackmailed. Nobody's allowed to say by whom, but allegedly it was Donaldson himself. *The* Donaldson."

She hadn't known there was a *the* Donaldson, but over the next few minutes she learned that Mark's father was in police custody, and it had been discovered he'd embezzled from *the* Donaldson. Now Mark was fighting to protect his mother's innocence, who'd also been drawn into the murky depths of underhand, nefarious dealings due to some money she'd won.

"All this happened overnight?"

"It only takes one little rumor. Don't forget, we fed the press, we pushed them to dig deeper. As soon as this story came out about the guy they'd just met here in town, they were like flies to a jug of cream."

"Is it going to be worse for Mark now?"

"Donaldson's lawyers are powerful. With hefty financial backing. The press is all over Mark."

"Where is he?" Lauren asked, knotting her fingers together in worry.

"LA, with his family. He's not giving interviews. He's saying nothing—which I personally believe is the wrong way to handle it."

"Perhaps he's got a plan."

"What are your visions telling you?"

Her eyes watered again. "I haven't had any."

She'd never forget the look on his face when he eventually understood what she'd been telling him. It was the look of a man who'd made up his mind. But that didn't mean she didn't care about him and what was happening to him.

"Can we help him?"

"He has to help himself. He's got the rest of his life to think about. He made decisions. He's the only one who can extract himself from all that. But the press is a different matter. I'm going to protect him."

"Mystically?"

"Why would I turn to mysticism when I have all the attributes necessary at my fingertips? I'm a reporter, sugar! I'm at the nerve center. Heck, with close to eighty-thousand blog followers this morning, I'm the mothership! All I have to do is ensure verification of noncredibility of that rag, the *Texas Portal* who are the ones spreading the gossip about Mark and his possible dubious involvement with crime. It won't be easy—I'm working in a post-truth era here. But, trust me, I know what I'm doing."

After dealing with the press yesterday, Lauren couldn't doubt Marie, although she had no idea what she had just said.

"I'll get the truth out. The rest of it is up to Mark." Marie stepped forward and hugged Lauren hard. "I have to go, there's a lot to do. Just don't stay cooped up in your house for too long. It's not good for blood sugar levels or your bruised heart."

Lauren collapsed on the wicker chair after Marie left in a cloud of resolve and Coco Chanel's famous No. 5.

The peacefulness from earlier now felt like solitary loneliness. What was she going to do now? Sitting around feeling sorry for herself wasn't going to work. If she was going to spend the rest of her life alone, she needed to pick up the pieces now, not hang around with a pile of tissues waiting for someone else to fix it.

So what if Mark never came back? So what if he hated her? That was life—unpredictable. Just because she was learning to be a soothsayer didn't mean she couldn't use her ordinary-woman skills. After all, they'd supported her for twenty-seven years.

First of all, she had to go into Surrender and show her face. They'd all have heard about Mark by now, and they'd all know he'd been in their town double-crossing them. She'd like to put them straight on as much as she could. Next, she had to create a list. A list of must-dos would keep her occupied. She needed a list so long it would exhaust her just getting through the chores each day. Then maybe she'd sleep soundly and forget everything else. And maybe, each morning would get easier, or brighter.

It was the only hope she had to go on.

FIVE DAYS LATER, she could explain the physical tiredness because she'd dusted and scrubbed the house inside out.

She'd cleaned all the windows and polished every stick of furniture. But the mental stress had been more than she'd bargained for. According to what she'd read, Mark was going through much more than she was, but even so, just talking to Deputy Lewis, and then more police from Santa Ynez about what her business partner had done, had been challenging.

She'd given them all the information she had. It was up to them to investigate and they'd said it might take months. So, once again, she had to leave another outcome up to fate.

The Buckner brothers caught her attention as they came out of the house with their tools. They'd finished fixing the bannister on the staircase. The hole in the wall would have to wait because their services were needed in town.

"Sure you won't stay for lunch?" she asked a second time.

"No, thank you, Lauren."

Doc led his brothers to their pickup.

It wasn't that they were cautious about being on the staircase or in the house because she'd checked and they said they had no qualms whatsoever about any of that and trusted the bad vibes had gone. They just didn't want to talk much. Nobody did.

Mr. Fairmont had done some plastering on the ceilings at Sage Springs, but he'd been constantly interrupted, having to pop back into town to receive various donations or loaned artifacts for the new marketplace museum. Mrs. Fairmont wanted to employ the Buckners to expand her flower plot, and was digging and planting furiously while she waited. Hortense was covered in dust from dawn to dusk as she cleared up her antique shop.

All of them had been reticent to talk about Mark.

It was as though there was a cone of silence around the whole situation. They knew the whole story now, but perhaps they thought being involved with someone who'd been entangled in embezzlement and blackmail wasn't the right tone for attracting tourists. Or maybe they were just taking it on the chin, in order to get over the fact that Mark had set out to cheat them, had then become friends with them, then left them high and dry.

As far as she knew, he was still in California. There was still nothing in the press about him, and she looked at all the online newspapers every hour. But what *would* she know? The gift of foresight had deserted her. No visions. No idea. No clue. Maybe she'd been a part-time soothsayer, although Ava had reminded her the gift wasn't for them, it was for others, but she hadn't even had a tingling of the skin. No eerie forewarnings. No popping in her ears.

She'd relied on her own womanly insights and strengths, and they were beginning to feel depleted too.

So were the rejuvenation plans.

The doors to the saloon had been closed and locked since Mark's departure. It was the business that brought all the others in town together, and now everybody had deserted it.

Her townspeople were misplaced again. Not that they weren't working or going ahead with their proposals, but the fight had gone out of their endeavors.

And what had she done? She'd been stuck in her gloomy world, furiously polishing everything in sight and making her list longer every day, but had she really given a thought to her townspeople? They too had lost something with Mark's leaving.

With an intake of breath, she left the porch and strode down the path to the iron gates that were always open these days. She marched right up to the brick archway where the honeysuckle aroma lifted her spirits.

It was time for order. It was time to get back to the task at hand—renewal of serenity in her beautiful hometown.

"Ingrid!" she called across the street. "Do you still have keys to the saloon?"

MARK SHUFFLED AN unopened bag of pretzels around on the table, not interested in eating but someone had left them. He'd be happy if he never saw another pretzel as long as he lived.

Neither was he hungry and hadn't been the whole two weeks he'd been in LA, even though his mom and sisters had plied him with food every second they weren't asking him numerous questions or, more lately, packing their bags.

He scanned the LAX departure area. His mom and sisters were airport shopping. He was taking them to Texas. He wasn't convinced of their safety yet, not until his father had been to court and sent to prison. What worried him was the possibility of retribution from Boomer—or Frankie or Bob or whatever the man's name was. The cops hadn't been able to locate him. He was just another notch on a long list of sightings and disappearances.

Apart from ensuring his family's safety, he was also heading to Texas to face the music—not necessarily to make amends, because he'd never be able to, but he was going to Surrender anyway, even if only to put a For Sale sign on the bar.

As for Donaldson himself, his lawyers were wheedling, and it was currently looking like he'd get away with it. He was being described as the victimized party, not the instigator. The poor multimillionaire whose honest and hardworking business and philanthropic reputation was being defamed. He knew nothing about a secret setup with a crime scene. He knew nothing about Mark Sterrett, the ghostwriter who'd written the murder scene, but he was pursuing charges of embezzlement against the senior Sterrett.

Fortunately, the cops were behind Mark and believed him. They just couldn't prove the blackmail. They couldn't find the crime scene either. Hopefully, it would be discovered. Or maybe the empty building it was set up in would suddenly and mysteriously burn down.

D'Pee and Slick were professing innocence and shock at what had happened. He didn't know what they'd do next, but was sure they wouldn't take their talons off Calamity Valley just yet. They might not have Hopeless and Surrender, but Reckless was still available. Mr. Donaldson would undoubtedly want revenge for having his name brought into the open like this. He'd want to see the valley's ruination and hopefully grab their land after all.

His heart clenched at the thought of the people he'd come to think of as his friends going through more trouble.

Once he'd sold the bar to some decent person—he'd be

double-checking the purchaser's credibility—Surrender would continue with its expansion, and maybe that, along with what Hopeless was doing, would help the town of Reckless get through whatever would be thrown its way.

It wasn't his problem, but he wished it was. Wished he'd be around to help out, if he could.

Not that they'd want him.

He was resigned and willing to do the one thing he had to do—sort things out with the bar, apologize, and make explanations if they'd let him. He'd hated having his face splashed across the newspapers and his family name muddied. He'd had his whole life dissected by the press. It was what he'd put into play though, so he could hardly complain, and they'd backed off now but only because Mark couldn't tell them anything more for legal reasons.

The last time he'd been in this departure area he'd been bored, until he'd spotted Lauren. This time, it was frustration that had him in a chokehold. The place was filled with too many reminders of Lauren and the time they spent getting to know each other in the VIP lounge.

He flicked the packet of pretzels.

He'd have to come face to face with her. Lauren Mackillop, the spooky woman with the smile that slammed a guy in the gut and the moss-green eyes that melted the heart.

When had he first started to like her? From the start, from the moment he saw her, but that was only animal attraction. She was a beautiful woman; any man would fall under her spell.

He brought himself up at that thought. He had to be

careful, in case some of the Mackillop spell was still in his system, making him think he liked her more at a certain point when in fact, he hadn't.

As for falling in love with her—

He'd liked the look of her. He'd felt some sort of empathy for her, or perhaps with her. He'd enjoyed her company in the VIP lounge to such an extent he'd almost forgotten the reason he'd approached her in the first place. None of that was anywhere *near* love. It was just the initial pull. Okay, so he'd been attracted instantly. That meant nothing in the scheme of things.

He'd gotten too involved, that was where he'd gone wrong. He'd fallen under a spell, all right. One for the town, its charming, slightly quirky characters, and its beautiful daughter.

He flicked the packet of pretzels again, harder this time. What he hadn't been able to work out was that if this had all been a scheme by the grandmothers, Wild Ava in particular, and no doubt Molly and even Marie had a hand in it—why would they put a spell on a man they must have known was up to no good? Why throw their daughter at a man like that?

A man like him.

"Mark! We're boarding."

He roused himself and waved acknowledgement to his mom, then stood and gathered his belongings. His return to Surrender wasn't going to be pleasant, but he wasn't a man who walked away from a bad situation without first endeavoring to fix the problem.

He made his way to the queue where his mom and sisters

were lined up, and tipped the unopened bag of pretzels into the trash can on his way.

MARK HELD HIS breath as he drove the rental car past the Welcome to the Serenity of Surrender sign. It was still early morning and the few businesses weren't open. But the junk shop had a new sign and was no longer an antique store but Hortense's Vintage Wares. The flower plot was in expansion mode, the blooms bright and cheery enough to make him think they weren't nodding in the breeze but laughing at him.

The information cabin had a new lick of paint on the exterior. Right next to it there was a new sign on another cabin. The Surrender Flapjack Kitchen.

Damn, this was hard.

The street was deserted so he had a chance to get his mom and sisters inside the saloon and settled before he faced everyone.

"Darling. If you think you've done so much wrong to these people, why are you returning?"

It was a question she'd asked many times, and he always gave the same answer. "I've got to make amends."

"What about Lauren? What are you going to do?"

"I'm going to wait and see what she wants from me." If she was going to slap his face or throw abuse at him, he'd let her.

His mom knew how his heart had gotten tangled up. He'd been so full of remorse, and so pressured with the cops and the lawyers, he'd thought he'd hidden his wretchedness from her, but he'd been wrong. She'd seen through him and forced him to talk about Lauren. Although she knew nothing about the staircase incident, or about the moments he had spent in Lauren's bedroom before he walked out and slammed the door on her. He'd told her they'd had an argument. They hadn't seen eye to eye on where the relationship was going.

She still didn't believe it was the whole story, but it was his problem. One he'd fix if possible, by apologizing for storming out on her. But most likely, he'd be told to get lost, that she never wanted to see him again.

He focused on the bar at the end of the street. No matter what happened to him, he was convinced the setup the people of Surrender had put in place for the family saloon would work for the town, would work alongside Lauren's business, and for the entire valley.

Was he really going to have it sell? Who would take it on? The saloon needed a special hand and creative management. Not just anybody could walk into Surrender and cope with that.

Perhaps he ought to give it away. Hand it over to them. It wasn't as if he thought about the money anymore. He'd make more money one day. Doing whatever it was he was going to do.

He parked the car to the side of the bar and ushered his family up the steps to the veranda, telling them he'd unload their suitcases later. He wanted them inside before people realized he was back.

He pulled the keys out of his pocket and unlocked the outer doors. His sisters pushed through the swing doors and went inside, but his mother stayed where she was.

Her bothered expression told him she still wanted answers and maybe she deserved the full explanation of why he'd come back.

"I once told someone that if I found myself in the same position as my father, I'd work it all out so that it was fair for everyone, and that if I couldn't do that, I'd hand myself in. That's what I'm doing here. Handing myself in."

She took his hand. "You're nothing like your father, Mark. You're like my father and my grandfather. You're a hardworking, honest man."

"Every man has to face something he dreads at some point in his life," he reasoned. "Something he might have done badly or hadn't worked hard enough to overcome."

"But what is it you're dreading? The apologies you have to make? Or how you feel about Lauren?"

She pushed open the saloon swing doors, and walked inside.

Mark exhaled. She was spot-on and still he couldn't make up his mind about what he felt. Duped? It served him right. Unsure? He should be used to that now. Lost?

Yeah. And a lot lonely, too.

He made his way inside and looked around.

His sisters were by the jukebox.

Jukebox?

When had that arrived? Who'd ordered it?

"What's been going on?" he said as he made his way to

the bar.

There were clean glasses in the dishwasher racks. Cutlery had been folded in paper napkins and the sauce bottles were filled and lined up.

"I don't understand." Only he had the keys. Who had been in here, operating the place while he'd thought it shut down?

Running footsteps behind him made him turn to the doors. It would be the townspeople. They'd probably want his hide.

"Mark," his mother said quietly, a hand on his arm as she looked through the doorway and down the main street.

"They won't hurt anyone. They just want to yell at me. Take the girls upstairs. It's going to be okay."

"Mark Sterrett!"

Ingrid.

"You've got some nerve!" Hortense shouted out.

Mark walked to the doors, his heartbeat pounding. This was it and he was suddenly a little afraid, a little worried how he'd handle the disparagement.

He steeled himself.

His mother followed him to the doors, although she stayed a few paces behind him.

Ingrid didn't falter in her angular stride, arms swinging as she strode up the steps to the veranda and right to him.

"Mark!" she said. "You're back!"

"Took him long enough!" Hortense grumbled.

Ingrid grabbed him and hugged him hard. "Boy, did we miss you!"

"Where've you been?" Hortense demanded, shoving Ingrid aside and throwing her arms around him.

"California," he supplied, bemused.

"It's so good to see you back," Mrs. Fairmont said, smiling and tearing up.

"We thought you'd done a runner, for sure," her husband added with a laugh.

"Like he would have done that," old Gerdin said, stepping forward. "It's all been happening here," he said, as he shook Mark's hand. "Never been so tired!"

"We've been opening from midday until sunset," Ingrid told him, nodding at the bar. "We've only got burgers, fries, and chili at the moment, but Kid has applied for a grant, and we're hoping our Surrender Flapjack cabin will be open within the month."

"Miss Flores has decided to use some of her savings to get the candlemaker's shop renovated. My Butch is doing that, with Kid and Doc so busy."

Mark's eye was drawn to the street where the Buckners were heading for the saloon, striding along the street with big grins.

"It's an exultant day, that's for certain," Doc said as he clasped Mark's hand.

He couldn't get his head around this. The smiles, the handshakes, the welcome home.

"Who's been running the bar?" It was the only thing he could think of to say. If he started thanking them or trying to explain, the pent-up emotion inside him might overflow and he'd make a complete fool of himself.

"Me," Doc said. "Along with Kid and pretty much everybody. We've been sharing the duties. We've had two busloads of tourists in the last week."

"How did all this happen?" Mark asked.

"It was Lauren," Ingrid said. "We were all a bit lost after you left, not knowing what to do next. Then Lauren turned up in town and demanded the keys." Ingrid winked. "I hope you don't mind that I gave them to her."

Lauren had put all this in place?

"You should see Sage Springs!" Mr. Fairmont said. "It's looking spectacular."

"We didn't do any more renovation work on the bar," Butch said. "We didn't think we should, not without your approval."

"We didn't mess around with your décor, either," Ingrid told him. "We didn't want to move things until you gave us the go-ahead."

"We've had a few more ideas though," Hortense said.

He'd bet they had. It warmed his heart, and it had been a dead cold muscle up until a few minutes ago.

"I can't believe it. Can't express my thanks." He'd never be able to find the right words. He was still choked up.

Ingrid swatted the air. "It was nothing. We wouldn't have gotten to the position we're in now without you."

"Best thing I did was sell you that lease," Gerdin said.

"What an awful time you've had," Hortense said. "If only you'd told us you were being blackmailed, we'd have rallied around sooner."

"Sharks," Gerdin added.

Mark faced the old man. He'd been at Mark's side many times in the last days. Sometimes at pertinent points. It was Gerdin who'd asked him relevant questions too. "Did you know I was up to no good from the start?"

Gerdin shrugged. "Might have had an idea. Might have thought about it for a while and decided there was something going on and something about you I liked."

"If it weren't for you, we'd never have gotten this far," Ingrid said, then spotted something over Mark's shoulder. "You must be Mrs. Sterrett. It's a pleasure to meet you. This boy of yours is something else!"

"Mom," Mark said, smiling and holding his hand out for her. "Come meet my friends."

It was such a strange sight, seeing his family standing on the veranda of the saloon they hadn't known he'd bought up until two weeks ago.

They looked good. They looked like they belonged.

"Oh, we can't have that!" Mrs. Fairmont was saying to his mom. "There's not enough room above the bar for four women."

"She's right," Ingrid added. "How about the cabins? We can all pitch in and clean a couple out."

"There's no need for that," Doc said. "We'd be delighted to offer you our home for the duration, Mrs. Sterrett. If the Fairmonts are in agreement."

"Absolutely!" Mrs. Fairmont said.

"Where are you boys going to sleep?" Ingrid asked.

"In our truck," Kid said.

"I'll stay with Hortense," Butch informed the group, going ruddy in the face.

"No way are you good men sleeping in your pickup," Mrs. Fairmont said. "We'll clean up those cabins."

Within minutes, the Buckners were unloading the women's luggage from the rental vehicle, and chatting about the house on Water Street. Hortense was telling them she'd organize some groceries and have them sent over.

Mark was alone with the Gerdins.

"Are you going to see Lauren now?" Ingrid asked.

"Um… probably not. We don't see eye to eye on a few things."

"Lover's tiff?" Gerdin asked.

"Let's just say we had different viewpoints on our futures."

"Let me give you some advice, son. Women who levitate are an odd bunch. You can never figure out what they'll do next."

"How many have you met?" he asked, genuinely hoping he'd say at least one.

"Half a dozen, easily."

Mark found a grin. "Good to know."

Gerdin winked. "You've got a good situation in front of you, if you want it. Don't mess it up, son."

Did he want it? Maybe, but how to reconcile with her before they held a conversation about where they might take things? And did she already know the outcome?

Chapter Twenty-Eight

"SUGAR, I'VE GOT news!"

Lauren smiled. "I should hope so," she said as she poked the last seedling into a pot she was planting up for the atrium, "since you spend your days wandering the valley looking for it." She hefted the container off the potting bench she'd put on the front porch and turned to her aunt as she slipped out of the blogmobile. "So what's happened now?"

"Mark's back."

She almost dropped the pot as her knees buckled. "Here?"

"No, he's moved to Reckless. Of course here! Put that plant pot down before you get soil all over that delicate ensemble you're wearing."

Lauren looked down at her gray track pants and the frayed hemline of her favorite workout tee. It was lilac, with the words *I should have been a Princess* on the front.

"When did he arrive?"

"Early this morning."

It was now close to midday. Obviously, she hadn't been the first thing on his mind.

"How did it go?"

"I knew our people wouldn't let him down. They're gushing at his return. They've already arranged for Mrs. Sterrett and his sisters to stay at the Buckners's place."

This needed some thought, but her mind was in a whirl. She put the plant pot back on the table. He'd brought his family?

"You should see our townspeople's faces," Marie said. "The fire is back in their eyes! All because of you and Mark. Of course, you won't see that fire, fiddling with plants on your porch."

"So, legally, he's out of the woods and he and his family are not in trouble?"

"That's what the papers are saying. Although they still have to locate Bob Smith, and don't talk to me about legal! I've got a head full of legalese."

"About Mark?"

"Donaldson's! They'll be up to something soon. They've still got one town left and Bob could turn up as anyone." Marie sighed. "It's a frustrating predicament for any reporter, let alone me and my heightened perceptions."

If the world of Momma's Hopeless Blog dot com ever got to know just how perceptive Marie was, and why, there'd be mayhem. The valley would be overrun with people wanting to see it for themselves.

Perhaps that was why she kept her gift to herself. She was protecting the valley.

Marie leaned forward and brushed a tendril of hair out of Lauren's face. "Why aren't you fixing your hair and washing your hands? He could be here any minute."

"He won't."

"Vision?" Marie said, eyebrow cocked.

"Uh-uh. No visions. I just know it intuitively."

"You're not going to search him out?"

"Absolutely not." She was firmly resolved on this. "He needs to make his own decisions."

"You think he hasn't made them all along?"

"If I do anything, it might tip more scales and fate might make another turn."

"Oh, fate's nothing. Anybody can shove that around."

"Well I'm not chancing it. I've done enough." Without really knowing *what* she might have done, or even *if* she'd had a hand in Mark's fate. But she was a Mackillop and that meant anything could happen.

"I'll leave you to your misery then, sugar. I have to go. I've got a new plan."

"For what?"

"Calamity Valley!" Marie marched off the porch and down the path. "What we need is organized and political leadership," she said, getting behind the wheel of the blog-mobile and slamming the door. "I may have to put myself up for the job." She beamed as she fired the engine. "Momma Marie for mayor! What do you think?"

Lauren smiled. Was there anything this smart, beautiful, intuitive woman couldn't do?

After a couple of minutes, she was left with nothing but the hum of a few bees and the rustle of leaves on the ivy and the sage bushes.

She fingered the heart-shaped stone in her pocket. She still carried it everywhere.

Would he be furious that she'd opened his saloon to paying customers? She'd been working in there as a waitress now and again too. She wouldn't be able to do that anymore.

How long would he stay? How long could she hide?

She hugged herself and tried to figuratively smell the roses but the only aroma in her memory was mint, and green grass, and the comfort she'd felt when he draped his bomber jacket over her shoulders that night they spoke by the iron gates. She'd been calmer this last week, buoyed by her hard work, pleased to see everyone find some renewed joy and energy as the town took shape.

Now he was back and it was going to torment her. It was pointless going over all the if-only arguments she'd had with herself through the sleepless nights. If only she hadn't lied at LAX. If only she hadn't presumed him guilty. If only she hadn't told him…

But she couldn't have lived a lie, not even for him.

Turning to the house, she stepped inside the doorway, new thoughts in her head. If he hadn't come to see her already, did it mean he wouldn't come at all? If he did come, would it be to advise her she had no right to open up his premises without his consent, and he'd be pleased if she kept her nose in her own business?

And worst of all—if he didn't come, would she have the courage to go to him so she could discover her destiny?

She held the stone in her hand and thought about her wishes before she closed the door on all the what-ifs.

I wish him love, wherever he might find it or wherever he might go. I wish him happiness. I wish…

She wished he was hers, but she couldn't ask for it.

MARK HAD BEEN back for two days and was ensconced in the rooms above the bar as though he'd never been away.

His mom and his sisters were content in Water Street. Even his mom had been impressed with the presentation and cleanliness in the Buckner's house.

He jogged down the stairs to the empty bar below, paused, and looked into the mirror. But all he saw was his own reflection.

Forget it. She hadn't come into town, but she'd have to at some point. In many ways, he wished he'd gone to her straight away because now, their eventual meet up would be even more difficult. He was primed for it though. He hadn't wasted his sleepless nights; he'd readied himself for her disparagement or perhaps her indifference or perhaps her resentment.

He didn't know what to expect, because she hadn't come into town, and he hadn't gone to her.

He opened the doors, latching them in place, ready for his staff to arrive to get the bar ready for midday customers.

The sun shone over the town and through the leaves of the plains cottonwoods, dappling the ground.

Kid was hanging around, close by. He and Mark's youngest sister were sitting on a wall outside Duggan's General Store, flicking through something on an iPhone.

His mom waved.

She and his other two sisters were about to go into Hortense's shop, and he had no doubt, given the stuff the women in his family liked to collect, that they'd be in there for hours and that the Buckners' house would be filled with their new purchases.

The Fairmonts were on the street too, sharing a morning coffee by the old marketplace, which was soon to open as a museum.

Was he really going to lose all this? Was he willing to walk away from it?

Doc was more than happy to take on the manager's role Mark had offered him. Mark would get a small return, and the bar would be in good hands. He wouldn't have to come back here again, unless he wanted to. He'd manage whatever needed to be managed from afar.

Except he'd miss her. She'd messed with his heart and he wanted her to do it again because it had made him feel alive, and whole, and worthy. He missed the light in her eyes, the warmth of her embrace, the power he felt when he was in her company.

Don't mess it up, son.

She'd told him about her abilities, and his options had been to listen and let her explain—or fly off the handle because he felt he'd been used. He'd flown off the handle, all right. Without thought.

But *he'd* been the one to make that decision. Not fate. The man.

People made choices, good and bad. He'd made a bad

one but nothing about him had been changed by others' hands. Not even by fate.

If he walked away from her without apologizing, he'd be the idiot he already thought himself.

He made his way down the veranda steps and strode toward the new museum. "Mrs. Fairmont!" he called. "I need to buy a bunch of flowers."

TEN MINUTES LATER he was knocking on the front door of Sage Springs house. Twenty seconds later, there she was.

He held out the flowers. Dahlias, Mrs. Fairmont had told him. "I wasn't sure what you might like. But these sort of called to me."

Her mouth was open, her green eyes wary. Her hair was coming loose from a ponytail, her T-shirt was frayed at the hem, her track pants so worn they were thinning at the knee, and he'd never thought her more beautiful.

She looked at the flowers, with a little choke of breath.

Maybe he'd gotten it right and she liked the orangy glow of the blooms in his hands.

He held them out to her. "Thank you for looking after the saloon."

She looked up, without taking the bouquet. "I broke in."

"You took charge of a situation I left to fend for itself."

"I took charge behind your back."

"I'm not angry and I'd like to apologize." Again, he moved the flowers toward her. If she didn't take them soon the paper wrapping around the stems was going to be ruined because he was crushing it in his grip. "You know the truth now." The whole of Texas did. "I don't know if you can believe me, but I was going to tell you. That morning, after we…" Woke up together and shared the dawn. Until he'd stomped on her with his accusations.

"What brought you back?" she asked, wariness in her tone.

"I didn't want to be known around town as a horse's ass."

Her smile broke, and for a second he thought he'd hear her laughter too.

His heart was in a thousand pieces and her smile had just mended it. "You have the most beautiful smile. I want to see more of it."

He offered her the flowers, and she took them, almost hesitatingly, but she'd taken them and her eyes were on his.

She put a spark inside him, just by looking at him, and it might be wishful thinking, but he thought perhaps he put a spark inside her too.

"Mark, nothing's changed. I'm still a Mackillop."

"Lauren—everything's changed."

LAUREN MET HIS eye and held his gaze. He'd come! But truth was of immense importance. "I knew you'd choose the dahlias."

He nodded, looking a little unsurer suddenly. "Your visions."

She held her bouquet with both hands so he wouldn't see

how much they were shaking. "I had them. I won't deny I thought that somehow it was all going to happen."

"Did you know I was going to turn up today?"

She shook her head.

"Do you know what the result of this difficult conversation is going to be?"

"No."

That seemed to surprise him. "I still have a bit of an upperhand?"

He had her very being in his hand!

"I don't know what my visions meant, Mark, and I haven't one since."

"You truly don't know what I'm going to say?"

"No." But she was beginning to sweat.

"Okay, well here goes." He took the flowers off her and put them onto the wicker chair, then rolled his shoulders and faced her. "The way I see it, if I *were* in love with you, it would have nothing to do with fate or whatever it is that your abilities conjured up in those…visions of our future together."

Her heart was in her throat. "Mark, I have to stop you now, because I want to apologize too. I shouldn't have—"

"How could fate know how my heart would feel?" he said, interrupting her. "How could fate know that I'd hate the fact I'd been deceived?"

"Mark—"

"It's not fate, Lauren. That's my conclusion. It's not fortune-telling or soothsaying—it's the power of love. Neither we, nor anyone else, can tamper with the power of love.

That's what I've discovered. That's what I came to tell you. I left you and I'm ashamed of doing so. After the way I treated you that morning, I don't know that you'll want to take me back—but I'm not going to let fate be the cause of my heartache or yours. Fate be damned. I love you. No matter the consequences."

Never trust a man who says he can solve your problems—unless he proves he can.

And he'd just solved all her problems. By returning to town. By coming to her when she'd been scared to face him. Her throat was clogged, her eyes brimming with tears, and built-up emotion tightened her chest.

"I was too nervous to come to see you," she managed, plucking at the hem of her tee as if it were her only lifeline.

"You, nervous? I thought you were a Mackillop."

"Oh, Mark."

"Could you just find the words to tell me whether or not you might also love me? Because I'm getting tense here."

Her smile bubbled over as well as her tears. She wiped them away with the back of her hand. "We still haven't cleared the air between us."

"Shoot. Because if we're going to have these children, we need to get on with this and make things formal."

Oh, God, he meant it. He loved her.

She steadied herself, taking a breath. "Do I scare you?"

He smiled then. "You scare the socks off me. Never doubt it."

He was teasing, but… "I'm still who I am. I can't deny it or maybe even control it. I don't know where my abilities will lead me, but I have to allow them to."

"Are you saying you won't have time for me and the kids?"

She gave a shaky laugh. "No! I'm saying I—"

He stepped forward and put a finger to her lips. "The power of love has nothing to do with fate or destiny. It's here, all around us. We can't escape it or change it. Not even you. You don't frighten me, Lauren."

It was the biggest gift she'd ever received.

He dipped his chin as he looked at her more closely. "Will they return, your visions?"

"I don't know."

"So we're both in the dark."

She nodded.

"Except for one thing."

Her heart all but exploded.

"Do I even have to ask you?"

Wonder trickled over her, like a shower of spring rain in Paris beneath the Arc de Triomphe. "I'd like you to."

He stepped close, took her fingers in his and kissed them. "You are my friend, my lover, my business partner, and my dream. I can't live without you. I can never be the man I want to be unless you're with me. I love you, Lauren. Will you marry me?"

She threw herself into his arms.

She felt his smile and held on tighter.

"It's a yes, isn't it?" he said, looking down at her with a tease in his eyes.

She nodded.

"I could tell without you saying. I'm catching on quick here, Miss Mackillop."

His embrace was all powerful, like the man himself. His warmth, his strength, and once again, she was inhaling the magic of him.

"If I could catch my breath, I'd say I love you with all my heart."

He dipped his head to kiss her. "Those are the only words I was waiting for."

Chapter Twenty-Nine

MARK HEFTED ANOTHER cardboard box from a stack surrounding him and put it onto the desk he and Butch had carried upstairs to the attic in Sage Springs house.

Dust flew around him, but he ignored it. All the space needed was a good polish, and it was about the last space left in Surrender that needed dusting. But it was going to make a fine study. A place where he could hide away and write his book. His own book. No more ghostwriting, and thankfully—no more ghosts on his back.

He'd never been filled with such pride and satisfaction. He'd had a hand in all the wonder going on, here in the house and in town. Damn right he was meant to have come here. Damn right he was meant for Lauren and she for him. They were a team.

Work was still going on in the house, but the wall had been rebuilt, with no scary moments, no falling plasterwork or spikes from the spire. Lauren had hired a team of workers to sort out the garden, which was beginning to look like it belonged to the house.

She hadn't levitated again, for which he was grateful, as any man would be. She hadn't had any more visions, either.

He wasn't sure what he thought about that but whatever ability she had, she'd use it wisely. He was happy to roll with whatever happened next, because he had a deep understanding that it was all focused on love and commitment.

The saloon was now fully under Doc's management, giving Mark the opportunity to write that novel. The candlemaker's shop and the flapjack kitchen were coming close to completion. The museum would open in a month's time with Mr. Fairmont as the curator, with help from Hortense.

And best of all, his mom and his youngest sister were planning to move to Surrender. His other sisters were going to live in the house in LA and continue with their jobs, but they'd visit often.

He pulled open a drawer in his desk, took out a jewelry box, opened the lid and smiled. A long string of pearls. Real pearls. His wedding gift to Lauren.

There would only be one wedding at the house. Theirs. They were going to marry by the lake and the waterfall and hold the reception for their family and friends at Sage Springs where warmth and love and care abounded. There'd be a rehearsal the day before, with dinner supplied for anyone who wanted it at the bar. Chili, no beans.

For a guy who'd had bad luck on his shoulders, he sure was blessed.

HE REPLACED THE jewelry box in the far depths of the drawer, then straightened the potted palm he'd taken from the bar and poked a finger into the soil to make sure it was damp but not overly wet. He was nurturing it. And so far, it was thriving.

He took a moment to look out the window.

From up here, he could see the road that first brought him to town. The road that had brought him back. It was his favorite view.

How could he ever explain his thankfulness for the life he'd been given, and the one he was going to live?

"Mark!"

He turned at the sound of Lauren's voice from the landing below. "Up here!"

"I know! Pepper just called me and Molly on Skype, so I'll be in our bedroom if you need anything."

The only pressing need was perhaps another lingering kiss. "Hey, Lauren!"

"Yes?"

Words failed him. He wanted to find some expression of his love for her. Different words. New words. A whole dictionary of words.

"I know," she called up to him, with a laugh. "I love you, too."

He straightened. Life with a Mackillop was going to be interesting. "I was actually going to say—what's for lunch?"

The sound of her tinkling laughter softened his grin to a smile.

"I love you," he said quietly, knowing she'd hear him.

"SO WHEN DO you two soothsayers-in-the-making think I'm going to get the call to come home?" Pepper asked as she ripped open a pack of caramel popcorn.

Lauren smiled at her cousins' faces on her laptop screen.

"Don't push the matter," Molly advised. "Let it happen."

"I'm raring to go!"

"Pepper," Lauren said in the responsible tone of an eldest cousin. "Given what I now know from my own experiences, I have to tell you it's possible you're going to fall so hard in love with this man that you lose your appetite."

"Isn't going to happen!" Pepper laughed so hard, she choked.

"She's got an unusual kind of loveliness, hasn't she?" Molly said while Pepper attempted to get her breath back.

"Makes me wonder about the man who'll come for her."

"Makes me wonder whether he'll turn around and head straight back to wherever he's come from," Molly said.

"I guess we'll find out."

"It's going to be fun," Molly said to Pepper when she'd gotten herself under control.

"What is?" Pepper asked, brushing popcorn off her shoulders before yanking out her hairband and shaking her head, making her riotous chestnut waves billow around her shoulders.

"Your love life," Lauren said. "If not your entire marriage."

"Marriage? Me? You two!" Pepper said, and started laughing so hard, she almost fell off her chair.

LAUREN MADE HER way up the stairs to the attic to let Mark know she was popping over to see Ava. She had a few lingering questions to ask her grandmother, and she wanted to see if she could pry some information about Pepper while she was there.

Mark must have heard her footsteps, because as soon as she stepped through the doorway, he caught her in his arms and swung her around.

She laughed as the dust swirled with them in little sparkles.

"Want to dance?"

"There's no music."

"Since when do we need music?"

His mouth hit hers as his arms tightened around her.

All their kisses were passionate, even the little ones. But she adored this kind of kiss. Where they were alone, touching, connecting, out of sight from the world. Only the two of them, showing the other how much they were needed and desired.

When they broke the kiss, it was reluctantly and softly, as though the earth stopped spinning and they had all the time in the world to just gaze at each other.

"We'd better make a decision on when we're getting married," he said, brushing his hand over her head. "And we need to decide where we're going for our honeymoon. How about Paris?"

"Perfect. It's the place we're going to meet our memories." And make more…

"I love you," he mouthed silently.

"I love you, too," she mouthed back.

There was no strange telepathic connection between them, only the real ability to know each other's thoughts, just like every ordinary man and woman in love.

It was more thrilling than any spell.

"I'm just going to quickly visit Ava," she told him.

"Something up?"

"Can't say."

She gave him one more kiss, and flew down the stairs.

"THERE'S LOTS I want to talk to you about," she said as she settled in the Adirondack chair next to her grandmother. "But the first thing I want to try to understand is why I haven't had any more visions of the future."

"You're getting to look more like your mother every day."

Lauren smiled. "Is that a clue?"

"No. It's a general observation."

She reached over and kissed her grandmother's cheek.

"You're trying to get me to work it out for myself, aren't you?" she said, relaxing back in her chair.

"And what are you thinking?"

She was reflecting on the cryptic things that her Mackillop women had said to her or told her when she'd first arrived home.

"There will be something nice waiting for you," Molly had said at the airport, *"after you've been through everything you need to go through."*

And the most telling of all. *Everything has an end. But you won't get there without going through it.*

"It's a beginning, isn't it?" She watched for her grandmother's reaction.

Ava smiled and reached across to take her hand.

"That's why I'm no longer having visions of my future with Mark. Because I'm at the end of that stage." She sat up in her chair, uplifted by the notion. "It's because I've come to a beginning!" The start of the rest of her life with Mark. It was *their* beginning. A new story, encompassing everything they'd both been through, and everything that still awaited them.

"The force of the gift is great when it first arrives," Ava said. "It needs to settle, so you learn about it and it learns about you."

"I get a feeling all my senses are growing and expanding. I feel I should know things about some people's future, but those things are not quite in my reach yet."

"Maybe the answers will come to you once others approach you with a question."

She had plenty questions of her own. "Why did I always think Mark was somehow integral to ending the curse, when it was me who had to do it?"

"Without him being here, none of what happened that night on the stairs would have occurred."

As simple as that…

"The great-grandfathers couldn't harm him because you were in love with him," Ava said. "Even though you didn't realize. Love protects people. So they turned on you."

And her own love for everyone around her had protected her. "Did this happen to Molly?"

Ava shook her head. "Not in the same way, although they were angry with her."

"If only I hadn't been so confused by everything at the start." Not to mention the middle.

Ava smiled. "Confusion is what makes the world spin out of control. Sometimes we look for the big reasons, when those skimming the surface are the real reasons. Don't forget that as you go forward with your gift."

Would she ever be as insightful, and somewhat exasperating, as the grandmothers? "Why did you all decide to renovate the houses six years ago? It wasn't just because you knew the developers were going to come snooping, was it?"

"Let's just say there were interesting future scenarios for each of you. But things didn't go to plan, thanks to the great-grandfathers. You girls left, so we boarded up the houses and waited until the time was right again."

"You were trying to shove fate around."

"It's easy to shove fate. It's getting it to work the way it's supposed to work that takes patience."

Lauren found a smile.

She thought about Molly and her happiness with Saul, and her own joy with Mark, and the many trials they'd been through to get to the end, and the start of their new beginnings.

"True love is invigorating, that's a fact." Not to mention tiring. She'd never imagined making love would be the first thing she thought about when she woke or that the man she was going to marry would be so happy to oblige.

"I'm worried about Pepper though, and how she's going to handle all this when her turn comes."

Ava chuckled. "I understand she thinks she's forewarned, and therefore thinks she's forearmed."

Lauren inched closer. "Who?" she asked in a whisper. "Who's coming for her?"

Ava whispered back, "Can't say."

"Oh, come on. Give me a clue. When is it going to happen? Has Aurora already set things in motion?"

"You'll have to ask her—but she won't say."

"Is he going to have a terrible time with Pepper?"

"Can't say."

Lauren slapped the arm of the chair in frustration. "What *can* you say?"

Ava pulled at the brim of her Longhorns cap. "Hang onto your bootstraps. It's going to be a helluva ride."

The End

The Calamity Valley series

Don't miss the next story of the Mackillop girls story!

Book 1: *Lone Star Hero*
Molly's story

Book 2: *Lone Star Protector*
Lauren's story

Book 3: Coming soon

About the Author

Jennie Jones loved everything romantic from an early age and still does. Give her a country manor with a debonair earl, a dusty outback station with a surly homestead boss, or a sprawling cattle ranch with a lonesome cowboy and she's in her element.

Born in a country town in Wales, all these romantic leanings in her youth led Jennie to the theatre where she worked as a professional actor for many years. It was a natural turning point when Jennie began writing fiction. She says writing keeps her artistic nature dancing and her imagination bubbling and she can't envisage a day when writing will ever get boring.

Jennie now lives in a country town in Australia, getting most of her kicks from books about earls, cowboys and all kinds of passionate book-boyfriend heroes. When she's not writing or reading she hangs out with Jonesey the boy cat, Zena the girl cat and Churchill the 50 kilo rescue dog. Plus the occasional sighting of her daughter. You can find more about Jennie and her books on www.jenniejonesromance.com.

Thank you for reading

Lone Star Protector

If you enjoyed this book, you can find more from all our great authors at TulePublishing.com, or from your favorite online retailer.